THE WEBMASTERS OF FATE
ORIGINAL SORCERY
BOOK III

ALEA HENLE

CONTENT WARNING

This story includes situations suggestive of assault and potential child endangerment.

%& I %&

The discovery of the ruins of Atlantis turned my life upside down.

Boredom drove me to surf news sites that Friday afternoon, starting with the most credible and reliable newspapers. I'd already completed all necessary tasks on my plate plus a half dozen unnecessary ones, but several hours of the work day remained. My sole desire was to find something engaging to keep my eyes from glazing over.

I preferred to present visitors with a ready smile and create a welcoming impression. In short, deliver the version of Rosalind Celia—aka Rose—Williams the firm hired as a receptionist and administrative assistant in the first place.

Anyone passing through the smoky-glass front door of the Webmasters of Fate's Philadelphia office would find a calm, sedate young White woman dressed in sensible black sneakers, black jeans, and a dark green shirt, her tall, lean body poised at a pseudo-mahogany workstation, in a chair with squeaky wheels. Seashell earrings dangled from my ears, longer than my medium-brown pixie-cut. And a smile, of course, pasted on my face.

As opposed to a wild-eyed creature bored out of her skull and ready to pounce on any source of potential amusement. Or a slumped figure snoozing over her keyboard only to wake with the imprint of keys on her face. I veered between the extremes on normal Friday afternoons, but more so on slow, hot summer Fridays before three-day weekends.

I'd already used up the one piece of chocolate I allowed myself per day on a luxurious double-chocolate truffle from the bakery on the first floor. Even with the rich taste lingering on my tongue, I needed invigoration of some sort.

Especially when my direct supervisor, the second-in-charge, turned the thermostat up as soon as the senior director—webmaster—left for the weekend.

"When the cat's away, the mice will play." Geneva's breathy alto tones rang out as she popped out of her office to give me the news. With a fist pump, she pulled off her thick, oversized cream sweater to reveal a thin red top tucked into her slacks, much more fitting for a humid summer day. A White woman a good two decades my elder, she ran a hand through short, light brown hair with only a few hints of frost at the ears. "No more freezing inside only to broil when we go out."

I smiled until she returned to her office. No sense irritating Geneva, who'd always been considerate to me . . . but she left me in a quandary.

Before, the chilly temperature ensured my fingers rattled away at my keyboard to keep warm as I shivered at the desk. Not fun, and I welcomed the first upticks as the air went from arctic-winter-day to balmy-equatorial-night, except it didn't stop. Within moments, we reached too-toasty.

My eyelids drifted downward, and my head rolled in lazy, drowsy half-circles. The residual caffeine in my bloodstream reduced the odds of my falling asleep, but I yawned and twiddled my thumbs while staring aimlessly at the images of different kinds of webs and networks decorating the pale gray walls. Founded in the 1980s as a subsidiary of Lachesis, Inc., the Webmasters of Fate produced video games and invested in art. Images from the games hung on the corridors and in the reception area and communal office spaces, along with photographs and visualizations of networks. Telephone networks, social media connections, anything web-like.

Even the custom, flat industrial carpet of light gray boasted black lines tracing spider webs and lifelike images of spiders here and there. All sorts of spiders, too, except magnified three or four times so viewers could distinguish legs, pedipalps, and spinnerets. At the start of my first day at work, all three of the local directors warned me never to kill a spider. If I found one anywhere I should to leave it be or, if brave enough, scoop it carefully up on a piece of paper and bring it to them or, if they weren't around, slip paper and spider under the door of one of their offices. I made a point of never letting my shoes step on a single spider imprinted in the carpet just in case it proved to be the real thing.

At least I had a job, and one at a firm that designed and delivered intricate games I'd regularly played—*Survive Vesuvius!, Long Live Palmyra,* and the grade-school-oriented *What's Under Your Feet?* The firm's products were admired for unparalleled degree of detail—helped in no small part by the owners, top executives, and at least half of the design and programming staff all being sorcerers.

Usually, work provided stimulation. As a regular matter, I got to buzz employees in and out and deal with visitors—not a lot, but some. Receive packages. Edit memos. Arrange appointments such as health, beauty, pet care, golf tee times. My title might be administrative assistant, but in point-of-fact I acted also as receptionist, concierge, and personal assistant to every employee working on site. This meant dealing with all sorts of tasks from mind-numbing number crunching to solving people's logistical problems.

Yet summer Friday afternoons stretched out, with every hour seeming to last three times as long. All around me people jumped and quivered to get time to speed up. Other Monday-Friday nine-to-five hourly workers probably spent the afternoon daydreaming about what to do with our rare paid holiday.

At least, I supposed other hourly minions daydreamed.

I didn't. The last thing I wanted was three days alone in my minuscule studio apartment. The alternatives didn't appeal either. Spend some of my very limited discretionary funds on a trip out of town to visit family and fake a smile while they worried over me? Take up an invitation from one of my few remaining friends and likewise get worried over and nagged to do something more "interesting"—in other words with better bragging rights—than my current job? Get out of my apartment and mingle with crowds of strangers at one or another of the street festivals?

Practice casting sorcerous spells even though I'd never managed to make even the smallest, most reliable spell work once, much less twice in a row?

No. No. No.

And NO.

Above all, I didn't want to dwell on magic.

The world had three kinds of people in it: billions of mundanes who didn't believe in magic, millions of sorcerers casting spells under the mundanes' noses; and the minute number with the worst of both worlds—we who believed in magic but couldn't work a spell to save our lives. I no longer fit easily in the mundane world, but neither did I belong in the sorcerous.

I needed a distraction. A challenge. A goal to accomplish that *meant* something.

Or a quest.

Considering where I worked, I should have known better than to say that out loud earlier in the day.

Because Fate most certainly provided what I'd asked for.

ATLANTIS FOUND! Inch-tall letters flashed at the top of the news site—breaking news! A five-second video clip filled the space below. A grainy brick wall half-covered with barnacles loomed in the distance. Water flowed around, along with bits of seaweed and plastic. The camera operator zoomed in, revealing a faint insignia on the wall. It resembled nothing so much as a mix of the symbol for anarchy and a stereotypical witch's hat.

Then the video clip jumped to a celebration aboard a luxe ship. People burst open champagne bottles right and left. In the middle a big, sweaty White guy in a too-tight blue sailor shirt and shorts jumped up and down. His badly dyed black combover flopped with every jerk.

"We did it! Am-I-right? Hoo-boy, we're going to paint the town red tonight. Atlantis or bust, baby!" He could barely be heard over the hoots and yells.

I hit the mute button, shaking my head. "What in holy hell?"

"What's so interesting?"

The lungs and vocal cords that produced the question came from a six-foot-tall Black man built on solid lines, dressed today in a close-fitting, midnight blue Polo shirt and matching slacks. He smiled more than frowned, although the smiles didn't always reach his light brown eyes. Black hair cut in a high top with a fade framed a long-nosed face, his skin a deep brown with sepia undertones. A hint of lavender and sandalwood hung around him, the dominant notes in his preferred scent.

I froze, my stomach turning into a lump of lead in my belly at the unmistakable growly bass of my third boss:

Maksim Irving. Fifteen years my elder, he ranked as the newest director—i.e. one of the people who ran the firm versus salaried minions, or hourly peons such as me.

Such a big man should thump around, but no. Today he wore soft leather sandals, but even in hard-soled boots walking across tiled flooring he could sneak up on a cat. He regularly slipped through the treated-glass front door without setting off the discreet bells attached. Routine glances up at the door and *not* getting caught up in anything on my computer were the only defense against him and certain others slipping in or out unnoticed.

I'd come up short and he'd snuck in.

"Well? What caught your eye?" Maksim tapped the top of my monitor with a long finger complete with a ragged nail edge.

"Nothing, sir." One hand hovered over the mouse without touching. "Just checking the news."

"That's all? You certainly seemed wrapped up. I could've marched right by you without being noticed." He chuckled and stamped a foot, making at best a soft thud.

Did he really think that sounded loud? Maybe he moved so softly because he physically couldn't make much noise. Allowing myself one look-over from head to toe, I refused to believe that. He had to be capable of loudness, and just amusing himself at my expense.

Prying apart teeth that had begun to grind together—the last thing I needed was a dental bill atop the rest of my debts —I wetted my lips and managed a small smile. Tilted my head and clasped my hands against my chest.

"There's breaking news, about the discovery of Atlantis."

"Jack Smith's excavation?" His hands clenched so tight his knuckles lightened. "The man's a—"

No surprise on Maksim's face. Nothing. Only his fists showed any sign of reaction.

I'd expected much more. Shock. Astonishment. Something bigger than biting his tongue over even saying the polite version of what Smith was.

Alas, my mouth opened and I filled in the blank. "Smith's a conman. A thief making a big, flashy show about finding Atlantis in the Bermuda Triangle while he redirects at least half of the millions he's swindling into numbered accounts. Oh, he puts on a good facade, getting one of his billionaire marks to kit out a diving vessel, but the guy's a walking, talking cliché! He can't even keep his accent straight, going from pseudo-Southern redneck to pseudo-Brooklyn in a single sentence."

"Don't hold back. Lay it all out, sister." Maksim settled his fists on his hips, teeth grinding. "I hate the man myself."

"He's bad, but the people funding him are as bad or worse. Buying into his stories of Atlantis being the pinnacle of White domination—they just want an excuse to feel superior." My jaw snapped shut so hard and fast the click reverberated along my skull. Seven months of keeping my own counsel and not sharing anything too personal at work, all blown in a moment.

"I don't disagree." The spark in Maksim's eyes and twitch of a tic in his cheek suggested much more than his words. "But walls sometimes have ears. Around here, the floors and ceilings do, too. And some of us are known to support causes others find . . . distasteful." His head tilted toward the open door leading to the senior webmaster's office.

"Point taken." I pasted a fake smile on my face. "I'm sorry, sir, but Mr. Anstruther isn't in this afternoon."

"Bounced out early, did he?" His eyes narrowed, and the tic sped up as his voice dropped. "I wonder if he's in Bermuda, celebrating with the rest." With a sharp jerk, he twisted his face in as fake a smile as mine. "So what's Smith latest find, the library? Another temple?"

I shook my head and patted my ears with my hands. "I'm sorry, I don't think I heard you right. Would you mind repeating . . ."

"What part of Atlantis has Smith uncovered now?"

"You believe this crap—" I swallowed hard and omitted other curse words, no matter the amused twitch of Maksim's lips. "I mean, that Atlantis even existed for Smith to find?"

"No one has ever been truly certain whether Atlantis existed, but to give him credit, Smith found clues the rest missed." His fisted hands banged against his thighs in a-synchronous beat. One foot tapped against the floor, sending minute vibrations that raised sympathetic resonance in the soles of my sneakers. "The man's an irritating, racist piece of . . . but he's stubborn. I doubted at first, but the artifacts he's brought up in the last three months would make a believer out of almost anyone."

Wait, three months? According to the news, Smith had only found Atlantis today.

Yet when I turned back to my computer, everything had shifted.

Hot New Atlantis Discoveries! Instead of a grainy image of a barnacled undersea wall, the video now showed a phalanx of white-legged divers swimming four-across along the remains of an ancient street. Broken walls of varying heights, none over six or seven feet, lined the way. At the end stood a jagged archway.

The camera cut away to show Smith beaming and waving his hands at tables covered with items, some cleaned and others still bearing barnacles and layers of sand. Immense pitchers, jugs, jars, and platters—both whole and in pieces, and all with elaborate decorations, some of the colors still recognizable. Youths portrayed in charcoal gray and brick red danced around and above a large bull on one platter. The artistic style reminded me of Ancient Minoan art from history class a few years earlier, but with blockier, squarer lines.

No way.

After all the changes, all the turmoil of the last year and a half, the world had finally crossed the limits of my belief. Life could crumble my plans to pieces and make me accept magic —but not the existence of Atlantis.

I refused to have my present alter as I watched.

"Atlantis never existed. Plato invented it. Everything I've ever read about Ancient Greece, before and after I discovered magic, insists on that—and it's certainly not in the Bermuda triangle." I ran a hand through my hair, yanking on threads until my head hurt, but the screen didn't change. "So how could Smith find it? And even if he did, how did he go from having found it today to finding it months ago in a matter of seconds?"

"Oh, Atlantis existed, it just . . ." Maksim blinked. Shook his head hard several times in succession as though a mosquito had flown into his ear, then rubbed his temples, although his foot kept rapping. "What did I just say?"

"Atlantis existed. Which, all due respect to you being my boss and all, it doesn't. Never did."

"No?"

"No."

"No?" He swayed as though I'd hit him. The wobbly movements increased until he rocked so hard, blinking all the while, that he toppled over. He hit the floor with a thud. No matter how soft the carpet, a body slamming against the floor made a ruckus.

He lay on his back facing up, jaw wide and tongue out and panting as though he'd run up the stairs from the first floor far below us. His arms splayed wide, hands flat against the carpet and fingers digging into the strands.

My chair wheels screeched against the rubber mat

covering the carpet as I pushed back from my desk. I nearly knocked the chair over in my rush to get down next to him. Except, what could I do? I'd taken a first-aid course, once way back in high school. Most of my medical knowledge came from novels and television shows, not exactly reliable sources. If he was having a seizure of some kind, should I call 911? Put something between his teeth to make sure he didn't bite his tongue?

Or call for help and let someone else figure it out? Not my preferred deal, I liked to handle things myself when I could—which partly explained why my life had tanked the way it had.

"Help! Someone!" I knelt next to him, hands fluttering uselessly in the air above him.

"No." Little more than an aspiration. He grabbed my hand with one of his. Calluses along the edges of his fingers scraped as he squeezed tight. His breath carried a hint of garlic. "Time. Space. Wait."

His eyes blinked rapidly, gaze distant and unfocused. Shadows danced across his face, almost under the skin. They had a flat look, as though an animated movie projected onto him. Yet a thrum of power emanated from his body, setting my wisdom teeth vibrating. I couldn't do magic, but recognized when others did . . . or had it done to them . . . This had all the hallmarks.

Unfortunately, nothing I'd learned about sorcery taught me what to do if someone else was suffering from a spell of some kind. But maybe it wasn't any different than what I'd do for anyone under other circumstances.

Prying my hand from his grasp, I dashed to the break room down the hall and around the corner. A head topped by a thick set of headphones bobbed from the corner of the big collaborative work area, but didn't turn my way. My shoes squeaked on the tiled floor as I skidded past the empty table to the mini kitchen. I grabbed a paper towel and dampened it with water chilly and straight from the tap, plus popped open the refrigerator and nabbed a cold bottle of water.

I sped back through the empty hall. He hadn't moved. Worse, his arms lay limp and head tilted back at an awkward angle. Only his heaving chest and the whistle of air escaping his lungs showed he still lived.

Dropping back onto the carpet, I laid the towel on his forehead. The water bottle slipped from my fingers and rolled until it stopped at an angle against his thigh.

He gave a sigh and the whistling sound lessened. I might've sighed myself, in relief because the whistling had hit me all the wrong ways.

"Sir? Mr. Irving? Maksim?"

He only reacted at the last.

His hands rose and clapped on either side of my face. Not pressing or hurting, just holding my head there above his. Sweat dripped down his forehead and small but visible gusts of steam wafted above the dripping paper towel.

"Rosalind Celia Williams, did Smith find Atlantis?" His gaze fixed on me. I couldn't look away.

An urge to agree rose and nearly filled my throat. The easiest thing would be to let it slide. Keep my job and not rock the boat. Not try to be a smarty-pants, know-it-all and above-it-all savior—to quote one of the first stones that had splintered my life's trajectory—especially since the matter struck him so oddly.

Too late. I'd already pushed the *no* line. Making nice would require me to take it back. Admit an error that I didn't believe in.

"How could he? Atlantis doesn't exist."

"You're right." His hands dropped away. He glared at me and snarled, a beastly sound. Shaking himself all over, he ripped the towel from his forehead. Sat up and burst into a coughing fit. He grabbed the water bottle and unscrewed the top. Drained the whole thing in a couple of long swallows. Then he slammed his hands together, crushing the bottle between them. The plastic cracked, and the remaining drops sprayed out. "More than you know. Atlantis never existed."

"Then why . . ." A couple of drops landed on me—face, neck. I wiped them off with a hand, rocking back on my heels.

"No time for whys right now." He shook his head and magicked the bottle away.

Clapping his hands together, he pulled them apart slowly. He'd held nothing, yet the air between his palms filled with an intricate tangle of strands as though he'd started playing a string game. All sorts of colors: bright greens and yellows, sullen blues and purples, flashy reds and orange, plus brown and gray and black.

I reached out a finger toward them, fascinated by the way they pulsed and seethed, glowing with light.

"Watch out." He pulled back. "Don't touch."

I recoiled as a brief flash of heat hit me. A faint stench flared in the air, as though a hair burned to a crisp. I patted my forehead, but nothing seemed wrong even though bits of ash danced in the air around the threads.

His fingers twitched this way and that, and the strands responded. Colors whipped along with rapid beats, then slowed. He studied the result for a long moment, then brought his hands together and the lines of light vanished.

Leaning over, he flattened a palm against the carpet. His fingers inched to the side until the tip of the long finger slipped under a strand of web.

I'd thought the webs printed on the carpet fiber. An artistic illusion. Yet as he pulled the filament of web away, additional lines appeared in the air outlining an intricate tangle of strands far more complex than those he'd held in his hands.

Worse, spiders appeared. Dozens after dozens surged out of the carpet to skip along the strands. Black. Orange. Brown. Tan. Gray. White. All purring. The vibrations pouring from them filled me, worse than anything else.

Creeping, leaping.

Swinging on strands from the web.

Jumping from the web to skitter along his arm. They seethed in an ever-growing mass wrapping him from fingers to shoulder. One made the leap from arm to the tip of his nose.

I hadn't a shadow of arachnophobia when I took the job, but then I hadn't lived through a mass of them seething around me. Small, medium, large, including three tarantulas as big as my hand, one of which passed a hair away from me as it crawled over to sit on Maksim's foot.

I fell over backward, inching away on my backside until I hit my desk and couldn't go any farther. Because of the spiders—and the sudden burst of magic.

Knowing the firm had a sorcerous side was one thing, experiencing it this way quite another.

At least a third of the employees were mundanes, or so a family connection—a sorcerer—who worked out of the New York office had warned me. I shouldn't expect to see much magic. She herself rarely used it at work, since as chief legal counsel she had other skills to bring to bear.

Guess she didn't anticipate this—magic on a level I'd never seen, not from any sorcerer under any circumstances whatsoever. The whole churning mass of spiders and the shimmering strands of web suffusing the air around me.

I pulled my arms in, hugging my knees against my chest. Made myself as small as possible.

The spider on Maksim's nose glowed, blinking in out of existence as though made of bytes or blacklight or something. More spiders crawled along the webs filling the air, until thousands covered the walls and floor and ceiling. They left a small circle free around me, but otherwise the only visible things not spiders were me, him, and a few flickers of the walls through the webs.

"Go, my friends, and help me undo this knot. Find and flag all mentions of Atlantis and Smith. In particular, Smith's discovery of Atlantis. Answer to none but me." He whistled, low and slow. "Take what you need, give what you can."

The purring increased—then ceased abruptly. A shock ran through me, as though an earthquake had hit the building. The foyer snapped back to normal with one exception: *no* spiders appeared on the carpet. Not real spiders, not ones imprinted on the fibers, none.

Maksim rolled on a hip and pulled out his cell phone. A few swipes, and a phone rang. He didn't have the phone on speaker, but the high volume let me listen in anyway.

"What hair's got up your nose now?" Bob Anstruther, the office's senior director, spoke with a rolling accent that practically dripped out of the cell phone—along with a metric ton of attitude. He'd stalked out earlier in a white Panama hat over his graying hair, white suit appearing freshly pressed as always and tailored to the body he took pride in keeping fit after fifty, and white shoes. The only touch of color, other than the flush on his cheeks and across his nose, was the tie in the University of Michigan colors.

"Quick poll. No need to put off starting your long weekend. A one-word answer will suffice." Maksim's eyes and nostrils flared. His intonation grew clipped and short, but remained polite. He always did, an admirable and irritating trait. "How long will it take Smith to finish excavating Atlantis?"

"That's what you're wasting a call asking? How could anyone know? Already the site is proving richer than anyone ever imagined." A heavy sigh. "Really, Maksim, perhaps if you put your mind to your work? There's another game to knock out and keep the money coming in."

"Who says this isn't for a game?" Maksim stretched his mouth wide in a grimace, a jovial note in his voice. "Enjoy your weekend."

He ended the call, then slapped his thigh.

It occurred to me that I was blatantly eavesdropping, a bit after the fact. Then again, I'd perfected the art of perching at my desk and appearing absorbed in my work. Perpetuated an illusion of privacy that left most folk, fellow employees and visitors, comfortable enough to use their phones in the foyer and talk about all manner of things.

Sitting next to someone while doing nothing but listening was going a bit far. I shifted, starting to push up from the ground, but Maksim wrapped a hand around my wrist as he triggered another number.

"Stay close," he whispered, voice low and harsh.

"Let go."

His fingers dug in for a moment as I pulled, then he let out a whistling breath and released me. I cradled my hand against my chest, though it didn't hurt, and glared right back at him.

"Sorry about that." He swallowed. Glanced away and back, without glaring although in no way happy either. A tic jumped near one corner of his mouth. "Wrong thing. It's not you I'm angry at, just . . . Stay close for a while longer."

Rather than outright agree, I gave a short nod.

"I stopped believing this alternate reality is the true one thanks to your disbelief, but it was a close thing. I need enough time for it to settle into my bones, so I won't get caught again." The tic jumped another time. He shook his head, then put on a game face—and called Geneva. The muffled tones of her phone rang out down the hall.

"What's up?" Her cheery tones echoed in the distance.

Maksim gave her the same spiel as Bob.

"It could be ages. I still don't believe we're getting the whole story out of Smith and his minions." An edge of irritation sharpened her pronunciation. "There was so much more to Atlantis, things they're likely suppressing because they don't fit their world view."

"Bottom line, though, you're saying Atlantis existed."

"That's what I said."

"Got it. Have a good weekend."

My muscles protested sitting so long on the floor, so I moved back to my desk chair. Not far away, but Maksim followed and leaned against the side of my desk as he made call after call asking everyone the same question.

In which case, I wasn't going to pretend not to listen—or to read what I could of the information his phone showed about each person he talked to. Most of the names were vaguely familiar, but he'd included their locations and ranks in his entries and those showed up clear and pretty easy to read even at an acute angle.

All sorts of directors up and down the Atlantic seaboard, Halifax to Miami, and even inland from Toronto and Chicago. Each gave varying answers from a couple years to decades to forever.

A junior from St. Augustine had a hesitant note in his voice as he said he didn't know, while a junior for El Paso and a senior for Seattle each burst into gales of laughter.

There might've been others called in between, because he made so many I had trouble keeping track.

Until the last, with someone not identified as senior or junior or city, only by first name. This time, he skipped any preliminary greetings or reference to a poll.

"Tanisha, do you believe Atlantis existed?"

"Now, isn't it interesting the way the world turns. If I were asked yesterday who might pose such a question, I would not have thought of you," a soft voice with a lilting accent answered. I had to lean sideways, but her words carried far enough for me to catch most. "Tell me first what you believe. One word, yes or no."

Maksim drew in a deep breath and let it out with a soft, low whistle.

"No."

"Good. It's about time someone along your coastline came to your senses." Distant rustles and bangs. "I've been tracking reports for hours of people believing Smith found evidence of a civilization we all know never was."

"Someone's changing history again." Maksim growled. "This time, let's catch them in the act."

"No one from the Eastern United States or Canadian Provinces has reported in. I haven't heard a peep even from Bermuda, although Smith's using Hamilton as a staging base. I floated queries to offices all over. The central areas seem confused and the West thinks it's a joke, so I assumed all of you were caught in the backwash and under the influence. The changes are still fresh." Several clicking noises nearly overrode her last words. "I'm glad I'm wrong about you getting caught."

"No, you were right. I was. How I got out is a puzzle."

"Danger?"

"No. The sleaze in the web is more important, but the puzzle?" He lifted his head and stared at me. "The receptionist here seems to be immune."

I snapped straight, arms pressing tight against my sides. My breath caught in my lungs. So much for casual listening in. The room became so quiet I heard distant ringing in my ears without any difficulty—until finally the person at the other end of the call broke it.

"Is she part of it?"

Maksim's eyes narrowed, then he shook his head. "I doubt

it. She can wait, with a minor precaution or two. I'll call you back in five."

My feet twitched, soles scuffing the rubber mat. An urge to flee flashed through me, burning out fast. I hadn't done anything, and running was the surest way to make that harder to believe. Since magic existed, so did truth spells. I could prove my innocence if necessary.

"I take it you heard all that." Maksim loomed over me even from a distance.

"I hear a lot of things here." I made a circle with a hand, indicating the reception area. "If you'd wanted to be private, you'd have gone to your office."

"Fair point." A flash of teeth, but the smile had a snarly edge. "Who else have you mentioned this to?"

"No one." The truth slipped out of me before I could consider whether it was the smartest thing to have said. A line of sweat dampened my back along my spine, making my shirt cling. The job wasn't supposed to be dangerous.

"Let's keep it that way, for now." Another baring of teeth. "You're not in trouble, sister, but . . . are you a sorcerer?"

I studied the tips of my shoes, and their squarish outlines against the carpet. "No."

"But not a mundane, either."

"No."

"Interesting." He stretched out his arms and pressed his fingertips together. His hands became a cage, the lines of his fingers the bars. "Few people turn halfway. Most who aren't born into sorcerous families either witness magic and turn sorcerer, or convince themselves they didn't see anything unusual."

"I believe in magic, ever since I witnessed my sister turning into a swan." Gritting my teeth, I snapped up my chin and stared at his left ear. "I just can't *do* it."

"That complicates matters. Do you remember that your employment contract allows us to enforce confidentiality?"

"Yes." Didn't most employment include clauses intended to keep trade secrets? I'd read the fine print. Going through two-thirds of a semester of law school had convinced me of the importance of that. Evidently there was some nuance I hadn't picked up—I had dropped out after less than a semester.

"Anything you've heard, suspected, or . . . let's say all information about Atlantis, is confidential as of now." He brought his phone up, fingers swiping over the surface and bringing up the phone app.

This time, he headed for his office before placing the call. But he turned back before he left my view and pointed a finger at me.

"Don't make plans for the weekend. We'll talk later."

❄ 2 ❄

The door to Maksim's office slammed shut behind him. Way to end a conversation.

Made me regret I'd so much as said good day to him. My chair wheels screeched as I pushed it back and leapt to my feet. Planted fists on hips, and gritted teeth to subdue the roar building in my belly. Every inch of my body heated . . .

Except for a cold spot at the top of my head—the source of an oily sensation. An invisible substance trickled over me, slipping through my hair and down my sides. Sifted through my blouse and jeans to coat my skin. No matter how I brushed and rubbed, it covered me and permeated every inch.

Itched, too, in the bargain.

The confidentiality clause must have already flipped on.

Atlantis. Jack Smith.

My lips refused to even shape the syllables.

I'd signed away consent in my employment contract, but that didn't make it right.

Energy flickered through my veins. My heart pounded and chest grew tight as adrenaline flooded me. Been a long time since every inch of me buzzed, but all the same it was oh-so familiar and welcome. The muscles and sinews in my back and neck creaked as I rolled my head and raised my shoulders high.

Chin up, I marched over to his office and raised a fist ready to pound the cream-colored door.

A spider on a thread whooshed down along the door to land at the bottom, stark against the clean, bright paint. It scooted under the door. An instant later, my ears popped as though I'd shot up to thirty thousand feet.

The door paint turned a light orange. Visitors might not notice, but it was a subtle sign to staff that an office's occupant had activated a privacy spell. He wouldn't hear me, or anything else short of a major alarm going off.

Trembling, my fingers slipped from a fist to weak curve. My energy fizzled and sapped. Chin and shoulders drooped. A sour taste flooded my mouth.

I turned around and slunk into the break room directly behind. The squeaky-clean floor lived up to its reputation. I nearly slipped twice before getting wise and slowing down.

Grabbing the cool plastic handle, I opened the refrigerator. This time I passed over the water bottles and nabbed a bottle of non-alcoholic ginger beer from the six-pack permanently stored on the bottom shelf.

Holding up the bottle to the light, I studied the detailed label with its gold swishes against a red background. Geneva made a point of keeping every permanent or semi-permanent staff members' favorite work tipple in stock. Technically I was the one who did the work, but on her authorization. She had me add my preference to the list at the three-month mark, as a sign I passed my probationary period. Ever since, I'd restricted myself to one a week—two if I had a really bad day—because merely holding it gave me the warm-fuzzies for a little while. Less and less each time.

Unscrewing the top, I gulped a third down at one go. The sweetness dispelled the sour taste, but despite the fizziness, the liquid sat heavy in my stomach.

From the break room doorway, I had a good view of the office suite. It was a fairly simple layout: three offices for permanent staff, all with equal allotments of square footage and windows plus another closed room for temporary office use that also served as a conference room; a sizable, shared workspace for brainstorming meetings and the one week out of every two months when varying assortments of staff came to town; never less than three accessible unisex restrooms and occasionally more; and the break room. All done up in light cream and pale yellow, with ample artwork on the walls and the custom carpet everywhere except the break room and restroom.

The three permanent directors had open-door policies. In Bob's case, this meant he left his door open most of the time but woe-betide anyone who entered without an appointment. Geneva and Maksim both kept their doors closed, even locked, but were a lot friendlier when anyone knocked.

I'd been in Maksim's office almost never, though I'd caught glimpses when he emerged to meet visitors, retrieve parcels, pick up lunch deliveries, or interact with the visiting virtual workers who all joked around with him a lot. It wasn't any different from anyone else's. He had the same basic furniture and setup, though instead of artistic renderings of networks he'd covered the walls with an array of family photos. Most were unstudied casual snaps, the main exception being a large photo from his wedding. This he'd given pride-of-place where he could glance at it when seated at his desk.

He had a desk in an office. Walls on which to hang art. A door he could close.

I didn't.

If anyone had asked me what kind of office I wanted, back when I was in college burning the midnight oil to make good grades and get into law school with a full scholarship, I'd have laughed in their face. I didn't pinch and scrape and push myself for an office. I wanted the *work* and what it meant. The chance to contribute. Make a difference. Put myself out on the front lines and move them with my bare hands if I had to.

My job, the first one I'd managed to hang onto since dropping out of law school, involved work. It was valuable, worth at least the hourly wage they paid me, and kept a roof over my head and clothes on my back and all of that.

But it was work others could do as well as I.

I'd worked here a little over a year. Time to pull myself together, without managing to fill the emptiness inside. As an adolescent, I'd set my eyes on getting a law degree to do battle with evil and indifference in the name of justice. My younger self hadn't taken into account the possibility I'd not only hate law school but be bad at it.

For a burning moment, I wanted his office—not the space but what it represented.

The heaviness in my belly eased. I drank the rest of the ginger beer with no sign of indigestion. Rinsed out the bottle and dropped it in the recycling bin, then turned to head back to my desk.

Only to come to an abrupt stop—again!—this time where the tile met the carpet. The empty lines of the web stretched out atop the woven fibers, with no spiders in sight. I'd crossed it a dozen times every day, five days a week, for more than fifty weeks . . .

Without ever realizing it was magical.

Balancing on my tiptoes, I managed to step in blank patches between webbed lines for all of five paces.

My calves ached as I lurched and dropped flat foot. Better to pretend I hadn't seen it rise from the floor or swamped with spiders—even as I ignored the itchy sensation slowly fading from my skin—and to shuffle back to my workstation.

I settled into my creaking desk chair and whirled so my feet rested on the rubber mat. My arms stretched out as usual, hands settling on the keyboard.

Before I managed anything, even so little as moving the mouse or depressing a key, a dark-brown spider rose over the black plastic edge of my monitor. Beady eyes glittered in the light. Two or three long legs waved in the air. The spider hopped down to rest on the space between keyboard and monitor, right on top of my phone in its bright blue case. Its legs stretched forward, giving it a crab-like appearance. With the legs extended, it was wider than my hand.

I froze, scarcely daring breathe. If I pulled my hands back too fast, it might pounce. It might not be deadly, but the mere notion of finding out the hard way made my belly lurch. After a few heart beats, my breathing restarted in slight, almost inaudible whistling pants. Sweat broke out across my forehead. My elbows clamped against my sides and my tongue hard against the roof of my mouth, repressing a scream.

Back when Geneva had told me to take any stray spiders and leave them on a webmaster's desk, I'd had small spiders in mind. As in, the size of a dime or less—something I could scoop up on a piece of paper.

Paper would crumple under this. Cardboard might not even be enough, not that I had any at hand.

"Ah, Rose, uh, I wondered if . . ." A warm, light tenor preceded a cautious peep of a head around the corner.

Dark-brown hair overgrown to the point of shagginess framed an oval face with the merest hint of five o'clock shadow. Matching brown eyes gazed through thick-rimmed black glasses perched atop a long nose. The tip twitched and a faint flush stained otherwise pale cheeks when his gaze met mine.

The panic on my face registered an instant later. His skin turned even rosier, but he leapt into action and his jeans-clad legs spanned the space between us in a leap and a bound. For a man of average height and build, he moved fast when he wanted and his bare feet made no sound. A heavy pair of earphones rested around his neck, the cord dangling against the buttons of his white shirt. The colors of his undershirt bled through—was he wearing a Spiderman T-shirt?

The young man's gaze swept over me and then down to the desk. His lips quirked.

"Good day, little cousin"—he bent and laid his palm next to my hand, arm warm against mine—"you've gone astray, haven't you?" He had a bit of a burr to his Rs. Rather nice on the ears.

The spider evidently thought so, for it skittered onto his hand.

"May I help you find your way?" He lifted his hand to his ear and waited. No sound came from the spider, or nothing registered on my ears, but he nodded. Kneeling, he laid his hand against the carpet. The spider zoomed off in a zigzag progression toward the hall and Maksim's office.

"Hmm." The young man followed as far as the edge of the hall, then turned around and flashed a smile. "Looks to be set now. Uh, are you all right?"

The shy curve to his lips triggered recall of his name. Neil something-or-other, one of a half-dozen White men in their mid-to-late twenties who'd descended on the office at the start of the week. Researchers and game designers working on a new video game, doing things at various area museums and returning regularly to the office for mass scanning, digitization, and arguments.

Such groups regularly worked here for a week or two at a time, though this group was unusually homogenous. The latest arrivals seemed to go everywhere as a package deal. Arrived together, left together, joked with Bob about colleges and fraternities together, ate together—might do other things together, though I knew they had separate rooms because I'd arranged six-week-leases on a row-house with ample bedrooms.

Neil had peeped at me from the middle of them on several occasions. I'd caught him in the act the other afternoon and smiled back, receiving a shy grin in return though he'd remained part of the pack. Until an hour earlier, when he'd entered the suite with only one of his fellow researchers, ducking his head and mumbling about work to finish before the weekend.

"I caught the tail end of the rush of spiders." He leaned against the wall, ducking his head. "That alone could give a person a turn, then you get to meet a huntsman spider up close. You're not scared of them, spiders, are you?"

"Not scared, not in the usual way." I waved at the carpet. The bare lines of the web stood out against the creamy background. The spiders I'd believed part of the pattern had vanished, but they might come back. "I wouldn't've taken the job if I didn't like them,"—a shiver rocked my shoulders—"though I'd rather they stayed off my desk."

"There's dealing with spiders and there's enjoying them." Neil didn't move away from the wall, shoulders at a slant and head tilted, watching me out of the corners of his eyes. He twined long, lean fingers together, thumbs touching each of the other fingers in turn. "I've not seen much sign of the directors here having great fondness for spiders. I'd say more tolerance."

"Is it different in other offices?" I'd never visited any before taking the job here, but the pack of researchers had dropped names of all manner of locales around the globe.

"Oh yes. Some offices have more than mere webbed carpet. Frames and special habitats built into the walls, and cleaners trained to leave be any web a spider chooses to spin up." He inched closer. "Then again, Philly is only a branch office. Something of a backwater. Not exactly an up-and-coming place to be for directors and those who would be."

"And which are you?" I shifted in my chair to face him full on, chin lifting.

"Neither." He straightened, squaring off opposite me. His stance mirrored mine, save that he stood and I sat. "Nothing more than a sorcerer who enjoys the working on the back-end of video games."

"That's more than me." My turn to tilt my head down and away.

"You're here and unfazed by the strangeness, that says a lot. The Philly office's got a reputation for bringing up good people." Neil didn't move back, although his long toes twitched against the flat carpet. "Sure seems that way here. You've been great, and both Geneva and Maksim welcomed us, and even though Bob went to the wrong school, I don't hold that against him."

The compliment eased a tightness across my shoulders. I rolled my chair back to make it easier to watch him.

"I might've heard something about that." When Bob came out to greet any employees passing through, he always asked where had they gone to school—in search of fellow Michigan alumni. He'd scowled on hearing Neil went to Ohio State, but all turned out well in the end because they'd pledged the same fraternity.

"I bet you did." He inched closer, glancing over at my desk. A chuckle escaped him, his shoulders doing a quick shake. "Are you following the Atlantis dig? Can we even call it a dig when it's all underwater? Maybe it should be an excavation."

"If there's any digging, then yeah, it's a dig to me." A lump formed in my throat, and every inch of me itched in sudden reminder of what I couldn't say. Even working around to offer that limited response made my head ache. With a flick of a finger, I rolled my mouse up and closed the browser. "But my break's done, so I'd better get back to work."

"Of course, of course." He padded a couple of feet away, then half-turned toward me. "I thought I'd play tourist and see the sights, from the outside at least. Wander around Freedom Park and the historic museums as a spectator rather than a researcher. I wouldn't mind some company, a local who knows off-the-beaten track places worth lingering."

Any other time, I might've jumped on the roundabout invitation, no matter how awkwardly delivered. My determination to avoid the press of crowds could melt under the right circumstances . . .

But what if the subject of Atlantis came up again? Or anything else Maksim had banned me from talking about? Maybe the spell would wear off over time.

Or I could avoid the subject. Maybe it would be better to push things off to the next morning. Give me time to recover, and get ready to spend a date out in a crowded city.

On the other hand, cute and shy as he was, I preferred a straightforward "will you" over a passive "wouldn't mind."

"I have plans tonight,"—to stay in—"and don't like crowds much." True, though I made exceptions, and my voice sounded anything but certain even to my ears.

"How crowded are things in the morning?" He tilted his head, watching me from the corners of his eyes.

"Are you asking me to go with you?" I crossed my arms over my chest and mirrored the angle of his head.

"Yeah." A head bob. After a several breaths of awkward silence, he broke and looked away for a moment, swallowing hard. "Would you come walking with me?"

"Sounds good."

We settled on meeting at eight o'clock in front of Independence Hall. He wrinkled his nose at the time and joked about keeping work hours on weekends, but otherwise made no argument.

"Text or call if you can't find me," he said after I gave him my number. He snapped his fingers, and my phone lit up a moment later. "And now you know how to get in touch." Wide brown eyes gazed directly into mine as he stood only a foot away, heat pulsing between our still forms. "If you ever need help with anything. Anything at all."

A hard thud, followed by a click, made us both jump. No footsteps sounded, but Neil leapt back. A decorous five feet separated us by the time Maksim strode down the hallway, as soft-footed as always.

The big huntsman spider perched atop Maksim's shoulder.

"Rose, Neil." He nodded at the two of us as he stooped low, angling his arm so his fingers brushed the carpet. The spider slid down, grabbing hold of one of the strands of web imprinted below. Then it flattened into a two-dimensional print on the floor.

As Maksim straightened, soft thuds echoed down the hall.

"Maks, wait." Geneva hove into sight, chest heaving. Her hands held a small, thin rectangular package. The wrapping paper bore a pattern of cheerful baby bears gamboling on a yellow background. Each bear wore a yellow ribbon around its neck, and a matching yellow ribbon was tied around the present. "Leaving so soon?"

"A few errands to run." Maksim's fingers wrapped around the doorknob, but didn't turn.

"Then you'll be back?" Geneva gave him a level look.

"After the weekend." His lips tightened. "I'm not on call this time round."

"Thanks for the reminder."

The two engaged in some kind of staring contest. Neither said anything, or moved, but the air started getting a little thicker, harder to breathe.

I swallowed, my own breaths harsh in my ears as silence rolled off them in waves. Neil inched way from them and closer to me, his posture shifting to cover the open side of my desk.

A beep from Maksim's phone broke the stillness. He and Geneva both recoiled backward a step. She smoothed her fingers over the wrapping paper, creating a soft whispering susurration, as he pulled his phone from a back pocket. Lines appeared across his forehead as he read the text.

I dragged in a deep breath as the tension in the air vanished, and a low whistle came from Neil as he did the same.

"Is Shauntelle all right?" Geneva gestured at the phone. "And the baby?"

"They're fine, for now. The doctor wants her to take it easy, so she's staying close to home." Maksim smiled, though a tic jumped in one cheek. "Her best friend has come over to prep for the shower tomorrow."

"Speaking of which,"—Geneva stretched out the hand holding the present—"I doubt I'll make it, what with being on call and you know how many things go wrong on holiday weekends under the best of circumstances. I've already called and given Shauntelle my regrets, but if you wouldn't mind?"

He regarded the present as though it was a snake.

"Would you prefer pink or blue?" Geneva waved the package, which briefly flashed each color in progression before returning to yellow.

"It's not a gender-reveal party." Maksim accepted the present, cradling it in one hand. "Thank you. We both appreciate it."

"Of course." She threw her head back and laughed. "I'll bet you manage to skip most of the party, one way or another. Should I have you on speed dial in case we get a triple dose of would-be time travelers?"

"No, I'll be there." Maksim twisted the handle, the door opening with a rare creak. "My mother and sisters are taking the train up from Baltimore at the crack of dawn tomorrow morning. Have a good holiday."

With an efficient, sliding motion he escaped through the door. It closed with a snick behind him. His form showed as a wavy shadow on the other side of the treated-glass panel for only a moment before it vanished.

I huffed out a sigh. A matching sound echoed mine. Turning my head, I grinned at Neil who smiled back, both of us relieved at the reduced numbers—and presences—in the reception area.

Geneva shook her head and ran a hand over her hair as though nothing had happened. Noting the sole spider on the floor, she knelt on the floor, touching the huntsman imprinted in the fibers. "Did he leave you behind?"

"There's a reason I'm not and never will be a director," Neil said under his breath, with a watchful eye fixed on Geneva. "Not half dramatic enough."

The huntsman spider twisted back into three-dimensional reality and crawled up Geneva's arm only to cross her shoulders and jump off her other arm back into the carpet about a foot away. This time it shrank to two dimensions and then vanished.

Geneva rose and dusted off her hands. A sharp glance in Neil's direction suggested he hadn't kept his voice low enough. Then her gaze slipped to me and wove back and forth between us as she raised an eyebrow.

Neil blushed and headed back to his desk, gesturing at my phone and mouthing for me to call him, or so it appeared.

"Planning to call him?" Geneva leaned against my desk.

"Maybe. We'll see." I folded my hands in my lap. "Not on work time, of course."

"That's all right. This is a very big company, and we employ a lot of young, single people. It's allowed." She brushed a finger across the top of my computer monitor. "You may not remember all the clauses in your employment contract . . ."

A puff of laughter escaped me. She spoke truer than she knew. One thing I planned to do over the weekend, while staying away from the crowds, was read over my contract for all the clauses I'd managed to bleep through before.

Geneva kindly overlooked my puff, apart from a brief twinkle in her eye. "Workplace romances are permitted so long as neither participant has any supervisory or evaluative role over the other."

"Ah, thanks. Good to know."

"On the other hand, coercion of any kind is not tolerated. No means no. Don't be shy asking for assistance or advice if you need it. After all, it's a dog-eat-dog world out there, and if women don't put ourselves first enough of the time, we'll get trodden all over." She cast a wry glance at Bob's open office door.

The quick spin from encouraging me to go out with Neil to warning me against getting caught in an abusive relationship made my head ache even more than before. But then, she enjoyed mentoring me and offering suggestions, which I, in turn, appreciated and considered. After all, she had a good job doing fulfilling work, even if it wasn't something I'd ever be suited to.

Though the odd cast to her face set me wondering about her and Bob.

I'd spent enough time at the desk to make the view of his office old hat. Prideful of me, for a moment later my casual inspection snagged on the digital photo display frame on his desk. It cycled through a growing array of images of Bob with famous friends, two-directional so he could share with visitors as well as gaze at them himself.

The display currently featured a photo of Bob with Jack Smith, both twenty years younger, in Michigan athletic gear and standing on a football field.

Something new. Bob was off this weekend. I'd heard something about sailing—maybe to Bermuda? Visiting Smith and the excavation?

Questions rolled through my head and teetered on the tip of my tongue, but I couldn't ask a single one. My scalp itched until I swallowed and stopped trying.

"You heard Maksim asking about Atlantis earlier, didn't you?" Geneva swung around, body blocking the view. Leaning in, her voice dropped to a hint above a whisper.

My whole body flared into one burning itch. An immense lump formed in my throat. Even nodding hurt—I managed the tiniest of acknowledgments.

"I'd keep that to myself, if I were you." She touched a finger against her lips. "The directors did some housecleaning when they added the second headquarters in Montevideo, but there are still a lot of pat-fanny blood brothers in the US and elsewhere."

After which she strode back to her office before I could say anything.

Or figure out whether she'd just given me some kind of warning or not.

Shoulders slumping, I dragged in breath after breath. The burning sensation along my skin subsided, but I grabbed my reusable water bottle from the desk, knocking my mouse off the pad in the process. Fingers trembling, I gulped half of the water down to ease the ache in my midsection.

My screen returned to full-color display from sleep mode. Though I'd have sworn I'd closed the browser, it remained open. The story about Smith and the discovery of Atlantis had shifted.

New Finds! The headline boasted. A big photo stretched from edge to edge, showcasing a gorgeous, bright blue sky and a fresh-scrubbed boat deck. Smith stood before a crowd of his backers, all in expensive casual boating attire and big grins. Bob beamed from the second rank, and a few other faces appeared vaguely familiar from passing through the office a time or two.

Curiosity bit, and I clicked on the link to the organization behind Smith: the "Atlantis True Believers." A new window opened showing a romanticized fortress atop a hill with billowing waves far below.

Boldface, italicized font proclaimed the organization's credo. Scanning it made me want to puke. Cliché after cliché about the supremacy of the White race, and how discovery of Atlantis would prove once and for all that everything good in the world came from the blessed hands and heads of White men made in the image of a White patriarchal god complete with flowing beard and a host of golden-haired angels surrounding him.

Talk about the kind of off-the-charts extremist organization that gave cover to well-off and middle-class White people. They could point at the Atlantis True Believers and say they weren't like that. Maybe they weren't—I wasn't—but there were a lot of stops on the continuum between the loony Atlantis-end and being an anti-Racist.

The website offered plenty of photos of members. At least three dozen people were willing to have their faces plastered across the website, although few of the photos had captions. Bob wasn't in the member photos, but he showed up in a different section: among glam images from a celebratory party on the yacht shortly after the discovery of Atlantis.

I'd never guessed the extent of his extremism. Though I'd noticed he treated Maksim as an errand boy and Geneva a glorified housekeeper, I'd not said or done anything. My position lacked the power, but . . . I could've searched for a different one in a better environment.

Instead, I'd stayed and accepted. How depressing.

I closed the browser, shutting it for good this time just as my phone buzzed with the arrival of a text from Maksim: <<Meet me at the Penn & Cup Coffee House at five-thirty.>>

<<Important developments. Tell no one.>>

3

A curse on Maksim for choosing Penn & Cup Coffee as a meeting place.

I should be elbowing for space down below and waiting for the right train to come through. Or walking south, rather than east toward the Delaware. Not heading for the Penn & Cup Coffee close to Independence Hall and half-a-dozen other historical and tourist attractions that ensured steady business.

Crowds came out in force, filling the sidewalks and surging into the street. Meeting him meant going the wrong away—away from home. I tripped on a crack in the sidewalk and stumbled. Wrenching sideways, I reached a brick wall and subsided against the rough surface. Warmth from the day's sun radiated out, heating me above and beyond the humid summer air. The sun still shone above, albeit at a stark angle as it headed down toward the horizon—with a couple hours to go before sunset.

Dozens of savory scents emanated from nearby restaurants and food carts, plus plenty of less aromatic foods frying in oil.

Not to mention the beer—lots and lots and lots of beer as tourists and residents toasted to anything and everything. Any one alone might set my stomach rumbling and asking for dinner, but together they edged hunger pangs over into nausea. Steam and exhaust wafting up from the underground lines made things worse as a train rumbled through below my feet.

My phone rang. I changed the ring tune for my mother at least once a month and I was overdue to alter it again. If she realized I used "Who's Afraid of the Big Bad Wolf" for her, she'd give me one of *those* looks.

Then again, she'd appreciate the dare wasn't meant for her but for me.

I swiped her over to voicemail. I had no desire to listen to any last requests for me to visit over the weekend.

Same with my father, and the seventeen collective texts from my younger sisters and two remaining college friends who'd hung around Philly.

I did read their texts, all loving and caring and offering good advice on getting out of my rut as if I hadn't tried. Having people focused on fixing me made my skin itch even more than the confidentiality spell. Even my father, who only tolerated his job, kept suggesting avocations to add meaning to my life. Such as joining an amateur theatrical troupe, preferably one with a penchant for Shakespeare, the route he'd taken to meet my new stepmother.

Exactly what I needed in my life, more Shakespeare.

If there was one thing my sisters and I agreed on with no argument whatsoever, it was running away from all things Shakespeare.

Mini lightning rays zapped through my brain, promising an incipient headache. I pulled a small, magical purse out of my pocket. A gift from my youngest sister, it held my driver's license, credit cards, a first-aid kit, flashlight, pepper spray, and e-reader. I popped an ibuprofen, swallowing twice to get it down my drying throat.

For the eighteenth time in ten minutes, a ding announced another text.

<<Where are you?>> Maksim assumed I'd follow his orders to meet at the coffee house.

Perhaps that explained my current proximity. <<Two blocks out.>>

<<Good. Things are going from bad to worse.>>

Way to be cryptic. Sadly, my curiosity ate his words up and urged me back into action. Only two blocks.

Arriving thirsty and cross, I stopped right inside the door and joined the line to order. Might as well get something first. The smells of coffee and cinnamon predominated, but the chalk menus listed a dozen teas and non-coffee drinks. Photos and stylized posters of coffee drinkers from around the world covered the walls. A mix of faux-leather-covered booths and mismatched wooden chairs and tables covered most of the plank floor in no discernible arrangement. Tall plaster columns marked with ample graffiti helped support the high tin-lined ceiling. Several whirling fans helped keep the air conditioning moving—and voices, too.

A couple in T-shirts and shorts directly ahead ignored me, carrying on an animated conversation in what sounded to be Chinese and swiping through guidebooks on their phones. Occasionally one or another screen flashed my way, showing dense, blocky characters. Ahead of them stood a group of five middle-aged White men and an older woman with a cane, whom the men kept urging to sit down and let them order for her. Both the baristas and the clientele filling most of the tables and booths were a mixture of ages and races.

Smoke-tinged glass formed the external walls, from two feet above the floor to the same short of the ceiling. Natural light mingled with artificial to make the space warm and inviting. All the same, people bustled along the streets outside with little more than occasional glances inward.

I shivered in the comparative cool, sweat starting to dry along my skin. Alas, the air dried my mouth all the more and made me long for a drink of any kind—well, anything cold.

Best of all: an iced ginger beer. Bonus points for my favorite brand, same as the bottle bearing a familiar logo and dripping with condensation sitting on a table half-hidden by one of the columns.

An empty chair had been angled as though someone had shoved it in without looking on their way out—yet left the unopened bottle behind.

Left their companion at the table, too, as a big mug of coffee with steam rising up rested on the other side of the table. The person behind the pillar lifted it and drank, returning it to the table and rapping their fingers against the side.

Maksim, though I didn't realize it until the line inched forward and the press of newcomers behind me, a foursome mixing English words with a language full of fricatives, forced me to scoot up. He'd chosen a perfect spot, with a good view of both doors, the front and the side.

He jerked his chin at me and waved a hand at the ginger beer.

Leaving the line, I squeezed my way through the maze of tables and chairs filled with chattering occupants.

Maksim had always seemed nothing more than a polite, distant boss uninvolved in my direct supervision. He gave me tasks now and then, always for work rather than anything personal. Plus given the expression on his face the couple times his wife called him, and the one time she visited the office, he was head-over-heels in love.

All the same, I had two younger sisters who delighted in creating spells to protect me. "Until you get the way of it yourself," they said, although by now we knew that wasn't going to happen.

So I took a precaution or two. Before sitting down, I pulled out a magicked handkerchief—blue with garish pink polka dots, my youngest sister's idea of a joke. Dusted off the chair, table, and bottle.

The colors switched to garish pink with blue polka dots. All clear.

"That's a nice piece of magic." Maksim's eyebrows rose and his mouth twisted. He lifted his mug and drank again.

The chair squeaked as I settled. The legs didn't wiggle, so it seemed solid enough. I popped open my drink and took a swig. The cool, fizzy taste cleared the last vestiges of my headache.

The same crowd clustered around the bar and filled the tables and benches, but the noise level dropped, way down, to little more than a murmur. Maksim must've cast a spell for privacy. Squinting hard enough revealed a hint of blurriness between us and the rest of the crowd—but also strained my eyes and threatened to bring back my headache. I blinked twice and focused on him and my ginger beer.

He kept his gaze moving constantly; now on me, then over my shoulder at the front door, and toward the side door, in a regular progression. The back of my neck itched. Might be the confidentiality spell or privacy spell.

"Well, I'm here." I swirled the bottle, watching the liquid slosh inside.

"Good. Thank you for agreeing to meet. I wasn't sure you'd show up." He wore the same clothes, but a new restlessness filled him. One or both feet tapped against the floor, the vibrations rippling through the boards.

Part of the time he rolled a finger along the rim of his mug, raising an almost inaudible note that made my back teeth itch. Elsewise, he kept reaching to stroke the phone laid on the table or inscribe invisible words on the scarred wood. Every couple of minutes, he glanced back and touched the dull blue backpack slouched against the wall behind him, as if it might grow legs and run off. It looked old and beat-up, but if it belonged to him was probably magical and capable of holding more than it should by the laws of physics.

Despite the movement, the edge of his right hand right rested unmoving atop the table. His thumb and forefinger extended about three inches apart with a length of cord visible between them. Overall the cord had an opalescent sheen, but on closer inspection bright colors ebbed and flowed, primary yellows and red near the thumb and blue shifting in to add subtle greens and purples toward the fore-finger. The ends weren't tied around either digit. They merged into his flesh.

"Thanks for the drink." I raised it in a toast before downing another swallow, and angled myself to get a good bead on the cord. "Am I getting overtime?"

"You'll be paid fairly for all your labor." The fingers holding the cord twitched, thumb rotating slightly. The thread undulated and grew thicker. The colors shifted. "If all goes well, on your next paycheck."

"And if things don't go well?"

"It's unlikely either of us will remember any of this, assuming we even exist."

Way to lay the heavy on me. He moved his hand, drawing my gaze to the thread with which he played.

Most of the yellow slipped away where the cord vanished into the thumb. Indigo and violet predominated—along two-thirds of the exposed length, then a sequence of three dull white dots broke the brightness. The white had a glacial tinge. After the dots, a faint hint of red or deep purple remained amid an otherwise ashy section rooted in the forefinger.

He played not with a cord, but a thread. The thread of someone's life.

Geneva had worked her fingers much the same, the day she hired me. Slid a paper onto the table between us and asked me to grant permission for her to check my thread of life. A condition of hire, and one I wasn't in a position to decline. She warned me then that the terms of employment granted someone in the firm permission to review my personal thread once a year without any advance warning, although subsequent checks within a twelve-month period would be conditional on my consent.

I'd seen her check other threads a couple times over the intervening months, not often but regularly enough to recognize and remember.

All threads appeared as mishmashes of colors. Nothing about this one differed from the others.

But my gut said it was mine.

He followed my gaze to the thread.

"Yes." He flipped his thumb, drawing the length tighter. "This is your thread of life, and counts as the yearly scan the firm is allowed. It means you're safe from anyone else checking without your permission until next year."

"Why?" I left it open ended to see how he'd take it, and because too many questions flooded through me to pick any one.

"I need help,"—his eyes flashed—"but not if there's any risk you're a leak. I had make sure you had no connection to any known Webmasters or Lachesis enemies, activist fate groups, or other red flags."

The sensible part of my brain insisted I watch him, weigh every expression and gesture, but the thread lured me. I hadn't managed to read or understand any other threads, but this was *mine*. No one knew my recent past so well as me, and I could name each of the white circles that shifted my colors from luminescent brightness to dull, ashy gray.

"And?" I swallowed, an acrid aftertaste stripping any remaining ginger from my mouth and throat.

"No indication of any intentional involvement in supporting White supremacy. You have a record of leading and advocating for anti-Racist initiatives—until you graduated from college. Ever since, you donate money but not time or energy. Care to explain?"

"No." The corners of my eyes burned. I gestured at the circles with the little finger on my left hand, careful not to get too close. A sharp cold emanated from the thread, chilling me all the same. "You could say I discovered magic."

"I could, but that's not the whole story, is it?"

Rather than make a futile attempt to rip the thread from his grasp, I wrapped my hands around the ginger beer bottle. The glass squeaked at the press of my fingers. I set my teeth, lifted my chin, and glared at him. "You mean you didn't read it in my thread?"

Vibrations continued to undulate through the floorboards, either from people walking around or him tapping, but otherwise he'd grown more still. His left hand no longer cycled between mug, phone, and backpack. His expression revealed nothing other than a hint of impatience.

"I choose not to look that close unless given explicit permission from you—or reason to suspect malfeasance. I don't know what happened except that something did. Based on your response,"—he lifted his free hand and pointed at my white-tight knuckles, tight throat and jaw, the corners of my eyes, and the drops of sweat starting to condense on my forehead—"it shapes you."

"It was a bunch of things all adding together. Discovering magic. Failing at it." And failing at law school before I dropped out. I swallowed, mouth dry. Lifting the bottle in a slow, deliberate arc, I opened my mouth to a rush of cool ginger beer. It washed away the sour taste and soothed my sore throat, but acid roiled in my stomach. I licked my lips to catch any last drops as I set the bottle back on the table. "You asked me here, not the other way around."

"So I did." A sharp nod. "How much do you know about how the firm operates?"

"Which one, Webmasters or Lachesis?"

"Both."

"Webmasters produces educational and historical video games, and has a couple offices in the mid-Atlantic. It's a front, owned by Lachesis, which has people everywhere, in every city or region on the planet whether official or operating under the table or a pseudonym. Lachesis runs mundane businesses, or seemingly mundane businesses, and brings in enough to cover payroll. Three is a magic number—an office doesn't rank even as a branch unless it has three directors, and the bigger the office the more powerful officials it boasts. The more officers, the more likely the office does arcane things they can't report on tax forms." I held up my hands, teeth sore from grinding them together. "What do you expect me to know? You're the boss."

"Bob is the senior director of the Philly office although both Geneva and I have more years in the firm and far better track records of leading successful projects. He blocked my request to transfer to the Philly office twice. I only managed to shift here because my predecessor wanted to get back at Bob and teamed up with Geneva to vote me in." He drummed his fingers against the table.

"That stinks. How long ago?" The question slipped out before I could call it back. I snapped my mouth shut, hoping it wouldn't disturb the flow of new information.

"Three years." His gaze grew distant and for a moment his mouth shifted into a smile. "One week after I met Shauntelle.

Tradition has it that new directors are selected by a trio comprised of the current directors including whoever's moving up or out." The smile slipped away as fast as it had manifested. His brows lowered. "One of Bob's friends also wanted the seat. Bob voted against me, and made sure I knew it when his friend lost out. He has not done anything *explicit* since. I have nothing solid enough to take to the directorship review board, particularly given the officers currently appointed. They're the sort who want blatant actions in public with witnesses. I believe he has a grudge against me, and I certainly now have one against him."

"Got it." I took another swig, leaving only a little liquid to slosh at the bottom of the bottle. Easy to imagine the kind of officers he meant. I'd been like that myself, though I'd thought myself better then. Now I spent a lot more time second-guessing myself.

"Lachesis organized to protect the Web of Fate from interference. Webmasters . . ." He wrinkled his nose as if he'd tasted something sour, and drank from his mug. A hint of warmth emanated from him, and the next instant the aroma of fresh, hot coffee rose from his mug. "I dislike the name, but efforts to change it haven't gone anywhere, so Webmasters it is. No matter what the firm supposedly does, we're part of Lachesis first and foremost. Our primary mission remains ensuring the Web stays inviolate, and people choose their fortunes based on their circumstances. I looked at your thread and others,"—his fingers rubbed together and a glimmer of gray and yellow manifested again,—"but there are those who would do anything to be able to play with them. Warp the tapestry to do what they want and to hell with free will."

A heaviness settled onto my chest, making it hard to breathe. That the firm oversaw the Web of Fate I knew, but I'd barely pondered the rest. Of course some people objected, and no doubt plotted and more, but this was all way above my pay grade, and hardly something I expected to hear in a coffee shop.

"Let me guess. There's a conspiracy to take over the Web and rewrite it."

"There's always at least one, usually several. Most fail, but some succeed—for a while. Others we guess at, but can never prove." A low growl escaped him. "And yes, there's one in particular that's succeeding now."

"Why are you telling *me* this?" I leaned back in my chair.

"Because you're here, you work for the firm, and you would make an excellent witness."

"Witness?"

"The current conspiracy seems bent on rewriting Fate to add Atlantis and use that change to make the patterns of history bend to their preferences. I suspect an organized group of White supremacists with a better-than-usual understanding of the workings of Fate. In one day, we've gone from Smith's expedition being the butt of a thousand jokes to his being compared to Heinrich Schliemann, who located the city of Troy. But Troy existed—Atlantis didn't, until now."

He sat back. Lifted his coffee cup and drank. Set it back down. Lifted to drink again. Down.

All the while waiting and watching me.

Smart man. Instead of overwhelming me with details and evidence, he let me work through it myself. Didn't hurt that I'd lived through so many changes today with the news shifting in under an hour from Smith finding Atlantis to being partway through excavating it.

I raised my almost-empty bottle in a toast. The tactic worked, but only partway.

"Okay, I buy that someone or some people are probably behind Atlantis becoming real. That it's a conspiracy. And that Bob may be involved or at least aware." I crossed my arms over my chest. "That still doesn't explain why you're here talking about it with *me*. Not a webmaster, not even a sorcerer. A magical dud."

"Yet you resisted the change to the Web, when directors up and down the Eastern Seaboard and in several countries succumbed. Although you're not a sorcerer, you remind me of Tanisha—she's another with a strong sense of what is and what isn't. Magical dud you may be, but you combine an acceptance of magic with a very strong grasp of reality." A flash of a smile again. "My mother would call it righteous stubbornness."

"My mom, too, the stubborn part at least. Not the righteous, though I like being right."

"All that, and you're also unaligned. Neutral." He passed his hand over his mug and the remaining coffee returned to steaming. "It can be documented that you and I never exchanged a single word out of keeping with our positions until now."

"Got it." No doubt other factors played a part. The Philly office might be a backwater in terms of the company, but the city hosted a lot of conventions, and over the months I'd seen a good number of Lachesis directors from around the country and world stop by. They came from all races, ethnicities, genders, sexes, and more—but White men had more than their fair share of those with senior titles. My being White probably wouldn't hurt if this required some kind of testimony or witnessing in front of the directorship. "I'm will—"

"Don't agree too fast." He held up a finger. "If it comes to needing testimony from you, people won't go easy on you. At least a third will be convinced you're under my influence. They'll strip any and all protections off you and roll your memories out for everyone to view. Being in the right won't be any comfort when every stray thought and feeling is yanked out and mocked."

The ginger beer turned sour in my stomach. An itchy sensation crawled over my arms, legs, and back, as though all the spiders from earlier were palpating me with their legs. My breathing quickened and a zing of energy zipped along my spine.

Bad and good. I hardly wanted the scenario he described to take place. Yet, the very risk accompanied this being worth doing. Protecting Fate—and keeping Smith and his conspirators from turning Atlantis into a reality to remake the world on White supremacist lines.

I'd always wanted a quest. Here was a chance to do something really worthwhile. Deciding required only a few minutes consideration, even knowing I might spend much more time regretting.

"All right." I swallowed. "If that's what's required."

"Better would be for Tanisha to arrive with at least one other director unaffected by the conspiracy or some of her staff. Three of us can stand joint witness and use our prerogative to blast the sleaze—that's the usual term for the physical manifestation of an attempt to change Fate—out of the Web." He scowled. "If I could find other unaffected directors close enough to get here fast, I'd drag them in—but this thing has legs and it's tainting everything and everyone."

"Tanisha?" The person he'd called who hadn't been taken in by the Atlantis scheme . . . a sorcerer whom I reminded him of.

"From Sri Lanka, though she lives in Uruguay now. She co-leads Lachesis's investigative service." He sipped from the steaming mug. "A thread-cutter, also known as a minion of Atropos thanks to the founders' affection for classical Greece."

"I haven't heard even a whisper of them." My fingers itched to run some searches on the web for more information, but I entwined them together in my lap instead.

"You wouldn't. They're the last resort."

"She's coming here from Greece?"

"Worse. The new second headquarters in Montevideo. She says her team hasn't located any nearby directors they can guarantee are unaffected by this newest sleaze, other than me." Maksim's fingers swiped over his phone, awaking an app that gleamed red and purple. "Her crew will fly up to Bermuda, access Fate, and hike back in time and space from there."

A visualization of glowing lights and sparkles rose above his phone, forming a globe the size of my hand. Radiating a soft warmth, it rotated and displayed an arcing purple line headed up from about half to two-thirds down the coast of South America.

"They can't just . . ." I waved a hand. "Dematerialize there and appear here?" Neither of my sisters had ever mentioned any special travel spells, other than the one turning into a swan and flying around on occasion, something I still couldn't watch without losing the contents of my stomach.

"Short story: no." He grimaced. "Tanisha may be too late. Supposedly we have one lunar cycle from when a sleaze is planted to unroot it, but the longer it sits unchallenged, the worse our odds. Seems as though we've got less and less time these days.

"It can't wait." He braced both hands on the table. "We're close enough I aim to slide in and slow down the sleaze enough to let Tanisha's team get here."

"And you need a witness." My head hurt. I popped a third ibuprofen as I downed the last of the ginger beer. The carbonated liquid infused fizziness into every drop of liquid in my body. I was numb, or reeling, or something. The world whirled around me, moving faster than I—but I'd catch up later. Tomorrow or the day after. Wake up and wonder what the hell I'd agreed to.

For now, however, all that mattered was that he needed *me*. Finally a chance to do something, take action even if nothing more than watching something and reporting back under questioning.

"I need you to come with me into the Web, find the source of the sleaze, and document it." The globe illusion vanished as Maksim drummed his fingers against the table. "I'll disable it if I can, or at least freeze it or something, but only after you've seen enough."

My heartbeat sped up. I was going to have an adventure and make a difference! Though, before I said yes, this time I meant to make sure I understood the fine print.

I opened my mouth, but stopped before I could let loose the first of a dozen or more questions.

He straightened with a snap. Every muscle tensed. His body appeared ready to spring into action, and his eyes had a feverish tinge as he stared over my shoulder.

Twisting around, I scanned to see what had caught his attention. The clientele of the coffee shop had turned over some since I entered to mostly sightseers in their twenties and thirties.

With a notable exception: a Black boy standing right inside the door. Thin and gangly and about five feet at best, so maybe early teens. He had medium-brown skin with cool undertones highlighted by the angle of the sunlight through the windows, his tight curls cut short. Worn black-and-green Philadelphia Eagles sneakers adorned his feet and the Black Panther decorated his oversized T-shirt. One hand tucked into a pocket in his black jeans, and the other rested on the door handle as though ready to leave at any moment.

Until he caught sight of Maksim and started weaving his way toward us.

"What's wrong?" Nothing about the youth suggested any threat or danger.

"That's what I want to know." Maksim texted furiously away on his phone, glancing back and forth between it and the boy.

A ding announced the arrival of a text and most of the tension drained out of him, leaving annoyance and, if I was right, a measure of resignation.

Maksim gestured, and the noise of the coffee house burst into full clamor. So too did the scents. I hadn't realized how much his privacy spell had blocked the aromas of coffees and teas along with voices.

The boy snagged a free chair from an empty table nearby and turned it around so he perched on it backward. Rocking forward, he leaned his elbows on our table. Dark-brown eyes to either side of a short nose in a round face glanced back and forth between us.

"Hi, Eli."

Maksim restored veil protecting us, reducing noises and smells to their previous negligible levels even as the new arrival made a face at him.

"Hey, step-pop."

❧   4   ❧

The Penn & Cup had the worst washroom, all chrome and glass and showing every fingerprint. Smudged mirrors everywhere, maybe to make it seem bigger. I could turn around well enough, and a good thing considering the room was marked unisex and wheelchair accessible, but that was about it. Bright as noon too since the florescent overhead lights reflected off of everything.

A potpourri jar in cheap glass sat on the counter in the far corner. The pierced holes in the chrome top allowed whiffs of lavender and rose to escape and cover less pleasant scents. The flower petals shone dimly against the semi-transparent sides, pale pink and purple.

I ran the water for a couple minutes, dashing cool droplets over my face and neck. My shirt sucked up any escaping rivulets of water, but the dark green hid the dampness.

The unrelenting brightness made my eyes smart. No matter often I blinked, flashes of color teased me—though I caught them only in my peripheral vision. A flicker of burgundy red to the right. I turned. Nothing to see but grays and my own reflection of black, beige, and green. A burst of gold to the left, but again it vanished when I whirled.

The contents of the jar shifted, a splash of orange appearing where I'd have sworn there wasn't any. A hint of citrus mingled with the lavender.

With a last splash of water on my face, I turned the faucet off and got out of the room while the getting was still good.

Only to have my phone go off in the tiny square waiting area between the restroom doors and the coffee house proper. "Who's Afraid of the Big Bad Wolf" rang out, and I meant to send her to voice mail but flubbed it. I slunk around the corner and leaned against the wall facing the back door, its glass covered with finger smudges and a fine layer of dust. Layers of old flyers were taped and plastered to the wall, crumpling beneath my back.

"Rosalind, I swear you're more stubborn with every day. How many calls did it take for you to answer one this time? A dozen?"

Chatter from the bar and seating area provided a distraction, but not enough sound to justify ending the call immediately. Especially given the cadence of my mother's voice.

"I've been busy."

"Sure you have, avoiding me. You don't have to come home if you don't want to, though there'll always be space for you, but answer when I call, at least every third try. It is it so much to ask? Your brother manages three out of five, and surely you can match him."

Her words washed over me—until they didn't. My fingers tightened around the phone, eyes fixed on the blurry mix of people walking this way and that along the street. Tourists seeing the sights. Business people heading home. Groups of twenty-somethings and thirty-somethings out crawling pubs.

"My brother?"

"One year and nine months older, minus a week, because a woman bears sons before daughters, of course." A sniff, the kind of sound I'd rarely heard from her. "Bane of your life growing up, him always having gone everywhere and done everything before you no matter how hard you tried to catch up. Remember him?"

"I don't have a brother."

A vague image began to form in my mind's eye. I clenched my jaw, gritted my teeth, and refused to let it manifest. Denied it and envisioned my sisters instead.

My middle sister, Viola, almost as tall as me, always pushing up her glasses as they slipped down her nose because even though she'd turned sorcerer, she'd hadn't found a good spell to keep them in place. She'd be dressed in natural fibers and nibbling on some godawful bean jerky since she'd gone vegan.

Then my youngest sister, Bea, a good six inches or more shorter and built on solid lines. Mom's logistics expert who enjoyed planning outings to the nth degree, and could pack anything more efficiently than anyone else. Strangers sometimes took one look at her and pegged her as a softie, but Mom always said Bea was *almost* as stubborn and pigheaded as me.

"Of course you don't. Things didn't work out that way, but I hope you never felt a great loss." Mom broke the long silence, her voice turning as cheery and determined as before. "Your sisters are both here and would love to see you. We're all hoping you can at least make it out to say hi one day. Monday, perhaps? I'll drive you back in."

"Maybe." Unexpected temptation swirled in my belly. What a shift, considering how recently I'd determined to stay away. "Let me think about it—but I promised to work some overtime this weekend. Can I get back to you?"

Of course I could. Mom was a firm believer in the efficacy

of water-on-stone methods of getting me to do her will. She'd take a tentative *no* now and follow up tomorrow if I didn't get back to her.

I slipped the phone back into my pocket but remained in place. On the other side of the glass, a trio of White guys in search of a good time paused. All dressed in soccer and football team T-shirts, jeans, sneakers, and with crew cut hair slicked back—and oddly familiar although I couldn't place them. One, daringly wearing the logo for one of the Philly Eagles' bitter rivals on his shirt, peered through the glass. Hadn't he seen the coffee house signs? The Penn and Cup didn't serve alcohol.

A hazy image of my nonexistent brother threatened to manifest—along those exact lines. Mom had really believed in him for a few moments, though she'd shifted back to normal fast enough.

I refused to believe. After-images of my *real, flesh-and-blood* sisters danced in my head, trampling the last vestiges of the brother-silhouette.

Turning away from the guy gazing through the glass, I forged through the maze of chairs and tables, now two-thirds occupied at best, to the corner where Maksim and Eli sat.

I'd been gone a good five or ten minutes, but they seemed not to have moved a hair or stretched a muscle, not even to smile or frown. Maksim had refreshed his coffee, and a glass of water sat in front of Eli. Even my ginger beer bottle remained.

I hung back, but Maksim gestured for me to join them. He hadn't cast any privacy screen, because I could hear Eli's high voice several steps away. Based on the lack of any hint of his voice starting to break, he seemed younger than I'd thought before. Perhaps only twelve or so, on the cusp of puberty.

"All I want's to go hang at David's. You tell Mom or Gramma I'm there, they'll be all smiles. That's all I'm asking."

"Weren't you having an overnight with Jason?" Maksim asked.

"Nah." Eli's chin sank toward his chest. "Not any more. He might've, kind of seen magic and did a fall back. Took back the invite."

I settled into the chair I'd left, still at the same angle, glancing between them because this didn't seem the right moment to rejoin no matter that I'd got the go-ahead.

"You already know about fall backs, don't you?" Eli gave me a side-eye, in between frowning at Maksim.

"Ah, not by that name . . ." Unsure whether he was looking for an ally or an ear into which to pour his troubles, I avoided making eye contact. Instead I squinted at the liquid in the bottle I'd drained. Picked it up and sniffed. Carbonated bubbles with a whiff of ginger rose to tickle my nose.

A new bottle or a magical refill. Either way, I lifted it and nodded at Maksim in thanks. His lips twitched in acknowledgment, but his eyes never ceased shifting between watching Eli and scanning the areas behind us.

"You don't already know . . ." Eli's shoulders inched up toward his shoulders. "You are a sorcerer, aren't you?"

"She did a half-turn." Maksim answered before I could. He drew a circle on the table, and the privacy spell snapped back into place around us so fast my ears popped.

"A what?"

"Turned enough to believe in magic, but not work it," Maksim said as he ran a finger along the edge of his mug.

"That's a real jawn, getting stuck halfway? I wouldn't've guessed. Thought people only ever were born sorcerers, born mundane and turned sorcerers, or born and stayed mundane." He sat straight up, face alight. "Hey, you think Jason might—"

"Not if he's already pushing you away." Maksim leaned

forward and gripped Eli's hand. "Be patient. He might get back to being friends with you when he finishes forgetting about magic."

One glimpse of the fading hope on Eli's face had me wishing myself further away. The less he knew I heard—couldn't avoid—the better. The face of a beloved childhood friend came to mind, one who'd shunned me when we hit puberty. We'd never talked again, but I could hope for better for Eli.

I shifted my seat so as to focus on the smoky glass and the crowds outside. Not so many tourists with young families anymore, more people in their twenties and thirties looking for a good time.

The loud urp of someone swallowing hard.

"It hurts, I know. He may come around in a week or two," Maksim said.

"But where does that leave me tonight?" Eli swallowed water and then slammed the glass down, rocking the table. "I can't stay home."

Seven or eight White men in T-shirts and jeans clumped on the other side of the glass. One cupped his hands around his face as he pressed close and gazed through. His eyes met mine for a moment, but then he moved on though he studied Maksim for several long moments. Nothing about him struck a chord in me, but one or two of his companions seemed vaguely familiar—as though I'd seen them but in sufficiently different circumstances to not easily make the connections.

"Why not? The shower isn't until tomorrow. Go up to your room and close the door." An abstracted note entered Maksim's voice. He held a spoon, angling the bowl this way and that. His other hand doodled on the table.

"Why aren't you there either?" Eli stamped his feet. "Shower mightn't be yet, but there're so many already there setting up they might as well have it tonight. Gramma, half of

Moms's friends, your mother and sisters even came up special for tomorrow starting now. They're everywhere with all sorts of glitter and ribbons and gift wrap and stuff. There's no room for me!"

A chill ran down my spine, having nothing to do with the cool bottle that slipped from my loosened grasp to settle on the table with a thud.

The man who'd checked through the glass pointed this way and that, sending the other men in different directions.

"What're you working?" Flickers of purple caught my eye. I turned to study the spell Maksim had drawn on the table with a bit of spilled coffee.

The liquid formed lines outlining a map of the blocks around the coffee house, clearly marked with the pen-in-cup logo. Blinking purple dots from up and down the streets converged on the coffee shop.

"That's—" Eli startled, nearly overturning the table. Maksim grabbed his wrist before he could touch the surface.

"I recognize some of them from the Atlantis True Believers' website. Them heading here can't be a coincidence—my calling Bob might have tipped him off . . . Eli, you get out the back door and run straight home." Maksim shifted to shake his stepson's hand and let go. He swiveled around, pointing a finger right at me. "Rose, in or out? There's still time for you to get away."

Twisting around, I counted the trickle of White men slipping into the shop and gathering at the entrance. Five, six . . . My neck and back muscles protested as I whipped around to check the side door—another there along with two women.

"I'm in." Might as well be known for the company I kept —and the enemies I made. I'd never desired the role of witness, as I'd always envisioned myself a champion helping forge a new path, but at least I'd be doing something for good.

"I'm in too." Eli's chair legs scraped against the floor as he pushed back a foot, but he didn't rise. "I'm not leaving you."

"You need to go home." Maksim snatched the backpack from the floor and swung it over one shoulder. "I'm counting on you to help protect your mother."

"Nah." Eli made a face. "With all the sorcerers at home, Moms's gotta be safer than you. Gramma could take on any army of sorcerers single-handed, you know she could, and that's not counting your family."

"You keep believing that." Maksim patted Eli's cheek, then his hand slid down to grab the boy's wrist again. "Your mother will be mad as all get out at me for putting you in danger. Too late for you to get out, though."

Even through the privacy shield, the clamor of conversation in the coffee house dropped. Ten, eleven men now. Bad odds. I swallowed, mouth suddenly dry and breath shallow.

"Rose," Maksim said.

I swung around to find him pointing at me again.

"We got to get out of here. Open your phone to a webpage, any webpage."

"On it." Fumbling, I drew my phone from my pocket. Nearly dropped it as approaching footsteps made the floorboards vibrate, but held tight. With a few flicks of my finger, I brought up the browser open to the usual search engine. "Ready."

Maksim's free hand wrapped around my wrist.

A flash of light made my eyes water. I blinked, but endless brightness met my eyes time after time. It took ten, twenty, thirty breaths before my sight settled enough for me to really look around.

Not that looking around mattered. The same view faced me no matter which way I turned, even when I pulled free of Maksim's hold and whirled around and around. Or stood and tilted my head back or studied the ground beneath my feet.

There was no floor, no ceiling, no walls, nothing except whiteness and a familiar logo straight ahead of me. A search box floated about even with my chest. Far smaller, a header hung up and left and a footer near my ankles. Everything moved with me, ensuring I saw nothing else.

And Maksim to one side and presumably Eli beyond, both also staying in the same position vis-a-vis me no matter where I moved—or rather tried to. I couldn't look at them straight on. They were always in a line, with Maksim's larger body mostly blocking view of Eli.

Almost all sounds ceased. My ears perked, straining for anything: the thump of footsteps or the clink of drinks poured and savored. Only hoarse breathing broke the quiet, my own and at least one other's by the faint whistle that didn't come from me.

My lungs struggled to drag in air, although I seemed to be breathing okay. No more scents of coffee or ginger beer, only a sour hint of sweat and a fading whiff of sandalwood from Maksim's cologne.

Neither was there any warmth or cold or anything. My fingers shook as I reached out to touch the multi-colored logo—only to pass right through it. Or occupy the same spot simultaneously.

"Where the Hell are we?"

From the other side, Eli's voice overlapped mine asking roughly the same thing.

No matter how I tried, I failed to turn around and glare at Maksim for dropping us in this strange place that made the skin along my shoulders creep.

Around and around I whirled—clockwise then counter-clockwise—without anything changing. This seemed the kind of place a person could scream forever and never be heard.

Maksim didn't reply at first. He was panting, and a sour sweaty smell started to override the last of his cologne.

Eli kept talking, babbling and running words together to the point I didn't understand anything except the general gist that he didn't like this any more than I did.

Nervous energy flooded my veins. My breathing sped, sweat streaking my face and chest. I gave in to the urge and screamed hard and long.

"ENOUGH!"

A louder shout overrode me and shocked me into silence. Echoes of Maksim's hoarse yell bounced around my head for a few moments. Chest heaving, I dragged in long, deep breaths.

"We're in the internet, on Rose's phone." Maksim made a harsh sound. "And if the two of you'll be quiet long enough for me to think, I'll get us out of here. Just give me a moment of silence."

With that lure, I kept my mouth shut. Barely let even a whisper of a breath out.

The promised moment stretched for minutes. Hands shaking, I turned my phone to view the screen. Three small, human forms did indeed fill a portion of the screen. There was magic and magic, and this beat the spiders popping out of the carpet for strangeness.

What had I gotten myself into?

Maksim had pulled out his own phone and was texting away.

"I'm telling your mother you're with me, and I'll do my best to keep you safe." He stroked Eli's head, as the boy leaned against him.

"Ready?" Maksim slipped a hand down to take Eli's, and grabbed my wrist with the other, fingers tighter this time.

Another flash filled my eyes with light as the world changed again.

⚘   5   ⚘

Warmth and darkness enveloped me. Layers upon layers. Softness beyond imagination. All discomfort faded away. No aches or pains, hunger or thirst. My body curled in upon itself. Knees nestled against my chest, arms wrapped over my legs, and head lolled on my shoulder.

Something rocked me, a slow swaying as though I lay in a cradle.

Or a womb.

Or spiderweb.

A frisson of ice rippled across my skin, leaving goose-bumps everywhere in its wake. Startled, I opened my eyes. A gray mistiness filled my sight—but not an everyday gray. This held an iridescence reminiscent of full-color photographs of distant galaxies and stars.

The softness supporting me fell away, leaving me unsteady but on my feet. The ground or surface or whatever was below me had a gentle give, rather like standing on a lawn of thick, vibrant grass.

Although I had no idea what I stood on, I didn't look down—too busy taking in the unexpected beauty above.

Rainbow-colored clouds of gasses formed spirals and curves. Shades of the Northern or Southern Lights, so bright and colorful beyond anything I'd ever seen. More varied than in any photo, and so close I could almost touch them. They simmered and flared, rising and falling in some rhythm I couldn't hear, mixed with a soft, deep crooning and the sense that if I stayed still and quiet long enough, I'd hear what they said even if I never understood it.

Between and behind the celestial illumination lay thousands, millions, of stars in differing colors and intensities overhead—white, blue, red, yellow. Here and there, faint lines stretched from star to star, as though a cosmic connect-the-dots.

Bits of cobweb, some thick as rope and others thinner than thread, dripped from my arms. They had a tacky feel when I plucked them from my skin, but when I shivered they dissolved into warm flecks of light that danced as if fireflies darting up to join the stars. Running a hand through my hair, I loosened more strands of web that likewise disintegrated in my fingers.

As before, the air held neither chill nor heat, though the womb-like warmth lingered in my bones.

A distant, celestial perfume wafted around, along with the sense that something breathed in an immense, slow drag and then exhaled four times as long. An occasional breeze fluttered around, occasionally running up my arm or leg, but otherwise the air was still.

My eyes began to adjust to dancing gasses amidst the endless reaches of space—and I made the mistake of looking down.

An infinite web of lines stretched out in all directions. The strands crisscrossed at any and all angles, going every which way. Most were transparent except for minor flickers at the edges of my eyes, while the thicker showed their edges as faint luminescence tinged with silver or copper, green or gold.

The one directly beneath my feet had enough breadth for me to stand without sensing any slant or slipping to either side. I bent down to touch it, to verify it existed, and my fingers stroked something as soft and warm as a baby's skin.

But beneath it . . .

The world lay so far below that I could almost see the curvature of the earth. Cities glowed with multi-colored lights, outlining the Atlantic seaboard while deep blue-black lines marked rivers and mountains, fields and seas. I pulled my arms and legs in, elbows pressing tight against my sides just in case I slipped.

Wait a minute. Why was the earth showing as though it were night? The sun hadn't even started setting when we sat in the coffee house.

A sudden chittering in my right ear had me turning my head so fast the bones in my spine crackled. A gray and brown spider no bigger than my thumbnail perched on my shoulder. It talked at me, then gave up.

The next moment, it ran down my arm and launched itself from my wrist. A thin strand of webbing floated in its wake as gusts of celestial wind carried it several feet to land on the same thick strand as I stood—but where Maksim sat cradling Eli in his arms.

The boy had his head buried in the older man's chest. His arms were tucked tight, and his body curled into the same fetal position I'd assumed earlier—but he appeared far less comfortable. Maksim's body too held an echo of the posture, with his shoulders curved as his head rested against Eli's and he rocked the boy in his arms.

"I know. I know. The sheer power hits us hard." A hint of moisture gleamed on Maksim's face, trickling in lines from the corners of his eyes. "I'm sorry I had to bring you here without warning. Breathe in and out. In and out. Let the magic flow through you."

Evidently, the place hit sorcerers a lot harder than duds such as me. I rubbed my hands together and rolled my shoulders. Didn't like feeling as though I'd missed things, but this was hardly the first time. I'd got used to it. Or not.

I waited, arms clutching my shoulders, as Maksim eased Eli. Breath by breath, Eli's body relaxed and unwound from his curved position. At length he pulled back, rubbing his eyes.

Maksim stood, offering Eli a hand up. The boy took it, then he caught sight of me and his face scrunched into a defensive scowl. His glare practically dared me to mention he'd been crying.

A low ache lined my throat, no doubt from my scream earlier. I broke into a fit of coughing, but managed a couple of key words and a glare of my own for Maksim. "Explanation time?"

"We're in the Web of Fate." Maksim opened his backpack and pulled out water bottles for each of us. "Drink and keep drinking. There are more where these came from. You need to drink a lot more water than you usually do."

"That's not an answer." I should've saved my breath, as merely speaking the words triggered flares of pain along my throat. The water—lukewarm and tasteless—helped, but it wasn't magic.

"Water?" Eli made a face. "Yuck. How about some Dr. Pepper . . ."

He started to gesture, but Maksim grabbed Eli's hand before he could work a spell.

"It stays water, the better to keep hydrated. We're at the magical equivalent of 10,000 feet above sea level. Do you want altitude sickness?"

"No." Eli unscrewed the cap and took a swig, wrinkling his nose. "But if you have to make me drink water, you could've at least brought reusable water bottles rather than this plastic junk."

"And where would we refill them?" Maksim drained his bottle in three glugs. He dropped the empty back into his bag as he slung it over his shoulder. Turning around, he raised a finger pointing this way and that as he studied the world below.

I mirrored his stance and head angle, but saw nothing other than the same glorious—and scary—world far below.

"How we always do. A finger snap to summon more water." Eli hefted his bottle as though about to throw it down between strands.

Maksim nabbed the bottle and wrapped the boy's fingers tighter around it. "We don't summon water in Fate, and we don't litter. Anything we bring in, we take back out with us."

Eli scuffed a sneaker against the thick thread supporting us, which showed no mark of any kind. He poured water into his mouth, gargling for several breaths before swallowing.

"I'm sorry." Maksim ran a hand across Eli's back. "I wouldn't've brought you here so sudden if I'd had a choice. But I wanted you safe, and this was the simplest and easiest. There's a thousand things I should've told you about being here beforehand, but we had no time."

"So, maybe get started on those thousand things?" I filled the brief silence, before the two could get sidetracked by water and spells again. "We're in the Web of Fate, but what does that mean?"

"The Web of Fate, or Fate for short." Stretching out his arms, Maksim turned around in a circle. He cast a wide shadow against the cosmic clouds arching and flickering behind. "Also known as time or history or a half dozen other things. At the moment, we're at roughly 39,9500 degrees

North by 75.1438 degrees West and 6:15pm Eastern time on the first of July."

Such precision, but he'd missed a detail or three. I recognized the numbers as longitude and latitude, but otherwise they meant nothing to me. Nevertheless, I accepted his description as accurate or almost. "And, what, a mile above sea level?"

"We're not above sea level. We're in Fate, where time is not linear." Smiling, he drew a line of light a foot long before his chest. Within moments, the light bent and curved before dissolving into nothingness. "If anything, it is similar to earth's geology with hemispheres and continents and continental drift."

I stood with my mouth open and round as a fish. Eli was much the same. He rubbed his arms and scowled as he kept chugging water.

Maksim's chest huffed with laughter. "Boiled down, that means we're in Fate above Philly right now."

"And the guys from the coffee house can't get here?"

"They can get here—if they have a fully-fledged director with them." Another grimace from him, very reminiscent of Eli's scowl even though they weren't biologically related. "But they'll have to go sideways as I did."

"You're sure?" A shudder ripped through me, leaving my muscles a little less tense. "So we might be safe?"

"Once we're in motion, they can't catch us until we stop— and they'll have to make it to the exact time, place, and space." He clapped his hands and stared at Eli until the boy stood straight, arms at his side. "Here's the plan: we hike southwest the equivalent of eight or nine hundred miles and back in time about two millennia to the location of the Atlantis that Jack Smith supposedly found and that should not exist for him to find. There, we will locate the sleaze.

Rose will stand witness. And with any luck, Tanisha's team will arrive shortly thereafter to help purify Fate. We clear?"

"Jack Smith? You mean we're going to see Atlantis?" Eli pumped his arms. "Cool."

"Nah. Atlantis never existed." Maksim crossed his arms over his chest. "Smith's part of a conspiracy. We're going to stop him."

Eli scuffed a foot against the surface below, which gave slightly. "Be more fun if it were real."

I bent down. Bracing myself with two hands on the strand, a warm, soft surface with a distant pulse, I peered over the edge at the city below. Being so far above the earth should make the hike across space—if not time—shorter.

Though what did I know about magic except that others could work minor and major miracles?

"And why do we have hike? Can't we jump?" Eli asked.

"Not from here." Maksim palmed his phone and held it up, the surface turned to a compass. "If we'd entered Fate through the Webmasters' office we could've at least positioned ourselves closer—but there wasn't time to get there safely. The fastest route into Fate was sideways through the internet, and that put us here."

"There's a . . . an entry point . . . in the office?" I blinked, flipping back through memories of the suite and coming up empty except for one of the directors' offices.

"The carpet. Maintaining it isn't easy. It takes three directors averaging sixty to a hundred hours a week in the office between us." Maksim weighed his phone, then sighed and slipped it into his pocket. "No use for this."

"Not even for a photo?" I extracted mine from my pocket, only to find the screen flickering inconsistently.

"It won't work in Fate. No externally-dependent technology does." Maksim said. "Now let's get moving. While we are not getting any older, every moment we waste talking and not walking risks the sleaze weaving itself deeper into the web—or the villains catching up with us."

Yet even he didn't immediately start off. Rather, he reached for the gray spider still clinging to his shoulder. He positioned a finger next to the spider, and it deposited a thin filament of webbing across it. "Thank you, my sister."

The spider leapt off, vanishing into the air mid-jump.

After that, Maksim started walking.

He got all of four feet before I snapped my mouth shut—I'd gaped so long my lips and tongue started to dry—and scrambled into motion. I followed with Eli alongside me at first. The thick strand of web remained broad enough for three to walk abreast without risk of slipping. All the same, Eli hurried until he was a couple steps ahead of me and caught up with Maksim first.

"I still don't see why not use a refillable water bottle," the boy grumbled.

"Magic doesn't just pull water from out of the air, it relocates it from somewhere else." The older man grinned down at him. "We're traveling back in time, and any spell to refill the water bottle would pull from the 'now' of whenever we are. It would be drinkable by then-current standards, but not necessarily ours."

"Which means what? It'll taste bad?"

"Or make you sick." Maksim pulled another full bottle from his bag and waved it at Eli, then me. "Keep drinking. I don't want any of you getting time sickness."

I followed, dutifully draining my bottle.

Time sickness?

"Is this going to be boring?" A heavy sigh from Eli.

"I can only hope." Maksim laughed, but he turned his head and made a face where the boy wouldn't see. His gaze met mine, only because he glanced around constantly.

Got me doing the same thing, skin itchy even though I

saw no sign of anyone else. Or anything else. We seemed to have the web all to ourselves.

All the same . . .

"Expecting trouble?" I kept my voice low, scarcely above a whisper.

"Always."

❧ 6 ❧

Thick strands stretched out as far as the eye could see. All we had to do was head for the horizon. Hiking in Fate should be a walk in the celestial park.

Hah.

The surface beneath us had a soft cushiness to it, bouncing with every step. As a result, no steps were level with each other. The translucence shifted as we walked. Sometimes it had a frosty tinge and other times only a hint of blue luminescence indicated it existed below our feet. Our journey combined the worst of glass floors and trampolines: I could see far below *and* failed to manage as little as two steady steps in a row.

Bonus: irregular pulses of energy that rippled along the length of the strand, sometimes in the same direction and other times reversing. Each pulse brought energy and a sudden burst of warmth flooding through me. None had knocked me down or even off-stride—yet.

Worse, the strand wasn't flat or straight. No matter how wide it stretched—and it expanded as needed—the sides curved. Those I avoided by keeping to the center as much as possible. I couldn't avoid the tiniest downhill slant. Although unnoticeable at first, the farther I walked the more my shins and calves ached.

All of that plus other strands that crossed this one. The smallest made no difference as they went beneath the larger but left a relatively flat surface for us to cross. One or two bigger strands wrapped around, forcing us to clamber over waist-high obstacles. Other big strands mashed together to form an uneven checkerboard. These proved particularly troublesome, as the surfaces varied from almost-level to a half-foot drop with each step.

The celestial aroma of stars and flowers, so lovely at first whiff, faded. No winds blew, but the air around us changed and the smell with it, so fast I couldn't keep up. One minute my eyes watered over onion juice, that turned to sea brine, then on to sweat and mud and dozens, hundreds of other scents.

In the silence, the sense of someone talking in the distance—a thousand, million, billion someones, and if I only listened hard enough I'd hear and understand what they said.

Maksim strode forward with the air of a man who knew where we were going.

I followed in his wake, trying to step where he did. Since he had several inches on me, I wound up either taking three strides for two of his or stretching my legs farther than comfortable.

Safer I might be, but in no way at ease.

Especially when watching Eli test the borders of the strand. First he tiptoed partway to the edge and peered over at the glittering lights far below. Retreated, only to edge out two steps further. For every three steps he took forward, he moved one further to the side.

"What if I fall?" He flashed a big grin at Maksim.

"Don't." The older man snapped his fingers, and part of the strand lifted.

Eli held his stance as the surface below him curved up enough to send him sliding down. Maksim's torso bent and an "oof" escaped him as Eli pitched into him.

"How'd you do that?" Eli dropped to hands and knees and inspected the surface.

Maksim grunted and marched on. I followed. Of the two of us, I was the only one to glance backward.

Eli let us get about fifteen feet ahead before he jumped to his feet and pelted after us. Within a few steps, he stopped. A pulse rippled through. His right foot slid one way and his left the other, stretching his legs almost into splits.

"Are you okay?" I stopped.

"What happened?" Maksim asked, turning around.

Before I could answer, Eli raised both hands in the air.

"Watch this!" He'd evidently noticed a pulse heading down the strand. He ran a short way, then lined up his feet on the very center of the line as though riding a skateboard—or surfboard—and slid forward on the pulse.

Kept on sliding. Passed us with a whoop, and a high-pitched whistling from where his shoes met the strand. The otherwise still air seethed and whirled in his wake.

"Stop at the next major cross-line." Maksim cupped his hands around his mouth and called after the boy. He shook his head, muttering under his breath, "I was hoping he wouldn't figure that trick out."

"You've done it, I take it?" The center of the strand no longer held quite as much appeal, not if it turned slippery under certain circumstances.

"A couple of times, until I overshot my destination by several centuries. It wasn't the inconvenience of trudging back—you can slide on fate-lines in any direction—so much as the mockery of my fellow trainees." His lips tightened.

"Few things can sour a person more than being laughed at in public."

"Being called out." I clenched my teeth together to keep any more words from slipping out.

Maksim sent a sharp look my way. "Is that what happened?"

I looked down rather than meet his gaze.

Big mistake. The strand—or rather fate-line—had turned almost completely transparent. Thousands of lights twinkled below. Before, they'd traced the eastern coast of North America, brighter for big cities but glowing in a facsimile of images from satellites or the space station.

No longer.

The lights gleamed in a couple dozen different colors and shades, and were scattered and clumped in ways that bore no resemblance to locations of cities and towns. The colors delineated the difference between land and sea—with the lights on the continent being greens, yellows, and browns while the sea boasted blues and purples.

"What's with the flickering lights?" I no longer walked in Maksim's footsteps but rather trailed to one side.

"Where?" Maksim waved his hands to either side.

With perfect timing, gouts of gasses burst into bright pulsing red lights to the upper left and vibrant blues on the direct right.

"Down there. Below us. I thought they were the cities, you know, blazing the sea coast from DC up to Boston, but they aren't glowing so strong there anymore."

"The lights?" He let out a long whistling breath, shaking his head with his lips thin and pressed together. "They're not showing where islands and seas are. This isn't a globe beneath us—at least, not a representation of land and sea. The lights are life-stars. Each represents a type of life— human, animal, bird, insect, fish. Plants, too. The more lives in any one place at a particular point in time, the stronger the light."

He paused long enough to throw a grin my way, then headed on to the cross-line where Eli explored the fate-line's trampoline properties.

Surfing the line looked such fun. Temptation rose within me, irresistible. I rolled my shoulders, making my spine crackle, and drew in a deep breath. A few quick scuffs against the surface of the fate-line, and I hopped into motion.

Only to stumble three steps and fall flat on my face.

My nose smacked against the warm surface, but my hands braced me in time to keep from hitting harder. This meant my palms took the brunt of my weight and smarted enough to wring a high "ow."

Evidently surfing required sorcery, bloody stupid magic power. My eyes grew wet, but I refused to cry. I'd gotten used to not being able to work magic. I *had*. I could smile when one of my sisters showed off their latest spell, and congratulate them with a heart full of happiness for them.

And sadness for me.

I wasn't going there. Too many tangled memories of falling short. What I couldn't do, I couldn't do. Better to focus on what I *could*. After all, dud or not, Maksim had asked me to serve as a witness.

Not treat Fate as a playground.

He'd turned around at my cry, and started back toward me but I waved him to keep on.

"I'll catch up." Once I pried myself off the fate-line. First I rose to my knees and inspected my hands. Bits of celestial matter flickered on them before winking out, bit by bit. My nose ached, if not as much as my hands. Getting up from my knees without putting my hands back on the line took a little time, and revealed additional aches on my kneecaps and ankles, but I made it.

A few moments later I caught up as Maksim and Eli navigated not one, not two, but three cross-lines in close proximity, all large enough that they'd mashed together.

Blech.

The intersections pulsed all the time, sometimes receiving bolts of energy along one fate-line or another, and other times sending them off. Even when not doing either, a residual aura set made my teeth ache and the hairs on the back of my neck stiffen.

I picked my way across the bumps and sinkholes where the fate-lines met, trying not to lose a shoe or my balance. Maksim offered a hand as did Eli, after a subtle nudge from his stepfather.

No. If they could make it on their own, so could I. I followed behind as we shifted from a fate-line heading southeast, to one canting off to the east, then a second tilting south, and back southwest but on a different line.

All that effort, and we ended up on a line paralleling the one we'd first taken except a couple of yards over.

I traded my empty water bottle for a full one as we paused after the last cross-line. Gulped a third of the new one down in record time. Before restoring the top, I dipped a finger and traced droplets across my heated forehead and cheeks.

Maksim gauged the length of fate-line stretching out ahead of us. There wasn't another cross-line for quite a ways.

"One, two. Reverse. One, two, three. Reverse." Eli crouched down, fingertips resting on the line and counting the pulses as they went forward or back.

"You plan to try surfing again?" The older man knelt next to the boy, but laid the flat of his hand against the line.

"Yeah."

The next pulse through took on a yellow-pink glow. The fate-line widened further in its wake.

"Fine. Don't go past the next cross-line—and don't fall."

"Got it." Eli beamed and took off, riding the crest of a pulse as it swooped down the line.

"I thought you didn't want him to surf the line." Since it remained wide even after Eli passed, I ventured to walk alongside Maksim rather than behind.

"Since that cat's out of the bag, he might as well enjoy it," Maksim said. "This is as safe as he can be. We can't be caught until we reach our destination."

"You said that before. Why not?" I watched the light show undulating in clouds around us, wishing I could capture it in some way. The beauty and serenity of our surroundings were so much at odds with why we were here.

"As far as anyone else who travels this fate-line is concerned—even ourselves, should we walk it in the future —we're nothing more than energy pulsing one way or another."

"You mean . . ." I jumped a moment later as power raced down the line, sending a zip of static electricity up me as it passed.

"That could be our pursuers. Or someone else who went this way, or will go." Maksim hadn't flinched at the pulse, and gained steps on me. He snapped his fingers and cast me a narrow look. "Forget anything you've ever read about time-travel, it's wrong or backward. None of it applies to the Web of Fate."

"Then what does?" I crossed my arms over my chest, gripping my elbows. "I never heard much about the Web, at least not so far as I remember. I thought it was virtual."

"Well, it is, or it couldn't connect up to the internet so easily, but it's a lot more than that." He rubbed a hand against the back of his neck. "I'm not a teacher, and I don't know what you need to know about being here. There's so much I can't even begin to think where to start, but I can at least answer questions. Lay them on me, my sister."

"Ah . . ." I had as much trouble figuring out where to start as he did. "Give me a sec."

Eli had evidently gotten tired of waiting for us, for he surfed back our way. A pulse traveled down the fate-line, going our way not his. He tried to jump over it, but stumbled instead. Whirling a half-circle, he tilted and swayed though he stayed upright. His unsteady steps tipped him close to the edge.

With a muttered curse, Maksim swooped up. He grabbed Eli's arm and planted him in the middle of the line. The older man set his hands on the boy's shoulders and shook, then crouched and wrapped him in a bear hug.

"Don't fall. Don't fall. I'd find you but I might not be in time." Low though Maksim's voice was, it carried in the celestial stillness.

"I would've made it. I got my feet under me." Eli wriggled within the embrace, but not to the point he broke out.

"You could've fallen, and we're going the wrong way." Maksim pulled back and cupped Eli's face in his hands. "People have lost their wits falling into time. Surf away, but only if you can take care."

Eli laid his hands atop Maksim's, fingers several inches shorter and a few steps lighter. He bit his lip, then nodded. "Okay, already." He squirmed, but after Maksim straightened up, Eli snuggled up against the older man's right side, glaring to make sure I didn't make any deal of it.

"Ask what you want about Fate." Maksim nodded at me as we started along.

Eli's eyes narrowed.

The rabbit hole of Maksim's reference to falling into time tempted me, but first I wanted something more basic.

"How are we going to find whatever it is we're looking for?"

Whatever Eli expected, I managed to surprise him. He

frowned and tilted his head to the side, then turned to his stepfather with an enquiring air.

"Good one. I should've thought you'd want to know that. Got a lot more respect for teachers now." Maksim nodded and shook his head at the same time. He drew in a deep breath. Without breaking his stride, he extended his left hand.

At first, it appeared as an ordinary hand. Standard issue: four fingers and a thumb, each with slightly ragged nails, attached to a palm and back of the hand, leading to the wrist

. . .

A moment later, a thick silvery-gray rope made of thousands of individual strings appeared. The rope wrapped twice around his wrist then ran across his hand up the index finger. From the tip of his finger, the rope divided and angled in dozens of directions all leading in the same way we headed although only a few aligned with our path. Even as I watched they kept splitting in two and multiplying, making the rope thicken. The near end trailing off his wrist was much slimmer than the section resting against his finger.

Maksim waited without saying anything, a smile playing around the corners of his mouth and growing broader with every step.

"What's that?" Eli squinted at the rope, then poked it with a finger. He didn't seem able to touch it, so he poked at it again before retreating and pulling slightly away from Maksim.

"Do you remember Bob? The senior director at Webmasters? He came to the wedding last year. The man in the light blue suit and the stars-and-stripes tie." Maksim waved his right hand over his left and an image of Bob appeared, matching and exceeding the description.

"You mean the jawn who joked about me having to share Moms with you and pretended to pull a quarter from my ear?" Eli rolled his eyes. "He could've at least made it something worth more."

"That's Bob all right," Maksim said. "The conspiracy to corrupt time has his stamp all over it. The involvement of one or more directors would also explain why it sailed under the radar for so long."

And why Maksim couldn't find any nearby directors not under the influence, and needed me for a witness.

"But he wasn't back there." The boy snapped his fingers, and the image of Bob vanished. "I would've recognized him as somebody I'd seen somewhere before."

"He's not working alone. It's a bigger plot than I thought —but I'm counting on him being a strong enough member . . . and selfish." Maksim gave me a small nod.

"Selfish?"

Eli turned his head this way and that, making faces, before turning back to his stepfather. "Yeah, how?"

"Most people who want to change history are selfish." Maksim hopped over a crossing line to continue on the same fate-line, Eli and me following suit. "They want to be alive to enjoy the changed timeline even though this constricts exactly how much change can happen. They specify this in the sleaze so that as it works on altering Fate, it can only make changes that don't prevent their ancestors from being born, meeting, and resulting in each successive generation. Assuming Bob is part of the conspiracy, I'm sure he'd mandate his survival in the alternate timeline.

"This,"—he paused and whirled around, holding up his left hand. The rope had thickened even more, now blocking half of the palm—"is the sum of all of Bob's direct ancestors at the moment we stand above time. Assuming the sleaze has to maintain his existence, that creates a connection between the two. It will help us locate it."

He didn't stay still for long. I had to jog to keep up with

him, veering around to his left for a better view of the rope. It doubled in thickness with every step Maksim took as each generation shifted and their parents took their place—except it also seemed to condense every four or five steps. The threads that fed into the rope grew ever thinner and hard to see. Still, without that magic all the doubling would have to make the rope too big for him to hold.

Yet something about his description nagged at me, a loose thread of some kind. I worried over it past another cross-line before I managed to parse it out.

"Guaranteeing they survive in the alternate timeline doesn't mean they'll be any better off, unless they include that in their magic."

A long moment, then I got a nod and a bit of smile.

"If they did specify they exist and come out on top in the alternate timeline, that further constrains the degree to which Fate changes and might reduce the odds that much was altered." He gave me another nod.

Eli twisted, shoulders rising close to his ears as he worked this through. Then he leapt ahead of us and gave the air a couple of punches. "That's not fair, changing the rules so you win."

"Exactly." A low growl escaped Maksim, his face turning stormy. "It's why I became a director, even if it meant smiling in the face of insults and working twice as hard to get ahead. I took those trades, pledging to keep anyone from cheating and changing Fate to their benefit."

"Yuck." Eli stomped forward a few paces, then glanced back over his shoulder. "Like what?"

Maksim laughed, a hollow sound utterly lacking in humor.

"Like what?" The boy whirled around and crossed his arms over his chest. "Like the talk Mom and Gramma give me about all the things I'm not supposed to do if there are police around?"

"That's part of it." Maksim said. "You remember last year when you won first place in the science fair and the father of the second-place winner accused you of cheating?"

"Billy's dad, yeah. But I didn't. Even Billy admitted it."

"I know." Maksim patted Eli's back. "But Billy didn't admit it in front of his father. What if Billy's dad had the ability to go into the Web of Fate? He could have changed things so that Billy won, or make it so everyone believed you cheated."

"Yuck. But we'd go and change things back, right?" Eli wiggled and stomped along next to Maksim as I trailed behind.

"We could, but then we'd all be chasing each other around—and life would be decided by whomever controlled Fate. That's why people—mostly White men, but not all—created Lachesis, of which Webmasters is part. We're dedicated to protecting Fate from external changes, so that when people fight for something and succeed they get to keep what they've achieved. It belongs to them. Or so our charter reads." Maksim hugged his stepson. "More changes won't be done on my watch. I decided long ago that *no one* should be able to undo other people's successes by sneaking into the Web of Fate."

"Yeah." Eli gave another punch at the air. "Me too."

I folded my lips between my teeth to ensure I didn't speak out of turn. This was their call to make, and my role to support or not. Besides, without magic I couldn't do much.

Lacking power didn't stop me from trying to touch the lifelines passing through and around Maksim's hand. Not the ancestors, for fear I'd spoil the spell, but the descendants who trickled back to the time we'd left. Alas, my hand went right through without me suffering so much as a prickle or twitch of energy.

We continued on in silence, making two more shifts

across fate-lines before I ventured to ask anything more. In particular, I waited until Eli'd gotten bored with walking along and surfed ahead albeit slower and with more care to stay in the center of the fate-line than before.

"You said most plotters were selfish. That must mean some weren't."

"Probably. Possibly. If someone is willing to sacrifice themselves to change Fate, and they make it, who knows how many people in the new timeline existed in the old to notice and try and change it back?" He waved a hand as though batting away a mosquito. "But most people aren't so selfless."

He directed a finger at the next cross-line.

"We're almost there."

The lifelines combining into the thread winding around his hand started to look . . . Dingy. Although never particularly numinous before, they'd had somehow gained a layer of dirt or dust—especially those leading off to the cross-line where Eli came to an abrupt and sudden stop. His body arced back, hands high and face twisting to the side in disgust.

"Ewww!"

❧ 7 ☙

No one could miss the sleaze. It didn't belong by any stretch of imagination—and sleaze turned out to be a far more apt description than I'd expected.

First and foremost, it stank. Not as bad as it deserved, but enough to override the celestial aroma and replace it with a staleness reminiscent of food gone bad.

A light covering of dust dimmed the translucence of the fate-line beneath us. That wasn't so bad for the first couple of steps, except some of the dust adhered to our shoes as though it were mud. Where once none of us had left signs of our passage on the impervious fate-lines, now it showed clear footprints and places where Eli'd stopped and tried to scrape off bits of muck as he surfed along.

Some of the dust filtered up into the air, adding a sour tang. Milk gone bad or worse.

The line became increasingly tacky, clinging to our shoes with a suck-and-gulp when I pulled loose. For all Maksim likely weighed more than I, he walked lighter. Or maybe his magic made the difference. I couldn't tell, but he never got stuck and I did twice. The first time I wiggled my shoe free, but the second proved tougher. Maksim grabbed my calf and helped me yank free. Globs of brownish-green matter splattered the fate-line around where my foot had been, exactly as though I'd stepped in a major mud puddle.

Cosmic gasses and celestial lights continued to billow around us, punctuated with the distant twinkling of humans and animals, birds, plants, and everything living far below. Unfortunately, the dust in the air thickened and dulled the otherwise glorious colors to shades of gray.

Oddly enough, our decaying surroundings failed to dismay Maksim.

"Why're you so happy?" I asked after he nearly bounced for three steps in a row.

"This is a good sign." Maksim clapped his hands. "It means the sleaze hasn't been completely absorbed. There's still time to extract it with only minor consequences."

"Oh. Good." Much as I appreciated his pleasure, I wasn't able to match it as we slogged forward as though walking through the yucky, grimy snow-muck that accrued in Philadelphia's streets in the wake of snow storms.

When we reached Eli, he'd planted his feet a good three feet away from the source of the sleaze. He bent his upper body inward, nose wrinkling, as he inspected it.

It was out of keeping with the gorgeous colors everywhere else and fit the growing dust in the air. Exactly what it was escaped me, something semi-solid but with a residual fluidity. A sickly brown color, it appeared to have been extruded in a large circle topped by ever smaller circles—a wedding cake made of sludge. Although the air five or more feet away held nothing more than a sourness, the object itself stank as though a sewer line had backed up.

Eli summed it up quite nicely: "It looks like someone took a dump."

"Whatever it is is still doing it." Maksim swallowed hard, the only evidence that the stench affected him too. He approached within one and a half feet, leaning in close. He moved his hand around, without touching anything, to show that a minute filament rose up from the tip of the pile—or trickled down onto it. The filament dissolved into nothingness—or vanished—in mid-air.

"So, what do we do now? Do I take photos? Scratch that." An instant after opening my big mouth, I remembered that phones didn't work. All the same, I removed my phone from my pocket and gazed longingly at the blank screen before returning it.

"Walk around it." Maksim moved back a couple of steps, encouraging Eli to do so as well. "Observe it from every angle you can. Your memories are what will matter. With your permission, other directors can review them."

"Right." More fun to look forward to. Too late now to request details about the memory extraction, though I'd seen my middle sister do something of the sort on occasion—without much wincing in pain.

I followed his instructions to the letter and proceeded around the sleaze an inch at a time. Would've been easier if they'd kept quiet and let me think instead of whispering back and forth. Whispers carried farther and were harder to ignore. I moved twice as slow because I kept pausing to listen in.

"What's it doing?" Eli asked.

"It's seeping into the fate-line." Maksim pointed to something, based on the flicker of movement in my peripheral vision, but I missed most of the gesture. "Wide and deep."

"Say what?"

"It's going wide because it's tainting the surface of the

fate-line. That's not good, but extends only a few centuries forward. What's worse is the extent to which some of the corrupted material has gone deep enough to reach all the way forward and start changing our present." At which point Maksim gave up whispering and went on in a normal voice as he shared about Smith's bogus-to-real excavation of Atlantis. I mostly tuned out, being familiar with the details.

Occasional pulses continued to pass forward or back through the fate-line beneath us. They paused, too, as they went through the corrupted area. One detail to pack away.

Along with the stench. Proximity should have helped me get used to it. Hah. If anything, it permeated my body more with every breath. I pulled the neckline of my shirt up over my mouth and nose to reduce the effect, and wound up untucking the shirt completely.

The sleaze's resemblance to feces increased the longer I examined it. Although brownish-green, neither color resembled any shade I'd seen in nature. There seemed to be an extra kick or tinge that gave it an unearthly appearance but in no way heavenly or celestial.

Alas, my glacial inspection triggered memories from earlier in the day. As a Friday treat, I'd skipped down the stairs at lunchtime and made a beeline for the chocolate shop on the first floor. Rather than darting right in, I browsed the shop window first. Inspected the display platters featuring a bright-colored macaroon tree, an immense milk chocolate urn atop a stainless and spotless steel pot, and an open box of assorted chocolates.

Only after I'd given them their due did I open the door and proceed inside. The first inhalation brought the glorious scent of fresh-made candies, as always. I filled my lungs and checked the ranks of truffles on option. I devoted my attention to the dark chocolates with their varied fillings. Raspberry. Buttercream ganache. Brazil nuts.

Four times out of five, I wound up with double dark chocolate.

The almost-spherical truffles bore little resemblance to this unseemly, stinky, and absolutely-positively-no-doubt-about-it inedible lump—yet I couldn't shake the notion that they had something in common.

That the trickle of . . . whatever . . . concealed something underneath.

It might be a while before I indulged in a truffle again.

As I finished my circuit, sensations rippled through the fate-line. Not the deep, arterial passage of a pulse, but rather surface ripples.

In an instant, a hundred or more spiders burst into existence around us. Some bubbled up through the fate-line, their legs stretching wide as they pried their segmented bodies from the thick surface. Others dropped out of the sky to dangle on threads whose originating ends vanished in the cosmic lights.

Each and every spider made noise of one kind or another. Mostly a high-pitched whistling that hit the top of my hearing range. Wincing, I edged backward and away from the spiders and the sleaze. Eli mirrored me, hands clapped over his ears.

Maksim leapt in front of us and stretched out his arms. The spiders left off their whistling and swarmed him. Every inch of his clothes and arms turned into a living mass of arachnids. Only his head remained free, apart from one large huntsman spider perched atop—perhaps the very one that had come looking for him so long ago, as in only that afternoon?

"Get back, as far as you can." The living spider-covered man turned halfway around and pointed far up the fate-line. "Whatever you do, don't fall off."

I grabbed Eli's hand, or he did mine. Our damp palms

nearly slipped, but fingers twined as we hurried backward several steps.

The spiders swooped off Maksim. Two-thirds spread out into a wide circle around the sleaze. The remainder formed a double rank several feet back, closer to Eli and me, in straight lines mere inches apart from each other.

We slowed to a stop. Dust whirled around our feet, the awful odors reduced to a mere sour aftertaste at this distance.

"Isn't he coming?" Eli asked, voice high and tight.

"I don't think so."

"What's going on?"

Before I could offer a guess or anything, a high-pitched whine filled the air. This blazing klaxon resembled a fire detector going off rather than the whistling of the spiders.

An instant later, a bulge appeared at the top of the thread dripping onto the sleaze. It increased in size exponentially as it slid down. The outside rippled and shifted, covering something within that fought or tumbled. Right before the bulge could slam against the pile, it burst open to release a man.

A White man.

A young White man.

A familiar young White man in sneakers, jeans, and a T-shirt emblazoned with the logo of one of the Eagles' most serious rivals.

"Hey, isn't he—" Eli pointed.

"Yeah." Something dull and gray caught my eye.

The new arrival moved his arm, revealing a snub-nosed gun in his hand. I couldn't see his fingers, but better safe than sorry.

"Get down." I yanked on Eli's arm as I dropped. He resisted for a moment, then followed suit. We both lay flat against the surface, but with our heads tilted to offer a ground-level view of the action. He coughed while I near choked from the brief whirl of dust our actions had kicked up.

As the dust settled, dozens of spiders rose up on their forelegs and shot silk from their spinnerets. The thin silvery lines glittered against the dull dusty air surrounding the sleaze. They landed in spits and starts, forming a loose array of webbing that covered the man's hands, shoulders, knees, and face.

And gun.

He yelled, writhed, and struggled to clear the end of the barrel. To see. To shoot.

Before he managed to do much more than scream defiance, Maksim grabbed an empty water bottle from his backpack and threw it.

Light flashed and the man vanished. The bottle floated down to the fate-line, sinking inch-by-inch. Before, the sides were clear and translucent apart from the label. Now a stick-figure of a human marked the plastic.

The whole thing took only a few breaths.

Maksim retrieved the bottle and screwed on the cap, restoring it to his backpack.

Only to pull out more empty bottles into a pile near his feet.

"Is that it?" Eli started to clamber up, but I grabbed his shirt.

"Look at the spiders."

Those near Maksim readied to throw more silk.

The high-pitched whine started up again, then doubled. Tripled. Quadrupled. Blobs shot down the thread toward the sleaze.

One after another the blobs burst to reveal men and women armed with sharp knives whose blades gleamed despite dull, dusty light—and more guns.

Six, seven, eight . . . how many people had come to the

coffee shop hunting Maksim? At least that many, but how could he fight them even with the spiders' assistance?

"We can't leave him to fight alone." I fumbled in the magic purse my sisters had given me for my special pepper spray. They'd given me that as well, promising me it'd work on any attacker. "You stay safe," I told Eli. "Don't go giving them a hostage."

Though I'd underestimated the spiders. The sky rained spider silk, turning the atmosphere into a blurry mass of stripes. Vague human forms moved amidst the thick air. Limbs occasionally burst free only to be swallowed again.

"At him!"

"Where're you?"

"There, I see him!"

"Kill!"

I lost track of Maksim amidst the ruckus. He didn't waste time on yelling.

But even with the spiders, he was vastly outnumbered.

I started forward with the pepper spray can ahead of me. The nozzle and body expanded in my grasp, shifting into the form of a fire extinguisher except with a bright pink canister instead of red. The simple spray top grew a foot-long, thin, gray hose. Thankfully, though, the weight didn't change. Still light enough I could heft it without trouble.

"I can't just sit here." Eli's footfalls thudded behind me.

"Then think." I yelled back at him. "What do you have that can be a weapon? I don't know, something you could throw." And stay safely back.

Two of the men glimpsed me through the whirl of spider silk and charged toward me.

Twisting the nozzle, I aimed the hose. A three-foot wide spray of bright pink fairy dust streamed from the end. The men coughed, choked, and bent over. Tears streamed from their eyes as they fell to their knees.

I inched forward, watching the spider silk for a chance to duck in and spray another attacker.

"Something we can throw." Eli said behind me. A heavy thud had me turning around to check on him. He'd dropped to the fate-line and yanked off his left shoe. Dust dulled the green-and-black fabric with Eagles emblazoned around the heel, but it looked pretty new.

He scrambled to his feet, standing one shoe on and one off. With no socks, his bare sole pressed against the dusty fate-line. I angled my body in front of him although no one had escaped the area around the sleaze. Spider silk continued to arc and make visibility difficult, but grunts and thuds suggested fists beating against flesh.

Had the attackers captured Maksim?

The next moment, all thoughts escaped my head except disgust. The unmistakable stench of old, well-used shoes made my eyes water.

Eli didn't seem to mind. He cupped his loose shoe in one hand. The smell doubled, tripled. "Not Maksim. Everyone but Maksim."

Then he reared back and threw it. The kid had a good arm. The shoe arced and slipped through a gap in the flying whirl of silk. It hit something, or someone, given the yelp of surprise.

With a big boom, gouts of ghastly lime-green gasses puffed out a good fifteen feet, carrying the multiplied odor of Eli's shoe.

The spiders skittered away in all directions. The humans weren't that lucky. Man after man dropped to lie prone as their bodies writhed, coughing and retching. Even I wound up nearly choking as the stench of stale shoe coated my mouth, thankful I was far enough back to have escaped the full effect.

"Stink bomb!" Eli pumped both fists in the air, then bent down to grab his other shoe and hold it at the ready.

"You practice that, don't you?" I kept my pepper spray at the ready.

"I can make the stinkiest bombs of all my friends." Eli ran a hand over his hair and strutted, chest up.

Fortunately, he didn't need his other shoe, or mine.

As the silk shower cleared, Maksim stood tall among the coughing attackers. Bits of dust dotted his hair, and sweat poured down his face, but otherwise he seemed untouched as he whopped them with water bottle after water bottle. Every time, the man hit vanished and a stick form appeared on the plastic bottle.

Seven, eight bottles . . . had we really drunk that much water? If so, I'd missed the usual effects.

Spiders zoomed in to the sleaze, navigating around standing and prone human forms and the array of water bottles. They didn't touch the pile itself, but slung gout after gout of silk around the drip until it was encased from the top of the sleaze to where the drip originated in nothingness.

"Maksim!" Eli ran full-tilt at his stepfather.

The older man wiped his forehead with the back of his hand, but turned around and opened his arms wide. The two embraced, holding each other close and saying words not meant for my ears.

I turned away and distracted myself by gathering up the water bottles from the masses of spider silk and bits of canvas and rubber that once formed Eli's shoe.

The bottles didn't feel any different to the touch, although the stick figures appeared embossed and raised above the plastic. When held, the bottles weighed more than they had empty but less than full of water. As I lined them up near Maksim's abandoned backpack, I noticed each figure differed slightly from the others. Three had both hands braced on hips or waist; four braced only one hand either right or left; and two held their arms wide both with guns at the ready. Each had at least one weapon.

"You *aren't* all right." Eli stamped a foot—the bare one—and a vibration made me jerk in response. I turned around in time to see the boy trying to peer under the spiderweb bandage on his stepfather's arm.

"I'll heal. We won the fight thanks to your assistance." Maksim gently pulled his arm away, then turned around to survey the mess. His eyebrows rose, then he winced and rubbed his left cheekbone. All the same, he managed a pointed look at Eli's left foot. "Is that why your left shoes disintegrate so often?"

"I might've practiced some." Eli doubled over and wrapped one hand over his remaining shoe and the other his loose toes. His stance evened out as the bits of fabric and rubber flew to reassemble as a whole shoe materialized around the bare foot. "See? Good as new."

"Until it falls apart tomorrow." Maksim rubbed Eli's back as the boy straightened up, but his gaze fell outward on the circle of spiders around them. "Thank you, my friends. Take what you need, give what you can. I would appreciate if some of you would remain near."

The spiders shifted, legs rubbing against each other in an almost inaudible whistling. Most vanished, but a dozen or two clustered a foot away from the bottles.

The caps were solidly in place, turning each bottle into a miniature prison. I touched one of the thick rounds of plastic.

Our attackers hadn't been dead when Maksim imprisoned them in the bottles. Did the caps keep out air to kill them? They'd gone after us without warning or even giving a chance for surrender, though Maksim wouldn't have accepted, but stifling them . . .

"Don't worry, sister." With a low groan, Maksim crouched next to me and started stuffing the bottles into the backpack. As he pulled the bottle from under my grasp, he patted my hand. "If they're alive when they go in, they'll be alive when they come out. It's a cheap, easy stasis spell. Though it does change the composition of the plastic in the long run. Can't recycle them after, have to throw them on a really hot fire or bury them in compost."

"Got it." Cheap, easy stasis spell—for him. Still, knowing they weren't dying of lack of air made me less wary of the bottles. There might've been an edge of vengeance, too— when brought back to the world, the attackers could be brought to justice . . . Or not. "So, we take them back to be hauled before a board of directors to testify about the sleaze?"

"It's not that easy. If they're employees of any subsidiary of Lachesis, Atropos has jurisdiction over them. It's in the employment contract. But if they're not, it gets murkier." Maksim rubbed his hands together, tilting his head as he glanced at me. "Did you recognize anyone?"

"The first one from the coffee house, but I don't remember where I'd seen him before. Probably from photos about Atlantis. The rest I didn't get enough of a look at, then or now. They look familiar, but they're sort of like that research group that's been in lately, so I don't know." I studied the bottles, but the stick figures had matching blank, round faces.

"Young White men dressed the same tend to look alike," Maksim said with a straight face, although Eli almost choked on a laugh.

"Especially when they're moving fast, and there's spider silk floating around." My lips might've quirked, but I managed to stay on-point.

"At any rate, turning them over to the Atroposi to answer

for changing Fate is not the most immediate problem." Maksim circled the sleaze, staring at the thread dripping down, and the spider silk encasing its length. "The trouble is, how they got here direct from the present without having to hike as we did."

"They took a shortcut?" Eli followed along behind, almost tripping on his stepfather's heels.

"That they did. Even accessing Fate from the Web-link in the office couldn't deliver people to a specific time and place in the past with such pinpoint accuracy." Maksim stopped and crouched, getting closer to the sleaze than I'd want to go. His nose wrinkled, as did mine in sympathy for the smell remained strong and awful. "But . . ."

With a grimace, he reached to where the spider-silk-covered thread met the pile of ooze. Ick! He pinched the yucky stuff and pulled out. The substance stretched, and a wash of colors appeared on the surface. The farther he pulled, the more colors and . . . images, letters, *words*.

He snarled, showing clenched teeth, and pinched another segment with his other hand.

Inch by inch, he expanded a rectangular section, until the colors resolved into the image of a website.

Pinching my nose, I scrambled over to kneel next to Maksim and Eli, for a better view. A romanticized island castle dominated the scene—the very scene from the Atlantis True Believers' website.

Maksim did something that set the image scrolling through the website to the photos section. "Baltimore's senior. Two from Boston, Miami, and, hah, London's new junior. Someone's been planning this a long time."

Maksim let the ooze slide back into the pile, face grim. He summoned wet wipes from the backpack and cleaned off his hands, rubbing the strawberry-scented wipes over his skin again and again.

"They've set up a shortcut. As long as the sleaze is linked to the website, they can jump into the internet and then back in time and space in two shakes of a lamb's tail." He dropped the wipes next to the bottle-prisons, and then stared down at Eli and me. "We can't wait for Tanisha and her team. We have to cut it now."

❧   8   ❧

Watching a man try to sever a thread proved boring really fast.

I dropped down onto the fate-line and sat with legs straight out. My calves ached from all the hiking, so I massaged them. Ran my fingers through my hair a couple times to settle it down. Then again, as my mouth grew dry. The air remained a constant comfortable temperature but had a dry edge that wicked moisture from me.

Maksim had pulled several additional bottles of water from his backpack—apparently he'd packed a flat or more—and set them in a distinctly separate pile from the bottle-prisons. I gave them the side-eye several times, because seeing grown men get sucked into itty-bitty bottles made me wary of drinking from the fresh bottles. The pile of protein bars in their foil wrappers attracted me more, but eating would make me thirsty so I ignored any rumblings in my belly.

Eli went for a bottle before me, though he didn't drink. He played with the top as he watched his stepfather saw away at the silk-coated thread.

The backpack lay open at Maksim's feet, seemingly empty

but able to produce whatever he wanted when he summoned it—and he'd evidently packed an armory.

First he tried a short, simple thing that resembled a plain dinner knife. It broke with twang. The blade went spiraling off.

"Come back here!" Maksim snatched at empty air with his free hand, and the blade came tumbling back.

Dropping both pieces into the backpack, he fetched out a pocket-knife. One of the bigger Swiss Army ones, where the blade and handle each were easily the length of his palm. The metal blade glinted until he touched it to the thread right below where the spider-silk coating ended.

Rather than breaking, the blade dulled within seconds. That knife, too, dropped into the pack. Hit the initial blade, or something else, given the soft ting of metal impacting metal.

The third try involved something more along the lines of a butcher knife. The big, rectangular blade had enough heft to disassemble a cow carcass in no time. I edged away, in case it broke and parts went flying. Eli had faith and stayed close.

He had it right. A few tries at the thread, and Maksim started to curse only to stop halfway through and turn it into a deep growl. The butcher knife had rusted.

Similar things plagued every blade he used, no matter what he tried.

The silver knife tarnished and got a nick in it.

The copper blade turned green and grew moss.

The solid iron knife flat out didn't work. Maksim sawed for several minutes before giving up.

Same deal with the cutlass, the Damascus steel knife as long as my arm, and the obsidian blade.

Ditto the diamond cutter.

Eli went over Maksim's backpack, but came back sulking because only Maksim could pull anything from there and every time he failed with a weapon, he restored it so Eli couldn't get it.

"How many knives did you bring?" I asked.

Maybe giving us weapons wouldn't be a bad idea in case we got attacked again.

"I brought a full kit, plus triple the usual allotment of water and food." Maksim returned the diamond cutter to the pack and brought out a lighter. "Cutting evidently won't work. Let's try a little fire."

When the lighter failed to do anything more than singe bits of spider silk wrapping above the exposed thread, Maksim tossed it back into the backpack.

"Move back." He waved at us, pointing several feet away.

Thirst drove me to grab a bottle of water as I scuttled along, Eli beside me,

Maksim bent down and physically removed a bottle of compressed gas wrapped in bright colors with all sorts of warnings printed on it. He attached a metal piece that resembled a hair dryer. Pointing it at the thread right above the sleaze, he pulled the trigger and sparked a lashing blade of fire.

Burnt sleaze produced a stench worse than it itself. Covering my mouth and nose with my hands didn't help. Eli coughed and pulled the hem of his shirt over his head. Maksim's face contorted in a series of disgusted expressions, but he kept the flame burning until it was clear this attempt, too, had failed.

He made one more try with some kind of acid that didn't interact well with thread or sleaze. Gouts of acrid smoke poured off, making my eyes water. Eli wound up with streaming eyes and a nasty cough. Neither of us had drunk from the bottles. I eyed mine, grunted, and finally lifted it to clear my face and mouth. Muttering a curse, Eli followed suit.

The water tasted fine.

Maksim tucked the bottle of acid away and grabbed a water bottle of his own. He wiped sweat off of his forehead, then squatted near us and drained the bottle in one go.

The sleaze hadn't changed much. Bits here and there showed slight pitting or scorch marks, but the thread still connected it to the internet and the real world.

"How would you usually get rid of something like this?" I asked.

Maksim took his time finishing off a second bottle and setting it aside. His shoulders slumped as he blew air through his mouth in a soft whistle. "I'd be part of a team of three directors representing a minimum degree of difference and we'd blast it away through a ceremony of common assent."

"Wha?" Eli sat straight, puzzlement clear on his face and his voice so high it hurt my ears.

I subsided to the side, happy for Eli to take the lead.

"We use the magic of threes, so there would be three of us directors." Maksim's legs wobbled and he sank down to sit next to Eli. "To be a director, you have to be Fate-qualified at the highest level, which means spending years of study on Fate. And you have to know yourself, your strengths and weaknesses. Because when we enter Fate—when I enter Fate—as a director, I'm representing more than myself. I speak for all the groups that I'm part of: men, Black men, married men, stepfathers, fathers-to-be, Baltimorean-by-birth, Philadelphian-by-choice, and so on. You got that?"

Eli pursed his lips and tilted his head as he thought it through, then started counting off on his fingers. "So I'd speak for boys and Black boys and Philadelphians-by-birth and . . . and . . ."

"And seventh graders, and skaters, and sorcerers." Maksim added, tapping his own fingers in turn.

"And you'd be women and White women and half-turned sorcerers and stuff." Eli pointed at me.

"And sisters, college graduates, receptionists, failed law students." I snapped my jaw shut.

"You get the math?" Maksim took mercy on me. "It's important that we have some things, some groups, in common but ultimately the more groups we reflect, the more diverse we are, the stronger our collective power. Even though there'd only be three directors here, we'd represent multitudes."

As Maksim helped Eli work through the implications, their voices washed over me. The underlying theories were familiar from my college days, not only classes but the various student organizations I'd belonged and contributed, led, and got booted out of. Though I'd hardly have guessed I'd end up hearing about them again while seated on a fate-line millennia into the past.

A harsh hand clap brought me back to myself. I startled, then subsided and took another gulp of water.

"If we're strong enough, we banish it." Maksim clapped again, then rubbed his hands together.

"So three put that thing there?" Eli squinted and pointed at the sleaze.

"At least. If people are alike, you need more of them to equal a diverse trio." Maksim growled. "There's still too many willing to lump it together. All those I saw in the photos . . . They're some differences between them, but they tick a lot of the same boxes."

"Do you got to be stronger to get it out?" Eli held up two hands, one with three fingers and the other four. "If they had four, you'd need four?"

"Fate doesn't want the past, or future, to be changed from the outside." Maksim patted the line beneath us. The imprint where his hand had lingered glowed for a few moments after. "It helps those of us setting things right, when it can. A good trio can work big magic."

Could it? I sat up straight and licked my lips. My fingers twitched, and nerves jangled in my legs.

"Maybe I'm talking out of turn, in which case forget I said anything, but . . ." I swallowed the sudden lump in my throat. "There's three of us here now. Eli and I aren't directors, and I'm not a sorcerer, but couldn't we make do?"

Maksim's first reaction was to shake his head, but he stopped halfway.

"Hmm. . . ." Eyes narrow, he inspected me then Eli, back and forth and forth and back. Then a check at the drops still oozing down into the line. "Worth a try. We've got age, gender, race, and power differences to start. But"—he held up a finger—"only if you're both willing."

Eli vibrated so hard he practically levitated off the line as he nodded.

I'd made the suggestion, so I couldn't—wouldn't—draw back. Not even when Maksim spent what seemed like ages positioning me and Eli as two points of a triangle around the sleaze. We had to be far back enough that we couldn't hold hands. Precision mattered. He kept having me go two-and-a-half inches this way, then back one-eighth until my back started to hurt from standing almost-still for so long.

Or maybe it was nerves, or flickers of power starting to flare around us.

Once Maksim took his place as the third point of the triangle, a distant whine and crackle marked the rise of not one but two circles of power. Energy whirled slowly in two directions: clockwise and counterclockwise. The fate-line warmed up, heating the soles of my shoes, as snapping sorcery twined around us, more felt than seen.

"Hold your arms out." He demonstrated, extending his to either side at shoulder height—pointed at the two of us.

Eli and I did the same. The warming air helped loosen my muscles against strain.

The remaining spiders formed a wider triangle. They lined themselves almost exactly a foot behind us, spread out with equally precise regularity.

The energy rose higher, up to my waist. It became all but visible, something I could see out of the corners of my eyes as flickering lights tracing circular paths and alternating which direction went inside or out.

Eli's eyes went big until they dominated his face. Evidently he saw more than me, as did Maksim. Their heads turned side-to-side, both watching the energy rise.

My skin started to itch waist down as the energy passed through and around me. It shifted from crackling to a buzzing as though a thousand bees swarmed around me.

"Follow my lead." Maksim shouted over the hum. "Choose your own words. Speak from your heart."

The power rose further, twining before and behind my back up to the shoulders. My peripheral view shifted, and we started to resemble a big ball of barbed wire tangled around three fence posts. Bits of energy pricked my skin and minute drops of blood speckled my arms. Points of pain bloomed along my back and legs.

A soft, orange radiance outlined Maksim. Pale green shone from Eli. I couldn't see anything around me.

The power rose above my head, making every single hair on my body, including all attached to my skull, stand out.

The twining strands of clockwise and counterclockwise force left an oval opening before my mouth.

I could barely hear when Maksim spoke again, but his words reverberated in my bones.

"Hear me, Fate. I speak for myself, and for many. I am a director of Lachesis and serve the greater good." He brought his arms together, palms facing the ugly mound of seething malfeasance. Orange light streamed from him toward it. "I denounce this sleaze. Let it be stricken from the record, and the former line restored. May the past be undisturbed, the better to build a brighter tomorrow."

He'd told Eli to go next, in hopes the two of them could build up a sufficient wealth of sorcery to make up for my inability to add any power. The boy seemed swamped, his body swaying in the opposite forces.

Eli swayed for a moment, then dragged in a big breath until his chest expanded. He aimed his hands at the sleaze and sent a steady flow of green light to mix with the orange.

"Hear it, Fate. I speak for me and lots of others, kids like me. Blast this to smithereens. Get it out of here. Be back like you were before. Be better,"—his voice cracked mid-word, and the remainder of the sentence came out half-low and half-high—"and make everything better for me and all of us."

My turn. I aimed my hands, mirroring Maksim and Eli, but nothing happened. Power flowed over and around my body, but not through me.

Licking lips turned dry again, I opened my mouth and nearly choked on the force swirling around my head. The crackling energy stole my words so even I couldn't hear them as they resounded in my skull. Nevertheless, they reverberated even as Maksim and Eli's had.

"Hear me, Fate. I speak for myself, and for many. I work for Lachesis and . . . Try to serve the greater good. I renounce this sleaze." Not what I meant to say, but I forged on and let the words pour out as they would. "I denounce it. Let it be blasted from the record, and the . . . the . . . what-was be restored. May the past be undisturbed, that we may build a brighter tomorrow."

The rushing sensation of energy crackling along every inch of my skin wound even higher.

"Begone!" Even as Maksim spoke, the curving power ceased to circle. It collapsed inward with a force that shoved me back a foot or more.

The sorcerous force covered the sleaze.

Coated it.

Froze.

Everything held still for a long moment. With a sharp crackle, the thread leading off to the internet broke first. It shattered into a dozen pieces that crashed outward—fortunately not so far as me or the others. The shards splintered further as they hit the fate-line.

Pieces of the sleaze started to break off. A bit here crumbled into dust, while another there slumped and slide off to dash to dust against the fate-line. In less than a minute, the yucky, poopy shell dissolved.

An inner core of bright, neon-green poison remained. No wonder it had reminded me of a truffle. A kernel about the size of a fist, it glowed, untouched or unharmed by the spell of banishment. The smoldering light flared.

A blast of heat burst from it, sending out visible waves of intensity.

The fate-line softened beneath it, and the green sleaze started to sink in.

"No!" Maksim leapt inward. He stretched out both hands, the right wrapping around the green object as it descended into the fate-line. His body landed on the tainted surface and sent up a gout of dust.

I covered my eyes with my arm and coughed, and Eli did the same. Maksim cursed through his coughing.

When the dust settled, he lay prone with his right arm embedded shoulder-deep in the fate-line.

❧ 9 ❧

For every step we took forward, we slid one back. Or more.

I dove for Maksim, grabbing hold of his ankle. Nearly bumped heads as Eli swooped down to grab Maksim's other foot. Dust puffed up from the fate-line as I dropped to lie flat atop it, but I was already so soiled it made no more difference to the lousy state of my clothes. I'd even grown used to the dust's taste, or more likely it had changed. Instead of a generic stale-food smell, the dust had a clammy, spoiled spinach texture. Yucky, but nothing worth screaming about.

Especially since Eli literally screamed "Maksim!" next to me.

The fate-line held firm beneath my body, but tremors shook Maksim's body. My fingers slipped as I clutched at his skin, so I gave up and clasped his pant-leg. The soft, worn jeans had a couple snags at the hem, giving me extra purchase.

The instant Eli stopped to breathe, I leapt in.

"Let's yank on three. Got it?" I pulled my knees up under me and dug the tips of my sneakers into the fate-line. Tried to, rather, for it resisted. Soupy, muddy parts remained but they'd begun to dry.

Maksim was a big man, but we should be able to shift him. Maybe get his arm free to the elbow at least?

"Yeah." Eli squirmed into a better position.

"One, two, three."

Gritting my teeth, I pulled and yanked. Clenched. Struggled. My knees slipped backward, but rather than dragging Maksim free, the fabric started ripping. I went back for his ankle, wrapping both hands around.

Sweat dripped from my forehead and all sorts of other places, and my breath came in pants. Next to me, Eli wasn't much better.

This way, that way, no way worked.

"Enough." Despite the hoarse note in his voice, Maksim commanded attention.

I stopped and readjusted my hold. My fingers had grown slick so I wrapped his jeans close around his leg and held onto the one over the other.

Spiders clustered around, several climbing atop Maksim's back and side, but none spinning any silk or doing anything more than standing.

"This isn't going to work." Maksim twisted sideways, glancing over his free shoulder at us. He flexed his legs, trying to shake us off.

"We got to get you free. Mom wouldn't ever forgive me if I left you stuck here." He wiggled into a better position and tightened his hold until his knuckles cracked. "Let me do it alone this time."

I kept my mouth shut, the better to avoid babbling apologies for having suggested we try the banishment in the first place. They'd both poured power in, but I'd had none to match and that must've left the door open for the partial failure. My whole body ached as though I'd run a marathon.

"Eli, I know you want to—" Maksim started, but Eli jumped in.

"It's sorcery. You want something to come free, you pull on it. Let me try." His voice stayed high until the last word, when it broke again. Maksim might not be able to see the desperation on his stepson's face, but surely he could hear it.

He stopped trying to get away. "Once more. If it works, great. If not, you do things my way."

Eli readjusted to grab both Maksim's ankles. His lungs heaved as he dragged in air. Back bent over and head down near his death-grip on his stepfather's jeans, a hint of pale green light played around his fingers.

"One . . . two . . . three."

I moved further away as Eli strained to free the older man. Maksim's body arched. His back curved and teeth glinted white as he grunted. Muscles flexed and contracted, but to no avail.

His arm remained trapped within the fate-line.

Eli continued to pull until Maksim cried out in pain. At that, Eli dropped. His back heaved as he panted, then he crawled up to lie next to his stepfather. His knees pulled up as he curled into a ball, suppressing sobs but not his broken breathing.

"Sorry." I sank into a similar blob a few feet away. "My fault for not having magic."

"It was worth a try. We almost had it! Not your fault it was a double whammy. We nailed the first, but the second . . ." Voice cracking, he grabbed for his backpack but it was just out of reach. I shoved it closer to him. He pulled out a water bottle, but had only one hand and couldn't open it. Before I could reach in to do it for him, he pounded the bottle against the fate-line. The top popped off, arching high and falling into the backpack.

He drank in slow gulps.

Most of the dirty dustiness of the fate-line had cleared up. The translucence glowed beneath us, bits of glitter washing over Maksim as though the line were trying to support him.

But deep within lay a trickle of light, neon green surging forward along the length of the fate-line. If I leaned and squinted hard enough, I made out a blurry outline of Maksim's hand holding the source of the green leaking into the line.

"What do you want us to do?" This was *so* above my pay grade.

Maksim drew in a deep breath, the air whistling as he dragged in. Head up, he looked at Eli, then me. "I'm sending you both home."

"No!" Eli shifted even closer to Maksim.

"Yes." Maksim laid the bottle aside and stroked the back of the boy's head. "To get help. Bring reinforcements. Tanisha may still be on the way with her team, but we can't rely on that anymore. Not with this second sleaze changing the time-line further. I need the two of you to go and bring back two or three directors, if you can convince anyone of what's going on. If you can't, then bring me other Webmasters employees or sorcerers."

"The banishment worked. Half." Eli turned his face up to Maksim, eyes big and pleading. "Can't we try it again?"

"We need a new third to form a triangle." Maksim inclined his head toward the arm locked in the fate-line. "I can't be part of it, not now. I'm holding back what I can of the remaining sleaze. I'll keep it as long as I can, but we need more people. More power. Elijah Jamal Jackson, Rosalind Celia Williams, I'm counting on you."

Leaving him here went against the grain. We were supposed to go as a group and return as a group, the whole bring-everyone-home ethos, after all. He was the expert, so I snapped my mouth shut on the objections bubbling up in my mind.

Besides, Eli offered protestation after protestation and got nothing out of it.

After he wound down, his shoulders hunched as he sat with his back to Maksim. He did not, however, move away. His backside remained in contact with Maksim's midsection.

Maksim wanted us to bring help back.

How?

"I need phone numbers. Directors who live close enough, sorcerers, anyone you think might work for a new triangle." I bit my lip. "I may convince my sisters, but they're visiting my mother who lives an hour out of the city when the trains run on time, so we'd be talking at least a couple of hours of travel time after I talked them into helping."

"You can ask my sisters, too. They're in town for the baby shower. My mother is as well, but I'd rather you didn't bring her along if you can avoid it. You probably won't, if you get my sisters. But before that,"—Maksim gave me a look-over—"where's your phone?"

"You said it wouldn't work." I extracted it from my pocket. A layer of dust covered the screen, which stayed dead even when I rubbed it against my pants.

"It will when you get back." He pointed at my phone and snapped several times. The screen stayed blank, but each point resulted in the same ding as a new text notification. "I've given you Tanisha's personal line. Call her first, as she may have some suggestions. If you can't get her, or if, God forbid, she doesn't exist after whatever changed in the time-line, then I've also included the default direct line to Atropos and whoever is in charge of the thread-cutters."

"What do you mean if she doesn't exist?" Blank and nonfunctional as it was, my phone seemed to weigh half again as much as I slipped it back into my pocket.

"This new sleaze is changing Fate. I stopped it. Mostly." Maksim scowled down at the line beneath us. "But something slipped through. I don't know what kind of world you'll find when you go back. Who exists, who doesn't. Better to be safe than sorry. If Geneva hasn't left town, get ahold of her. That'll give you one to bring back to start with."

Just what I needed, more things to worry about. As if figuring out how to explain the situation to other directors I'd never met, or Maksim's sisters, wasn't bad enough. Because, sure, they'd listen to me and believe when I told them he was stuck in Fate and they had to go with me, whom they never met or probably even heard of, to save him.

Then again, Eli would be with me. If we needed to enlist Maksim's family, surely Eli would take the lead in the convincing.

Though, once we'd got enough sorcerers on our side, other problems would loom.

"How are we supposed to find our way back to you?"

"Good question." He rubbed at his forehead with his free hand. "Give me a moment."

The more I sat, the more I pondered, the more problems occurred to me. As a distraction, I got to my feet. Standing wasn't enough. Every nerve in my body twitched. Pacing hardly helped, either, but I accidentally knocked one of the pieces of the overlaying sleaze. It crumbled as it rolled over, then slid down the slope off the fate-line. Hardly much physical exertion required, but watching it roll off eased the tension in my shoulders a little. So I proceeded in a rough circle kicking the remaining detritus off the fate-line.

Maksim noticed what I was doing and gave a small head-shake, but he didn't tell me to stop.

He summoned me over before I'd finished clearing off the crumbling piles.

"Give me your non-dominant hand." He extended his, palm up.

I laid my hand atop, shivering at the touch of his cooler flesh.

Two small spiders—with golden bodies marked by black spots—clambered up and over Maksim's arm to sit on his wrist. His fingers wrapped around mine as the spiders spun silk. First a thin bracelet for Maksim, then a matching one for me. Both in beautiful lacy patterns that glittered when first made, though the illumination faded quickly to the point they turned almost invisible. A thread connected them, but it resembled the thread that linked the initial sleaze to the internet in that it vanished an inch away from either of our wrists.

But when I stepped back, I felt a tug in Maksim's direction. Running a finger along the length of the bracelet, it seemed soft and fragile to the touch, but strong enough to stretch a little—and not break.

"Close your eyes and turn around." Maksim slumped back against the fate-line. "Do you know where I am?"

No matter how much I turned, how dizzy my head, a tug at my wrist indicated where he was in relation to me. As a test, just in case, I stumbled to a stop and kept my eyes shut as I shifted so that I should be facing him. When I opened my eyes, there he was.

The spider silk bracelets worked this close, but . . . "Will this work across time and space?"

"It should. We might even be able to speak now and then when the winds are right." Maksim grimaced and brought his free wrist to his mouth to whisper to the spiders. Those words I didn't catch, but a moment later he extended his arm again and spoke louder. "There's a fall-back, too."

One of the spiders clambered into his hair.

The other scrambled from his wrist, across the partially

invisible silk connecting our bracelets, and onto me. I started as the segmented legs climbed up my arm, setting the hairs on my skin upright. The arachnid continued all the way up my neck and along the side of my face into my hair before I managed to react. A squeak escaped me.

"Try not to disturb your hair too much. It'll stay with you until you get back." His eyes softened as he turned to the boy crouched against him. "Now, Eli, let me do the same for you."

"No! I should stay." Eli wrapped his arms tight across his chest, glaring not at Maksim but me. "What about the guys who attacked you? There could be more of them!"

"We destroyed their shortcut. They'll have to go the long way, and unless they remember exactly where they left the sleaze, it'll take them extra time to get here. If anyone does come," his teeth flashed in a snarl, I'll be able to see them coming."

"You'll need me." Eli whipped around, wrapping both hands around Maksim's bigger one.

"Rose may need your help," Maksim said, then, lower, "and I need to know you're safe."

"But . . ." Eli's voice rose in a whine, then cut off. He cast another angry look my way.

"I'm counting on you." Maksim twisted his hand within Eli's grasp so that he was holding onto the boy. "You know how to cast spells of invisibility, inaudibility, intangibility, right?"

"Yeah." A nod.

"And spells to ensure any incident is accurately recorded on all available cameras and phones?"

"Yeah, yeah, yeah." Another nod, and eyes rolled in the long-suffering way only teens and adolescents managed. "Mom made me practice all those spells even before she first started giving me the talk. I can do them in my sleep."

"Then go back with Rose, and you can tell your mother I

might be late, but I'm coming home for the shower, okay?" Maksim held up their linked hands and shook them. "Tell her I love her."

"I don't . . ." Another wail cut short when Maksim gave Eli a level look.

The boy's head drooped. His chest rose and fell in two deep breaths, then he brought his head back up, eyes flashing. "All right, already."

A second pair of gold-and-black spiders descended along Maksim's arm. They spun a set of matching bracelets, for him and Eli, then one scrambled over to hide in Eli's hair. The boy patted his head lightly, shoulders writhing and face scrunching into different expressions before he let loose a gust of a sigh.

"Anything else we should know?" I ticked off the different matters already addressed on my fingers. Contact information. The number and type of people to bring back. How to find our way back here . . .

Maksim closed his eyes, face taking on a drawn look. After a moment's thought, he shook his head though he didn't say anything.

Eli was cuddled up against him again.

"Right, then. We'll bring help." I held out a hand to Eli. He sat for a moment, staring at it, then matched his palm to mine. His fingers clutched me as he pulled himself up to stand and gaze down at Maksim. The older man lay prone, almost sleeping apart from his free hand opening and closing as if to release the tension from being unable to do the same with his other.

At which point, Eli and I exchanged glances as we realized an important detail he'd neglected to address. Eli beat me to asking: "Um, how do we get back?"

Maksim opened his eyes and glanced over at the remaining spiders. The big huntsman stepped forward.

"Follow the spider. It will take you to Friday in Philly, and not just anywhere . . ." He managed a sardonic, even sadistic, grin. "You've both been chugging water the whole time we've been in Fate, without any consequences. They'll hit you as soon as you leave Fate. I'm sending you back to the office, right outside the restrooms. There's a reason the suite has a minimum of three."

❦ 10 ❧

For the second time in under twenty-four hours—depending on how long we'd been in Fate—a public restroom changed on me.

Maksim hadn't been kidding about dropping us outside the restrooms, or how much we'd need to use them. The huntsman spider led to the present and aided our exit very precisely outside doors bearing signs for unisex occupancy. Eli dashed into one, and me into the other.

After washing my hands and tossing water on my face, I faced the world with a little more energy. Only a little, for dark lines had already started to appear under my eyes. I gripped the edge of the sink and faced myself in the mirror, toting up the tasks ahead. Too many. I gave up and focused on my assignment to find directors or sorcerers.

I blamed fatigue for my not noticing the differences until then.

The basics hadn't changed. I'd been in all three restrooms at one time or another over the year and a half I'd worked at the firm, and they were exactly the same. Sink on the left, cupboard and toilet on the right, and everything adjusted to match the height of whoever went into the room first. Off-white walls with no art whatsoever. Stainless steel and off-white porcelain fixtures. A plain, vinyl-edged rectangular mirror over the sink and black-and-white diamond-shaped tiles covering the floor.

An industrial rose-plus-other-flowers soap smell kept the air fresh. That remained the same.

On the other hand, the floor colors shifted to blues, midnight and a pale shade only a step or two from white.

Most notably, blue-flowered fabric hanging from rings off of a rod exactly like in a shower lined the back wall. Or rather, divided the room in half.

Because when I pulled the soft calico fabric aside, there stood a full walk-in shower. The blue tiles on the wall and floor would direct any excess water flow down the drain, so it didn't require a separate curtain. Opposite the shower sat a bank of lockers, metal covered in light blue enamel except for the handles and locks. The room also boasted a shelving unit bearing piles of folded blue towels with the Webmasters of Fate logo emblazoned on them, and a basket with an assortment of soaps.

All the comforts of home.

These fit because the room was twice as big as before. Squeezing in the additional space didn't bother me that much —after all, the office suite had only come with one restroom in the first place and the two extra ones were shoehorned in through sorcery.

But sorcery didn't explain the restroom changing within hours.

Maybe sometimes people leaving Fate needed a fast wash.

Alternatively, Maksim had warned us that we might find the world somewhat changed. He'd halted the poisonous sleaze, but not stopped it. A good chunk had already filtered into the fate-line and into the world.

I'd wonder if we were in the right place at all, save for the logo on the towels.

Such a small thing to rest security on.

Opening the hall door, I peered out and focused first on the carpet. That at least hadn't altered. Second glance told a different story: instead of shades of gray this was shades of blue with the webbing in midnight to match the bathroom, or vice-versa.

The hall bore a lot of artwork, most vaguely familiar but not worth investigating because a different element made clear it had changed as well: the length doubled. Regularly spaced doors lined the bulk, but at the far end it opened into a wider area from which spilled light and laughter.

Eli stood flush against the wall across the hall and a couple of feet further from the open area. His arms pressed tight against his sides, the occasional water drop still falling from his hands to the carpet. He seemed a lot smaller and younger in this setting, and harder to see. I had the sense he belonged there as much as the wall did, to the point that if I hadn't looked for him in particular, and known he was there, I'd have missed him.

"I'd say we're in the wrong place, but this is the office. It's just not the office I remember." I rubbed my hands against my pants, though I'd dried them off already. Even when I took a couple of steps in his direction, he didn't glance my way. His attention was fixed on the far end. "Are you okay—"

He pressed a finger to his lips. "You can see and hear me, right?"

"Yeah, same as always." I kept my voice low, watching to make sure he heard.

"There're a lot of people around, but nobody seems to see me." He hunched his shoulders. "I was all ready to explain why I was here except folk walk right by me without even looking my way."

"Maksim did say we'd find changes, but that's odd." I turned around, counting the offices on the corridor. So many, when there'd only ever been three before. At least half of these had permanent nameplates alongside blinking swipe pads. Or were the offices set up for handprint authentication?

If the suite had altered this much, everything was up for grabs.

"Do I even work here anymore?" A chill ran up my spine.

Eli pointed at an office door two down from the restrooms. "Isn't that you?"

I tiptoed across the carpet, heading in the wrong direction as in closer to the noise.

A gold-enameled number on the plain, maple-finished door designated the room as number 519. The metal name plate bracket held a paper slip rather than a permanent plate.

The paper slip featured a head shot recognizably of me, along with my name and title: Rosalind B. Williams, liaison to Atropos.

"Wrong and half-wrong. I'm an administrative assistant, not a liaison." I ran a finger over the middle initial. "And Rosalind Celia. C., not B."

Before Eli could respond, a light tenor called down the hall.

"Hey, Ruby, you're back!"

I recognized the voice, had heard it earlier in the day— but speaking to me, not some Ruby. I resisted whirling around. Hands shaking, I brushed any remaining dust motes from my shirt and pants.

The carpet muffled the sound of steps, but not enough for me to ignore the man's approach.

"Ruby?"

Or did he mean R.B.? Rosalind B.?

I turned around slowly to meet a pair of warm brown eyes. No glasses atop that long nose, but the pale face hadn't otherwise changed—still oval with a five o'clock shadow bristling along the edge of his cheeks and chin. Shaggy dark-brown hair brushed the top of his shoulders.

His clothes varied from earlier. He no longer wore a white, button-down shirt over a T-shirt but went with a dark green Polo and jeans. At least this time he'd put on shoes, albeit worn black sneakers with no socks covering those bony ankles. A hint of sandalwood clung to his skin, along with a touch of sweat to combine into a scent uniquely his.

"It's good to see you." He moved in, giving me ample time to draw back. I didn't, largely because I couldn't quite believe he intended to kiss me.

Wasn't he a shy sort who'd barely gotten to the point of asking me out—and even then, I had to push him beyond doing it sideways.

Yet his arms wrapped around me and lips brushed back and forth over mine in a fashion that struck me as both familiar and overly familiar. After all, I'd only just agreed to go out with him. Sort of. Then again, that was hours and another timeline ago.

But I'd figured out in college, after extensive experimentation, that I preferred kisses and caresses only when I'd reached the point of comfort, of having a strong emotional connection. Evidently we had a relationship in this timeline that had progressed far beyond an initial date—to the point he felt comfortable kissing me in public—in stark contrast to my memories. My body seemed torn between the two, both welcoming and not.

I froze, arms clamping against my sides. We were at work. He might be into that kind of public demonstration of affection, but not me. My last serious relationship had self-destructed—more on my part than his—before I graduated from college, all of two years ago plus change. Even then, I had strict rules about what my boyfriend could—or rather couldn't—do in any class we shared or in front of any professor.

And since when did I have a nickname other than Rose? My life in this timeline was on the verge of freaking me out. Blinking, I pulled back and shook my head—remembering too late about the spider in my hair and hoping I hadn't dislodged it.

Neil instantly gave me space, and a rueful, almost shy smile.

"Was it one of *those* cases?" He tucked a loose strand of hair behind my ear. "I wondered, when you didn't come home last night or offer any details."

"I . . . I . . ."

"Can't tell me. I know, I know. That's what I get for working on the mundane side of the business. Though even if I switched, honey, I'd hardly reach your classification level anytime soon." He stepped back, but his arms slid down my arms to hold my hands. His skin proved warm against my chilly fingers, his expression earnest and trusting. "I'm not asking where you were or what you did, but you're okay, right?"

"I guess?"

"Did you get any rest?"

A laugh escaped me, one that spiraled upward and had a hint of panic. Snapping my mouth shut, I swallowed hard. He expected me *home* last night, so either I lived with him or regularly stayed over. "It's been a bit rough. Not quite over yet."

"Got it." His gaze flickered at the door to my office, completely passing over Eli standing next to it. Neil shook his head and heaved a dramatic sigh. "I take it you're not here to join us?"

"Join you?"

"The Friday Pre-Holiday Foosball Tournament?" His

eyebrows raised, but the curve to his lips suggested he didn't really expect me to remember. "I came in third-place in the single contender ranks last time, and I've got my eye on winning it this time round. Unless you change your mind and want go in as a team?"

"No." That, at least, was an easy call.

"Neil, you're up next!" Bob's voice rang in my ears and Bob's face and body lurched into view down near the open area. This was hardly the Bob I saw in the office regularly. The same height, looks, and fit-after-fifty body, but no white hat, suit, or shoes. The man I knew took his position as head of the branch overly seriously. This version of him wore jeans and a Michigan T-shirt. At least his collegiate love hadn't changed, but his attitude! His expression so open instead of his usual superciliousness.

"*Bob's* in on this?" I blinked and looked and blinked and looked. Nothing changed.

"Of course he is." Neil said. "And a decent foosball player too, even if he did go to the wrong university."

I managed a grin, no matter how shaky, as Neil rolled his eyes and made a mocking face. "But he's the senior director. I'd have expected him to only show up and the end and pat the winner on the head."

"Bob the senior director? Never." Neil wrinkled his nose waved a dismissive hand. "He's a decent artistic designer, and a dab hand at embedding sorcerous integrations, but definitely not on the managerial track."

All of which meant there were a lot more differences. It might take ages to investigate, time I didn't have.

Eli remained on the far side of the office door. He glanced at me and Neil on occasion, but held his phone and was busy texting, and frowning. Then again, he didn't know enough about the firm to catch the nuances in operations.

"So who is senior?"

"Did you hit your head while you were gone?" Neil traced a line down the side of my face, finger triggering jolts of energy in its wake. "Geneva, of course. She got the promotion six months ago. Rumor has it she's fast-tracking toward a berth on the Lachesis Governing Board one of these days."

Geneva up and Bob down. That better fit my sense of a just arrangement, since he left a lot of the management and oversight to her. Artistic design and sorcerous integration might well suit him a lot better.

Was that what he'd wanted, though? In the other, the real, timeline where he'd set the sleaze?

Then again, Maksim had said something about changing Fate being tricky enough just ensuring people still existed in the new timeline let alone rose up in the world. The more requirements built into altering Fate, the less the world would change.

The current situation bore this out if Bob had wanted to still exist but have more power. He'd ensured Philly was a bigger part of the corporation, but not wound up on top of it.

I should probably be glad, as the fewer major changes, the easier it would be to get around—and the more likely Tanisha was still on her way to help Maksim.

But the changes that did exist left me uneasy for some reason I couldn't put my finger on.

Or, rather, I could but I didn't want to because I'd liked that kiss, surprise as it was, a lot more than I'd expected.

"Brydall, last call or you forfeit your turn!" Bob waved from the end.

"Gotta go. Call me if you need me, and get some rest before the fireworks." Neil jogged back down the hall.

Leaving me exactly where he'd found me, but with nervous energy doing tap dances in my belly.

"Is he your boyfriend?" Eli slipped across the hall, shoes making no sound on the carpet.

"He wasn't before, at least not yet, but it seems he is here. Then again, he's also a lot different. More confident and outgoing than I'd have thought." I shivered and sucked in air through my teeth with a soft hiss. "There're more changes here than I'd anticipated. We can probably find directors willing to help us, but we'll have to convince them and . . . It's probably faster if we go for Maksim's sisters at your house."

"Yeah, with Mom and Gramma. They showed up after only calling a little ahead of time, but Mom said no matter since they always leave the place better than they found it. And she likes them well enough, when they're not reminding her over and over what the doc says she can and can't do." Eli pulled in closer. "But no one's answering their phones. Not even the landline. Can we go now?"

"Soon. But let me call and see if Tanisha still exists first. And maybe we can get a little more information."

Hoping my hand hadn't changed, I placed it flat against the pad next to the door. Light bloomed around it, blue in keeping with the overall color scheme.

With a sharp click, the door unlocked.

Ducking into the office, I shut the door with a click and leaned back against it to let the wood hold me up.

Eli'd slipped through before the door closed, took one look around, and plopped down on a blue, faux-leather sofa. The cushions creaked beneath him as he swiveled around to lie back and toss his legs over one of the arms in a classic kids-don't-have-bones style. His fingers swept and tapped away at his phone, without cracking his frown so much as a hair.

A sofa. In this timeline, I ranked an office with a sofa. Only a two-seater, but still a sofa.

And a window.

With a view.

What in tarnation had the other me done to deserve this?

Ignoring the rest of the room, I scooted across the soft carpet to press my nose against the glass. The window wouldn't open, being nothing more than two panes of glass at least four feet wide and as much or more high. On the other side stood City Hall in all its ornate glory. The sun remained high enough in the sky to minimize shadows and maximize my ability to soak in details of the bell tower closer than I'd ever seen before.

Here stood another difference between what-should-be and what-currently-was. The office I'd always worked in was down near the Delaware River, but without any nice views of anything better than the hotel next door—that view belonging to only the directors, who had offices.

This office of Webmasters filled a whole floor, if not more, and sat right in Center City.

Equipped with sufficient space to allocate a whole room—and view—to me.

Turning around, I breathed deep—in, out, in out—and looked around, and around, and around.

A low, two-drawer filing cabinet in one corner with both drawers slightly ajar, and empty by the look of it. The chair looked nice but a bit weird, being a steel-and-mesh affair in place of the standard, cushioned chair I'd inherited from my predecessor. It sat at a desk, turned slightly as though someone had just risen and walked away and left their silver laptop behind. The desk was really nothing more than a computer table, lacking drawers and any kind of front panel, a stark change from the reception desk I worked at. The walls were bare except for a digital clock on one side wall and a poster for the firm's *Survive Vesuvius!* game on the other.

Nothing gave me any sense of who I was in this timeline. Most of the furnishings appeared sufficiently neutral to belong to the room regardless. My nameplate had been temporary, only paper. A new addition? Or implying I was just passing through.

Though Neil complicated that.

Correction. One item had a bit of personality: a glass reusable water bottle set within a bright turquoise rubber covering to keep it from breaking.

Half-filled.

Why had I not asked Maksim about the existence of another version of me in this timeline? I hoped not. One of me was quite enough to deal with. Neil's not having seen Ruby or R.B. in a while gave me hope I sufficed for the time-line, but ignorance in this case was not bliss.

All the more reason to get in, get sorcerers or directors, and hop back into Fate.

Even if I desperately wanted a nap first.

Then my eyes scanned the clock again as I kept making rounds, and the time registered. I stopped, hands on my hips, and stared.

"Hah."

"Wha?" Eli pried his gaze from his phone and squinted at me.

"It's only four." I pointed at the dark, solid lines on the light gray clock face. "We got back here earlier than we left. The spider should've taken us a couple hours further along."

"Maybe that's why no one's answering." He waved his phone at me. "If it's four, Maksim's family is just arriving. Does that mean I'm here twice? How would the phone company handle that, do my texts get assigned to the other me's phone?"

"I got no answer for that. I'm hoping it's just us, but . . ." I grimaced and edged over to the desk. "It's probably better if we don't run into a version of you that hasn't gone off to find Maksim. Do you remember when you left your house?"

"Five-thirty? Six? Something like that." He rolled his eyes. "We didn't eat a sit-down dinner, you know, 'cause there was just so much food everywhere that even if we nibbled on stuff, almost nobody'd ever notice."

"Then we'll stick here until after six, just in case. I'd say we could go to my place and catch a quick rest, but . . ." I studied the door. The room had excellent sound-proofing and

I couldn't hear anything from the play area. All the same, I preferred not spilling details where anyone could hear. "I'm not sure where I live in this timeline."

"So we're going to ask Maksim's sisters or some of Mom's friends to help out." Eli nodded, scrunching further down into the sofa. "Cool. They'll be sure to."

"Yes, but first I'll try calling Tanisha." I settled into the chair, which proved more comfortable than I'd expected. Quieter as well, with no squeaks as I rolled it up to the desk and back. "See where the official team is at, and make sure they're still headed here."

Though if it was late afternoon Friday, would they have even left? I'd been so sure we'd get back in the wee hours of Saturday morning, when they'd be on their way.

"Okay. Alright if I nab some zees over here?" He turned sideways on the sofa and curled up, one hand rubbing his stomach. "I don't feel too fine."

"Are you hungry?" If this office suite had a break room suitable for playing foosball, it had to have a kitchen or snack area too.

"Nah. I'm good."

"All right." I pulled my bottom lip between my teeth as I gauged the laptop. Eased it open, but the screen asked for a password to access the contents and I had no idea what I might use, or rather I had too many ideas.

The room didn't come with any kind of phone, not even a cheap landline in a corner. I slipped my phone out of my pocket, letting out a short sigh as the screen lit up. One thumbprint authentication and a few swipes later, and I was faced with a ton of unread messages and voicemails.

Eli's phone might have trouble connecting up, but mine didn't seem to have any issues whatsoever. Then again, our phones came from separate ecosystems. Maybe one handled alternative timelines better than the other? Or we had different carriers and mine switched over okay, but his didn't exist.

Too many problems and possibilities, none of which evidently troubled Eli as he slipped into sleep. His mouth lay open and the occasional snore emerged, unnerving me until I got used to it.

But the phone thing, plus the differences between reality and this timeline, made my skin itch. The other me clearly had a position of some power or influence. Just what I'd always wanted? Or not.

My fingers hovered over the phone app, because I should make the call first as promised. Alas, I was weak and inched over to swipe into messages instead.

The first thread of messages up was from Neil. Clicking into it entered me into a long conversation between him and my other self.

Him early this morning: <<Hey honey, it's your morning check-in.>>

One minute later: <<You didn't come home last night. You okay or do you need me to raise holy hell with the firm? >>

Ten minutes later: <<Countdown initiated>>

Me, shortly after: <<Cancel countdown.>>

Also me: <<Case blowing up in my face. Sorry I didn't call. All gone hell-and-back.>>

Still me: <<Miss you so much.>>

Him: <<Countdown to cuddle-time tonight?>>

Me: <<All systems go!>>

And more along those lines. My cheeks grew hot, and I swiped back up into the list of unread messages in case Eli should wake and come peek over my shoulders. Not that he had and would, but . . . I hadn't only been texting Neil, I'd been *sexting* him.

None of which I remembered. Except . . . Neil's kiss in the hall had seemed familiar, no matter that it wasn't.

I closed my eyes and leaned back, a kaleidoscope of memories of him flashing through me. The kiss in the hallway ranked as pretty tame in comparison.

No! I bolted straight up and punched the air with my fists. I'd never kissed Neil, until now, and I'd only just agreed to go somewhere with him in the real timeline, not even an official date.

A glance at the phone showed the next unread message trail came from my mom. I didn't want to deal with her in the real world, why do so here? I swept my hand across the phone to close the scroll of personal messages.

Once in the phone app, I scrolled past all manner of contacts I didn't recognize to the Ts, only to not find Tanisha there. When I broke down and searched, she showed up under A, for Tanisha Aponsu. She had two listings there, the second one noted as "direct."

My chest rose and fell as my breathing shallowed. Nervous shudders rippled through me and left every nerve alight.

I clicked on direct number.

Sounds of blowing wind or maybe an engine crackled in the background, but a smooth, resonant voice overrode them. Sadly, the speaker didn't use English or any language I recognized.

"Hello?" I lifted the phone closer to my mouth and ear. "Is this Tanisha who works with Maksim Irving?"

"Who is this?" The voice shifted into English, in an accent I couldn't place.

"Um, I'm Rose. Rose Williams. I work with Maksim. If you're Tanisha, he told me to call you for help." Sweat made my palms slick. I shifted the phone from hand to hand, wiping the free hands on my pants.

"Ahhh . . ." The speaker didn't admit or deny the name. "When did he tell you?"

"When and where or how long ago from now?" I asked.

Tanisha—might as well presume the name belonged to her—half-covered the phone and yelled something in another language, this time Spanish. Maybe. It was muffled enough I couldn't make out what she said, but several of the sounds were familiar. Then she uncovered the phone again and addressed me. "However you want to answer."

Right. How to compress everything into a short, comprehensible narrative. Or, rather, how to try.

"We were at the site of the sleaze. He tried . . . We tried to banish it, because there were three of us though only he's a director. But Eli's a sorcerer too, and I believe in magic even though I can't do it." I swallowed. Every word came out a hair faster than the one before. "But it went wrong, and we only half-banished it and now Maksim's still back there with his arm stuck in the fate-line because I couldn't power the spell or something, and we undershot returning to now so he'll only have called you a couple of hours ago butsomuch-hashappened."

A sharp clap on the other end made me jerk.

"Slow down." Tanisha's firm tones made that an order. "Breathe deep."

I did, hands shaking as I held the phone.

"Again."

This time, I let out a deep, shuddering breath after. My upper back ached and arms were tight against my chest. It took several moments and focus to force my body into a semblance of less tension.

"Let's begin closer to the beginning," she said. "I am, indeed, Tanisha. You've reached the right personage. My team is headed to Bermuda to deal with the sleaze. Maksim knows that. Why did he go ahead of us?"

"He was, um, concerned you wouldn't make it in time. That things were changing too fast."

"Well and even if so, much change wouldn't keep us from our appointed tasks. He should know that by now. Perhaps a little bent pride played a part, that he was taken in for a while as well, though so has been half the seaboard." She heaved a deep sigh, then her tone shifted. "Rose Williams, you said. Would you be the receptionist he mentioned, who was not caught in the changing Fate?"

"Yeah." I nodded even though she couldn't see.

"Well done. I could wish there were such as you in other offices as well."

The unexpected praise sent a wave of warmth through me. My lips curved into a grin, one I quickly wiped off and bit my lip instead.

"Now, why did he ask you to go with him?" Tanisha asked.

"As a witness."

"And you said there was a third who accompanied you?"

"Eli, Maksim's stepson." A glance over at the sofa showed him still curled, still rubbing his stomach, and still snoring. "He was there in the coffee shop when . . . I think Maksim was worried we'd be attacked, so he took us into the internet and then Fate."

"Where is he now? Eli, that is."

"He came back with me, because he can do magic and I can't." The last vestiges of warmth from her praise seeped away, leaving my fingers and toes chilled.

"Good. How old is he?"

"Eleven or twelve. Or maybe thirteen." Another look at him still left me in doubt, though his voice had started cracking in the web—and hadn't done so since.

Tanisha muttered something in syllables that blended together, with a lot of long a-ahs. Switching back to English, she gave a small sigh. "Tell me, slow and with details, what happened when you reached the sleaze."

The muscles in my back eased as I loosed the burden and shared everything I could. In between spates, I made use of the reusable water bottle atop the desk. Surely my alternate self wouldn't begrudge me, as she had the same taste as me.

All the tension swooped back into me when Tanisha asked about Eli and my return to the present, and what had and hadn't changed.

"I don't know how much yet." A hard push with my foot sent the chair swirling around so I could re-absorb the details of the room. "But the firm has a much bigger outpost in Philly now and . . . Apparently I'm living with one of the other employees, someone I'd barely said hi to before. Do I need to look out for an alternate me?"

I held my breath as I waited on the answer. It came quick enough, and started with a soft laugh.

"Oh no, that's one fear you need not have. There are other worlds, of that many of us are sure, but there is only one Fate for us. And only ever one timeline in the present, although it may be experienced very different ways by different people. That's why it isn't represented by a simple line or plane in Fate but rather a celestial web. All those fantasists and scientists positing infinite alternate times—we have no record of any such ever existing. Perhaps in other dimensions, or it might be that our Fate is one of many looping about and always remaining inviolate from each other. " Tanisha chuckled again. "It's simpler if you think of the real timeline as the goal and this alternate timeline as an accidental stopping point. But there will be only one *you* here."

Of which I only understood half, and stored the rest away to ponder in the future, assuming I had one. The last sentence reassured me.

Just in time for her next to send a cold chill down my spine.

"There are changes reaching here. One of the members of my team has already switched over to someone I refuse to remember." A clicking sound. "But we are on our way, by private jet. It will still take many hours for us to reach Bermuda, nearly a day, and another hour or two to get into Fate and hike back. Maksim will have to hold until then. Do you believe he can?"

"Ye-es." I squirmed in my chair, then noticed Eli had woken up. He sat hunched over on the sofa, staring at me. He could definitely hear me, and probably Tanisha as well. "He didn't look too good, though."

"Maksim?" Eli mouthed.

I nodded.

An instant later he did so as well, vigorously.

"Eli agrees with me that Maksim would appreciate as early a rescue as possible."

For which I received a shaky smile in reward.

"If you can convince at least one other director and a few sorcerers, whether affiliated with Lachesis or not, to go with you that would be well," Tanisha said. The background noise intensified for a few moments. She paused until it had died down, then continued. "I do not say this is necessary, but it is always preferable to have more options."

"But who?"

"I will text you a list of people in the area who've worked with Atropos in the past, or whom I or others on my team have met and consider trustworthy. Might take a little bit to compose, but not so very long. Though mind, with the shifting of the timelines, I cannot guarantee that the versions of them you meet match our memories. Take care who you trust, but there will be those you can."

"Right. With no magic to know if they're lying or not." Though maybe Eli had picked up a good spell.

"Sorcery is not a cure-all," Tanisha said.

"Yeah." A bitter belly-chuckle escaped me. "Easier to say when you're a sorcerer and people aren't looking down on you."

"Have you never met another person who believes in sorcery but does not work it?" she asked.

"No, though I've been told some exist." A long pause, that I finally broke. "Are there many?"

"Oh yes," came her instantaneous answer, "thousands at the least computation. It's a Western idea, this division of the world into sorcerers and mundanes. Born, I believe, of Enlightenment sorcerers who chose make disbelief more powerful in many Western circles. There are other ways. Ask me on the other side of this, and I will introduce you to some."

"Thanks. I appreciate that." It had a distantly familiar ring. My middle sister's boyfriend might've spouted something along those lines the last time I saw her and him, but I'd blown him off. Worthy of thought, but not during the current situation. "So you're going to send me a list, and I'm going to convince two or three to go back with us, or just with me if Eli wants to stay here."

He looked up from his phone and shook his head hard.

"But that's just a precaution in case you don't make it in time," I continued with more confidence than I felt. "Which you will."

I turned the phone to speaker mode so that Eli could definitely hear her reply.

"Exactly so. Hold to the timeline you remember, and we'll see it restored."

All the same, once she hung up I stayed in place. Even

kept holding the phone at the exact same angle, and reran the conversation through in my mind.

Until Eli coughed.

"No one's still answering me. Not even Mom or Gramma on the landline." His face had a plaintive cast. "Can we go home? I don't care how they fuss over me, I just . . . "

"Yeah." I tucked my phone away, refusing to glance at the still-unread messages. I had hopes for Tanisha's list, but enlisting allies from people who cared about Maksim seemed a better bet. "Let's go."

❧ 12 ❧

In the large scope of things, leaving proved a minor bobble because I didn't know my way around the building. We had to explore, especially with respect to finding a way to get to the elevators without passing the foosball tournament. No sense risking another exchange with Neil, or anyone else who thought they knew Ruby or R.B.

The soft carpet helped, muffling our footsteps, as did the noise from the tournament complete with people chanting "Brydall, Brydall, Brydall." I misinterpreted this as brittle until I remembered Neil's last name—after he burst out with a "Take that!" over and above the commotion.

He probably wanted me to watch him win.

Another time, another timeline.

Luscious aromas drifted out from the area too—coffee and fresh popcorn—but I held my breath and slipped around with Eli to enter the elevator. Wood paneling covered the bottom half of the walls, but above the railing gilt-edged mirrors surrounded us. The two men already in the elevator plus the two of us turned into a veritable multitude with the mirrors reflecting ad infinitum.

We got second and third glances from the other people in the elevator, or rather I did. My shirt had held up pretty well overall. Maybe there were more wrinkles than when I'd started the day, hours and hours ago, but it didn't look too bad to my eyes. My hair wasn't too tousled, though I was hesitant to do more than run my fingers through it loosely for fear of disturbing the spider lurking there. In all, I might appear to have started celebrating the holiday weekend a bit early.

An older White man in an expensive, custom-fitted blue business suit and a slightly younger White man in an off-the-rack version clearly meant to look the same—and failing—rode down with us. The younger glanced at me a couple of times, paying no attention to Eli, and started a desultory conversation about holidays bringing out all the riffraff and tourist element.

When the elevator reached the ground floor, the two men departed leaving me for last.

And Eli, of course.

An odd sparkle outlined his body as we moved through the plain gray-tiled, gray-walled foyer and out glass doors into the world.

Instead of the heat and humidity we'd left in the previous timeline, we emerged into a balmy evening. Exactly the kind of weather that brought out everyone who enjoyed eating and drinking outside. All the sidewalk cafes would do well tonight.

Sadly for our purposes, that meant more foot traffic to wade through if we went in the wrong direction. Some restaurants with sidewalk areas had already started filling up near us. Philly was a pretty mixed-use city, with most of the central areas combining commercial and residential spaces alongside each other. Even though we'd exited a business, savory aromas floated over from the Italian place to the left and the

Lebanese to the right, both of which I'd visited or ordered from in the past even though I lived and worked farther away.

Alas, this wasn't the time to stop for dinner.

The motor traffic wasn't that bad either. Occasional hold-ups, particularly when some pedestrian tried to beat a light across a crosswalk, but otherwise the mélange of buses, trucks, and cars moved along at decent clip.

Plus taxis and ride-share cars—one zipped by with a familiar logo leaning against the dashboard.

Slipping a hand into my special pocket, my fingers verified the smooth rectangles of my driver's license and credit card still existed alongside my phone.

Not that I knew where we were headed, but it had to be somewhere within an easy walking distance of the coffee house. Otherwise, Maksim might've given Eli more grief for straying far from home. Therefore, they lived near the Delaware River.

"You want us to catch a taxi or summon an Uber?"

"It's not too far." Eli rolled his shoulders. "Let's walk."

"Your call." Didn't seem such a good idea to me. He still rubbed his stomach now and then, and his complexion had a hint of grayness in the bright sunlight. Then again, he started fidgeting and bouncing up and down. Walking might work to ease out some of the tension clearly humming in him.

I'd stay ready to flag down a ride if necessary.

He set the pace, a brisk measure that required a certain amount of weaving around and between other pedestrians. I followed a half-step behind.

Almost immediately the hairs along the back of my neck started to prickle.

People noticed me, but no one seemed to see Eli. Time after time, folk passing us gave me room but bumped him without ever apologizing or showing any awareness of what they'd done. Most of the pedestrians appeared to be White, especially those in business attire, though this being a Friday in summer there were fewer of those than in other seasons.

The two of us walking side-by-side didn't work. No matter which side, or how close together, somebody inevitably tried to pass and knocked him in the process.

"I don't like any of this, so I'm going ahead." He bent and tightened his shoelaces. "Follow me, okay?"

"Got it." I kept my voice low. "But where are we going? No guarantee I'll keep sight of you."

"Elfreth's Alley." And he took off. Still walking, though his pace verged on a jog.

I started slower, letting him put distance between us. A third of a block seemed a good length, especially now that I had a destination to aim for.

The balmy weather made slower walking a pleasant matter. Time to smell the roses, when living in the outer suburbs where my mother still resided. Or check out shop windows and dining options, in the city.

Over the years, I'd made a virtue of being able to walk separately, either on my own or with my mother while my father and older brother went on ahead. Or just my older brother, leaving me to hold hands with both our parents. For whatever reason stuck in his brain, he hated being associated with the family from age eleven until after he went to college.

Though, really, it wasn't so much our parents he minded as me trailing after him. He'd sacrifice the company of either parent to be able to pretend he wasn't related to me, no matter how much we resembled each other. I had a tendency to flop around, limbs nearly as loose as a rag doll, that he hated. The more he tried to get away, of course the more I sought to keep up even though my one-year-younger legs never quite managed.

Wait.

All wrong. I didn't have an older brother. *I* was the oldest of three girls with my sisters always trying to keep up with *me*. My father had remarried after he and my mother divorced, and produced a baby still in diapers. So technically I did have a brother, but he was about as far from being older as possible.

The other me's memories pressed on my brain.

I picked up my pace. Folded my trembling hands against my abdomen to reduce the shaking. Gritting my teeth, I shoved any and all thoughts of brothers out of my head. This wasn't my timeline, and I refused to allow it to suck me in.

A muffled ding from my pocket announced the arrival of a new text.

I wasted a whole block fretting over whether or not to check it. Arriving at an intersection just as the light changed, I caught Eli's heels disappearing ever-farther down the block. Good thing he'd told me where to find him, as I'd not catch up now without flat-out running.

The light stretched, and stretched.

Another ding.

It might be Tanisha, sharing contacts to approach if Maksim's sisters declined. Or offering other suggestions.

At least people weren't watching me anymore. The folks strolling and striding along the busy sidewalk seemed less uniform, more mixed. Perhaps the approach of high tourist areas—or just the passage of time and space. All the same, I had elbow room to spare.

A third ding.

The urge won out. Snatching my phone from my pocket, I put myself in multi-task mode with constant glances to-and-from the screen to my surroundings.

Nothing from Tanisha.

A text or two from my mother, but after the false memory of an older brother, I didn't want to go there.

A very recent series from Neil.

First: <<I won!! Wish you could've seen it live, but some of my friends got it on camera.>>

Then: <<You off on another case?>>

And, three seconds later, a follow-up: <<No vacation?>>

Memories tried to well up within me, of lingering over shared breakfasts or him stopping by my office with lunch on the days he knew I wouldn't eat otherwise. The two of us dancing in clubs, in the street, and at a fair once. Worst were false recollections of dancing to music in our apartment. Our shared apartment that I'd never been in and had no idea where in the city it was, yet somehow had memorized the layout.

My speed slowed, and I slipped through groups of other walkers to the mix of restaurants and shops lining the street. Paused in the shade where one melded into another.

I rejected the memories, carefully replacing them with recollections of meeting Neil for the first time *less than a week* earlier. Him sending shy looks my way while hiding among the other young White guys in town for a research jaunt. Him talking to me one-on-one *for the first time* earlier *this same day*.

Yet even as I did so, my fingers tapped away at my phone sending Neil not one but two texts. <<Important errand. Might run late. Might not.>> And: <<Wait for me??>>

His reply appeared within a matter of seconds: <<Always.>>

I didn't know Neil, not yet. I repeated the words over and over until I walked to their beat.

At least the texts should keep him from texting again for a while.

Just in case.

All the same, I stuffed my phone away and vowed not to check again until I'd reached Eli's home.

Picking up my pace, I didn't bother searching for him in the crowds ahead. I'd lost him and had no idea which way he headed home. No doubt he knew all the shortcuts in this neighborhood.

So I took the shortest route I knew. Kept repeating the denial of knowing Neil well as I wove in and out amidst the sidewalk traffic. Even with the added press of tourist crowds as I approached Independence Park, I made good time. Passed buses and bus stops, skirted around the regular stairs down to SEPTA stops with the tattered and colorful advertising posters plastering them. Skipped around kiosks selling newspapers and stuff.

Everything resembled the timeline before—except when it didn't. The headlines were off, and half to three-quarters of the names unfamiliar to me whether politicians, sports stars, or glitterati.

A loose newspaper blew my way at one point, smashing against my chest. I fought my way clear, discarding bits of paper this way and that, but in the process a photo caught my eye. A lineup of living presidents attending the funeral of someone or other. I only recognized Carter—no one else. There were no Bushes or Clintons or Obamas, only strangers. Two of them were women, and all White. I spared the time to skim the caption and leading paragraphs, but still found only unfamiliar politicians' names.

With all that distracted me, Eli would've arrived first even if he hadn't had a head start. I only knew I'd find him somewhere along the alley, not where, so I slowed down as soon as I reached the super-narrow street.

For the first time, our surroundings really dawned.

Elfreth's Alley was one of the coolest and most private historic areas in the city, comprised of old row houses dating way back to the eighteenth and early nineteenth-centuries. Most remained privately owned, other than two that had become a museum, and only people with the right connections ever got to see the insides of even one of the other houses.

And now I'd join their ranks! Not that I'd wish for the whole catastrophe to happen just for this, but at least I'd get a small benefit out of it. I'd certainly walked the alley enough times in the real timeline to appreciate how special it was.

Row houses lined the street to either side, all covered with brick. Brightly painted shutters hung to either side of every window, colors carefully matched to doors. Double lines of removable posts were inserted into the brick sidewalk on either side, ensuring the cobbled street was narrow enough to discourage motorized traffic.

A sweet, light breeze blew down the narrow expanse. Although the area was popular with tourists, no one else lurked around at the moment. We had the whole area to ourselves.

I'd have expected Eli to go inside, but maybe leave the door open or hang half-in and half-out waiting for me.

Rather, he leaned against one of the waist-high poles lining the sidewalk to either side of the single-lane cobbled drive. Arms crossed over his chest and chin low, he stared at the house opposite.

The residence in question wasn't the biggest or smallest house on the street, from the front at least. In decent repair, it boasted blue shutters on either side of the windows and a matching door, plus nearby basement access though that was likely blocked from below. Although some of the other houses had modern, double-sash windows, this featured an old-fashioned style comprised of several square blocks of glass.

The alley was in enough shade with the approach of evening that, despite the sun remaining well above the horizon, I'd expect to find lights shining from within the house. All the more so since Eli had gone looking for Maksim to get permission to spend the night away from the press of people.

This particular house featured only shadows. No lights visible inside, none, nor sounds of people talking or laughing. Yet given Eli's fixed stare, this had to be the place.

My life had changed markedly between timelines—why hadn't we considered his might have as well?

I bit my lip and tried to figure out something encouraging to say. Nothing came to mind, so I waited instead.

"I knocked." Eli grunted. "No one answered."

"Maybe your family doesn't live here in this timeline?" I stretched my arms, then twined my fingers together so as not to twitch over-much.

"Gramma would be here. Someone would be. We've owned it for ages." He canted his body a little forward and wagged a finger in the air, voice going high. "Gramma always says we lived here long before anyone started talking about priceless heritage and national landmark, and we'll be living here long after." He straightened and gave a sour laugh. "She'd never move."

Digging a hand into his pocket, he pulled out a key. The dark bronze rested evenly against his palm.

Turning his head to the side, he glanced up at me. His breathing sped up, chest heaving, and fear shone in his eyes.

"Your call." In so many things, but especially whether or not to try to enter his home.

Eli's breath whistled for a few minutes as he shifted to panting. Then he rose, chin high, and strode over to the door.

Inserted the key. In the quiet alleyway, it clicked as it turned.

He pressed his free hand against the door, stroking it. A faint shimmer of blue-tinged light manifested along the front and then dissipated.

A moment later the door opened, and he beckoned for me to follow.

13

Caution glued my feet to the cobbles for several moments. Only the memory of the key shining in Eli's palm, the key that had unlocked the door, allowed me to pick up my feet, climb the sole stair, and enter the house.

Apart from the clop of Eli rushing through the first floor, all lay still and quiet. Even the rush and blow of an air conditioner was absent. A gentle hint of roses and peonies hung in the air, which held a hint of morning cool. It was certainly not so warm as outside, especially with curtains and shades pulled. Someone, likely Eli, had flipped a switch and an electric light overhead provided ample illumination.

Although I let the door swing closed behind me, I stayed in the front of the house. No matter how I wandered around the living room, I tried not to touch anything. Eli had invited me in, with a gesture, but I didn't belong. Goose bumps prickled along my arms and legs.

The door opened right into the living room, narrower than it was long. It ended with a door left ajar, revealing narrow stairs leading up. The next room over might have been a dining room once, but the doorway offered a glimpse of a brass bedstead topped with unmade mattress and box spring. Likely a kitchen and perhaps a washroom lay beyond, but I opted not to venture so far.

A fireplace—wide but not particularly deep, dominated one side of the living room. Cream-colored paint covered the ceiling, walls, and chimney—all but the wood mantel over the hearth. It glowed with polish, matching the old, wide floorboards, of some reddish wood, where they peeked out from under the rug at the corners and in the rooms beyond. A simple rectangular mirror edged in black and gilt hung over the mantel, which supported several framed photos both casual and posed.

Two rocking chairs, upholstered in a deep-burgundy fabric, sat near the window at the front, with a narrow table between them. It held a pierced jar from which came the floral scent, and nothing else atop. A shelf below boasted rolls of yarn and at least two unfinished pieces by the number of knitting needles protruding from masses of yarn and stitches.

A long, narrow sofa in a lighter shade stood opposite, on the far side of the fireplace, and a large braided rug in a thousand colors covered most of the floor, with additional multicolored floor mats under the rocking chairs.

At least two dozen family photos, old and new, black-and-white and colored, adorned the wall opposite the fireplace. Among them hung framed documents as well, mostly old.

Every piece in view spoke of love and care, but not much money. The upholstery had sunlight stains no amount of labor could cure, and signs of rips or loose sections carefully tacked back together. A few patches of moth damage marred the braided rug, though they had a blurriness that suggested the moths had been treated and stopped.

The signs of wear I could understand. My parents had lived with beat-up furniture and rickety tables for years out of sentiment—and the shared ability to procrastinate dealing with it or agreeing on what to buy to replace it, hence their staying married way past when they could've split.

Yet the unmade bed in the next room over nagged at me. That wasn't just putting off tasks.

The first thing it brought to mind instead was that someone had needed it, who couldn't climb stairs, and that person needed it no longer. Maybe something had happened with Shauntelle's pregnancy, to leave the house dark and unoccupied. All food for the shower covered and put away, so thoroughly as not to scent the air, and the decorations hidden from sight.

Unfortunately, other possibilities also suggested themselves to me.

Because nowhere in the living room, despite the ample use of cheap, standard frames obtainable at any drug store or dollar mart, did there hang any artwork. Including the kind of art children did and parents cherished.

At least mine and most of my friends had. Or maybe that was me universalizing from my own experience in the wrong way.

Eli returned from the back of the house, which evidently extended farther than I might have thought. After one glance my way, eyes wild and hands shaking, he bolted up the stairs. Thumps overhead marked his progression through the second and third floor.

My hands firmly entwined behind my back, I headed for the wall. Much as the documents would interest me under other circumstances, I skipped them in favor of the photos. These portrayed members of a family, given the resemblances.

Many of the faces reminded me a bit of Eli, a detail which eased some of my discomfort at being in the house. His key worked, and the photos showcased his family, which meant he had some right to invite people in.

Problem was, none of the pictures included him.

Or Maksim.

There were no recent wedding photos, and certainly none even remotely resembling the one Maksim displayed prominently in his office—of him and Shauntelle with Eli.

Fingers cold and a lump forming in my throat, I crossed the rug and checked the photos on the mantel. Still no images of Eli or Maksim.

Did Shauntelle live here or had a relative wound up in the house instead? I'd only seen her a few times in passing, plus the photo in Maksim's office on occasion. She appeared in many of the pictures, but perhaps as a relative and not the resident here.

A step caught my attention, coming not from far overhead but nearby. Just outside, in fact, for when I swung around the door appeared ajar—not much, yet enough for thin lines of light across the top and side.

I untwined my hands, ready to hold them up and offer . . . whatever explanation I could until Eli joined me to do so.

The door opened no further.

A blast of power pulsed through the room. It knocked me over onto the floor. My breath rushed out of me in an "urp" as I landed on my side on the rug with a solid thump. My shoulder and hip took the brunt of the fall, and immediately began to ache. I curled into a ball.

Spirals of blue energy wound around my wrists, knotting them together. A similar spiral pinioned my ankles. A third, wider, covered my mouth but not my nose. The energy fizzed and burbled along my skin, although only slightly warmer than room temperature, doing no damage but keeping me a prisoner.

It resembled the light that had flared briefly across the

front of the house when Eli unlocked the door. He must've disarmed a spell of some kind—related to the spell that whipped through here.

Far above, a heavy thump suggested it had caught Eli as well.

With that the door opened. A woman entered, mostly in shadow until she moved into the pool of light from the chandelier.

She seemed tall, though since I lay on the floor gazing up at her she could've been short and looked otherwise.

She had a definite resemblance to Eli. They shared the same medium-brown skin and cool undertones. A small nose marked the center of her round face. She wore her hair short in tight, textured curls, furthering the likeness to her son, although her eyes were bright amber rather than dark brown.

In most of the photos on display, she wore ample jewelry —layers of bracelets around wrists, glittery dangling earrings, and strings of beads at her neck.

At this moment, she wore no jewelry save for post earrings with blue and green beads held tight against her ears. The colors went well with the blue-green medical scrubs covering her body. Yet the clothes pointed to another discrepancy between the real timeline and this, for Maksim had mentioned on occasion, and I had reason to know, that Shauntelle was on the law faculty at Temple.

So why wear scrubs? Or the odor of ammonia hanging about her—and definitely emanating from her sensible black shoes.

Because despite the odd angle from which I observed her, I had no doubt this was Shauntelle, Eli's mother and Maksim's wife.

Despite the curves of her breasts, belly, and hips, she appeared anything but eight months pregnant.

"Intruder." Shauntelle rubbed her hands together, the

light blue haze coating them a perfect match for the bonds holding me prisoner.

The substance over my mouth thinned. A pressure on my head pushed my teeth and lips apart, another force bore down against my diaphragm. Was I supposed to answer?

I managed to utter a rough but coherent word. "No."

"Thief."

Again external forces encouraged—forced—me to answer but I managed only the same word. "No."

"Trashing my house, if I hadn't stopped you." She bent down and bared her teeth in snarl. "Tell your bosses to give up. I'm not selling."

I tried to respond, but only mangled mutters emerged.

"No screams." She gave my mouth a hard tap.

"I'm not here to trash your house or rob you or beat you or do anything to you." I dragged in a hard breath at the end, having gotten the whole thing out in one wind.

"Then what are you here for?" Shauntelle rose, glaring down at me from her full height of at least five and a half feet.

"I need your help to save your husband."

"Husband?" This earned a full belly laugh. Hands on either hips, she let loose peal after peal.

"Yes. Husband." I couldn't scream, but my loudest speaking voice still got her attention.

"You believe that." For a second time, she crouched down next to me, examining my face as though that of an alien being. "Or you're a better liar than any I've met. How'd you get in, and tell the truth this time."

"Eli let me in." Distant thumps suggested he'd gotten free and was heading downstairs, and about time, too. Unless his arrival realized my new worst fears.

"Eli?" She blinked, then gave her head a hard shake as though a fly had flown into one ear.

"Your son."

I didn't say anything more, because he pounded down the stairs. She rose and stepped away to set her back against the wall, hands glowing with blue light.

"Mom!" His cry rang out across the room, then he ran straight into her. Wrapped his arms tight around her, not seeming to notice that instead of wrapping around him her arms extended out to either side. "I'm so glad to see you."

"I have no son." She stared down at him with half-puzzlement, half-horror—though at least she saw him, unlike the people in the streets.

Eli hugged his mother without pause, no matter that she wasn't hugging him back.

The angle at which I lay on the rug offered an excellent view of both their faces. I'd have turned and offered them privacy, but I couldn't move. The bonds around my wrists and ankles, although appearing pure energy, weighed me down and prevented even wiggling or rolling over.

I'd have given almost anything not to have to witness Eli's face when he pulled back to stare at his mother.

Dread dawned, but not yet complete.

"What's . . ." He laid a shaky palm against her gently curved abdomen.

"Let go!" She jerked back, out of arms reach.

He didn't move, the hand still outstretched shaking in the air.

"Where's the baby?" His voice started in a whisper, growing louder with each syllable. "Where's Gramma? Why's her bed not made? There's no sign of the shower anywhere, not the food or decorations or . . . Why are you . . . Why aren't you . . . You're wearing scrubs? Were you in the hospital and you didn't tell me?"

"I don't have a son." Her hands moved, one possibly headed for a pocket holding a rectangular object patently visible through the thin fabric. No doubt her phone.

I summoned every inch of air I could, because my mouth remained covered. "You don't need to call the police. We're not here to rob or hurt you in anyway."

"A likely story."

"You don't need to call, not for her, Mom." Eli perched on the edge of the sofa, one foot dangling loose and swinging. A casual pose, except his chest rose and fell in uneven heaves. "This's Rose, who works with Maksim. She came with me. We need your help. It's Maksim. He's stuck in Fate and we got to get him out of there. We need sorcerers—his sisters, wherever they are, or some of your friends. The ones who're supposed to be here, helping set up for the baby shower tomorrow."

"You believe it." Shauntelle traced a glowing circle in the air. It floated over to rattle down around Eli, as though she'd thrown a hula hoop over him. The light remained constant all the way, then flared at the bottom. "Every word you say, you're sure is truth. You think I should help you."

"Who better? It's for Maksim. I know, I know,"—he waved a hand—"I didn't like him for the longest while, but he's not so bad after all."

"Maksim?"

"Your husband? Father of the . . ." He gestured at her, then his head drooped and he scuffed at the rug with the non-dangling foot.

Or tried to.

For he'd started to turn insubstantial. He become slightly less solid—less *there*.

"Where's Gramma?" His voice dropped. "Why isn't any of her stuff around? Where's my stuff? Why'd you clear out my room?"

Hints of moisture glittered in the corners of his eyes. He knew, he had to have guessed even as I had.

He didn't exist in this timeline.

Hard to deny, with his mother right there shaking her head.

On the other hand, she hadn't left or done anything more to us although clearly a capable sorcerer and able to toss us out on our heads or toes. Me at least. But she had yet to do so. Although she refused to accept what we'd said, she still listened.

Maybe some part of her remembered.

Could be reached.

"Get a mirror." Uttering the words clearly despite the thinned-down gag took way too much energy, especially enunciating enough for them to understand. "Look at yourself and him."

Eli glanced my way, then did a double-take. An instant later, he waved a hand and the power binding me dissolved.

I sagged into a heap, panting as I massaged my legs and wrists.

"How did you—" Shauntelle asked.

"You already know. You showed me how to get out of ropes and binding spells." Eli's voice cracked on the last word, but he forged on. "You taught me how to go invisible, inaudible, intangible. Put temporary bonds on people and stop guns so they can't go off. Trigger or release the ward spells on the house. And how to undo all that. Don't you remember?"

"No." She barely aspirated the word. Surely she did recall. She had to.

"This isn't how it's supposed to be in reality." A sob escaped Eli. "So much's changed."

"Tell her," I urged him. "Show her. Help her remember."

"The house should be filled with light and sound and laughter. Gramma in her chair with her feet propped up on that ugly, old footstool in gold and purple. You got rid of that?"

A harsh indrawn breath from Shauntelle, followed by soft words. "It fell apart after her death."

"She's not dead!" The cords in his neck stood out as he yelled, though his voice had less power than before. "She's alive and living with us and still gets around, even if she does complain about her legs hurting all the time. And it was her idea to have the shower here, when you got told to stay home and take it easy and your friends were worrying about how to get it done. They should be here too. Monique who always pinches my cheek, and Eloisa with her baby who screeches down the house when she wants to nurse. And Maksim's mother and sisters came up from Baltimore special to help set things up tonight and be here tomorrow. This is the wrong timeline. We're going to change that, back to the real one, but we need help."

"No."

When I glanced in Shauntelle's direction, she'd started to cry, too. Only a few tears, but he was reaching her.

"I figured I'd find you lying on the couch, since the doc doesn't want you doing too much, and Gramma maybe fussing over you while you fuss back about her taking it easy too," Eli waved his arms this way and that. Faint illusions popped into life, peopling the room with other presences and objects. "And lots of food delivered already, the refrigerator stuffed with BBQ and slaw and trays of cookies in the shape of people, dressed in blue and pink and yellow and green."

Competing aromas filled the air, making my mouth water and stomach rumble. Barbecued chicken and beef. Chocolate chip cookies.

"Everybody talking all the time,"—hints of laughter and people's voices manifested, too distant to understand—"and tomorrow when your other friends and coworkers come, them all patting my head and saying how I've grown while I carry around trays of food because Gramma ordered me but

Maksim's mother's bribing me, too, and she pays well though I wasn't supposed to let that out."

He managed a weak grin, that didn't conceal the extent to which he'd faded.

"Look at him." I rolled onto my knees, pointing at the mirror. "You're so much alike."

"You do resemble my nephews. You've got the same silver tongue they do." Her lips turned up in a fake smile that lasted only a few seconds. "But I've never had a child. I would know!"

"You had me." Eli dashed closer, grabbing her hand and clutching it to his chest. "You were only twenty, and your boyfriend hot-footed himself off into the Army and left you pregnant. You've told me that often enough, and if you hadn't, your mom does every time she comes down to visit. Gramma offered you room to stay here and do some errands for her, and with her help you scraped by. Finished college right on time—there's a photo of you in your graduation outfit almost ready to pop as you always say." He waved a hand at the wall of photos, but didn't check.

Good thing, because it wasn't there, not when I'd checked and not now.

"What photo?"

"You traded favors with friends and spent way too much time studying while nursing me or rocking my cradle or swapping play dates so you could finish law school, and even get a clerkship." Eli pulled closer, nestling in. "That graduation photo's got me hanging off your robes." Another wave at the wall, but his arm didn't work as well as before.

"Law school?" She retreated, back against the door. Worse, she pulled her hand from Eli's grasp. "I'm a nurse."

"You teach, now . . . at Temple . . . That's how . . . you met Maksim . . . He came up . . . with his littlest sister . . . when she toured . . . asked you out first thing." He gasped for breath, shoulders curving as his body started to shrink.

"*Look at him!*" Lurching to my feet, I pointed at the mirror over the fireplace again. "He's your son and he's fading. If you don't believe in him . . ."

Tremors rocked Shauntelle, and tears streamed down her face. "How can I have a child and not remember?"

But her hands reached out, folding one of his between them. Holding on.

"Mom?"

My eyes ached from crying. I grabbed hold of Eli's other hand, jerking as his fingers met mine. It was like trying to hold onto cold jelly. "I can't do magic, so I swear I'm not running any magical con on you. We believe it because it's the truth."

His head turned so intangible that the spider hiding in his hair floated through the air down to the rug, and then scooted over to climb up me and hide in my hair.

"Please," he said.

Shauntelle kept shaking her head, but she held on.

Bright blue light limned their entwined fingers and surged halfway up his arm.

No such magic flared where I kept hold. A few sparks heated my skin where I clung to Eli, but I couldn't hold on the way she did—with magic.

"Mom!" Eli's hand fell through mine.

Eli himself remained—at least his seeming.

But utterly intangible, except for where Shauntelle gripped his hand tight.

14

One sorcerer on board, one to go. Or something along those lines.

But at the moment, I had no energy to go anywhere. I slumped in one of the rocking chairs, the runners creaking below although I barely rocked at all. The thin, burgundy cushions provided a little padding between me and the wood. A tall blue-and-white mug filled with steaming coffee rested on a coaster on the table near me, complete with a whiskey-laced tang.

I'd taken the liberty of going into the kitchen to make us tea. When I couldn't easily find any tea bags, but noticed the prominent coffee maker, I made up a pot instead and prepped two mugs of coffee.

Only to find Shauntelle right behind me. She grunted, grabbed a half-filled bottle of whiskey from a cupboard, and poured a good finger in one.

"You want some?" she asked.

"Sure." She started to do the same with another mug only to stop after a couple of drops and kept that, pushing the other toward me.

She sat on the sofa, a matching mug in one hand and Eli beside her. He clutched at one of her hands, squeezing it between both of his. He'd let go of her at first—long enough to figure out that the farther he went from her, the less solid and coherent he became. One wispy, near-dissolving step had sent him three back toward her. A second test, and he'd retreated to her side from whence he'd hardly strayed.

He'd told Shauntelle his tale twice, and I'd shared mine once. Shauntelle had nodded her way through all three renditions. Exactly how much she'd taken in remained in doubt, but she had the high points down.

"Gramma's alive and well. I'm a lawyer not a nurse. I'm married with one child and expecting another." Shauntelle lifted her mug in a mock-toast. "Go me."

She knocked back a slug of coffee, then set it down and rubbed at her forehead.

"Or not. I shouldn't drink too much coffee if I'm pregnant. I'm a nurse, I know better. In which case I'm not pregnant. Or I am pregnant and I'm not a nurse."

"You are, or you will be again." Eli leaned in closer, laying his head against her shoulder. "I wasn't any happy about it, but I'll be a great big brother. Promise. We just got to get Maksim back first."

"Maksim." Her eyes closed and she shivered, but kept massaging her temples. "I remember bits and pieces."

I could imagine the pressure there. The life of the other Rose—Ruby—pressed against me. A heaviness demanding acknowledgment. The flash of memories that didn't belong to me. A hesitancy to the self I knew and remembered, because nothing here quite fit me.

Gritting my teeth, I shoved it all back and away. Refused to allow anything except a pounding at my temples from the pressure to live the other life and be the other me.

Shauntelle didn't have the same fortune—or privilege.

We'd burst into her life and begged her to open her mind to another self.

No doubt she needed time to adjust, time with Eli and vice-versa.

Although the unseen bracelet around my wrist—and the two spiders snuggling in my hair—offered ever-present reminders that we might not have much time to make sure things were restored and Maksim freed.

He'd sent us here to bring back three sorcerers, at least one of whom needed to be a director or Webmasters employee or some such. We got one in Shauntelle, surely, but might've lost one in Eli. He hadn't done anything I could pinpoint as magic since nearly dissolving—though I wasn't about to push the matter either.

"It's hard facing memories of two lives. Take it easy, give yourself what you need to adapt." I frowned. "Is there anyone I can call, who you'd want to be here?"

"Call? I'm still trying to figure who's who in my other life." She cast a quizzical glance at me. "Do I know you? In wherever my . . . Eli . . . lives?"

"Not really. I'm the admin at the Webmasters Philly office in the real reality. I only remember seeing you visit the office once. But Maksim's got a photo from your wedding in his office. He talks about you sometimes." I leaned forward, scanning my memories for anything that might help. "His face always goes soft when he does. And it's clear he loves Eli, too."

"Yeah, Maksim's a right dude." Eli bounced on the sofa, which made no noise. The cushions showed no dent or indication of his weight resting on them. "You'll help get him back?"

"Right." Shauntelle's head bobbed loose on her neck.

"Then that's one sorcerer. We need one or two more.

Maksim said bring back three sorcerers." Eli frowned. "Without Gramma . . . who of your friends'll do it?"

"Monique." The name dropped from Shauntelle's mouth an instant later.

Eli scrunched up his face. "She'll pinch my cheek."

"It'll take time to convince her. She's headed over here anyway. She swore she'd drag me out drinking and swanning through a half dozen bars, leaving broken hearts in our wake." A chuckle made Shauntelle give a slight hop. "Won't she be surprised at the change in plans. And to learn I have a son."

"I'll find us a director or other webmaster sorcerer, and we can meet up tomorrow morning to head back into Fate." I took a swig of coffee, the whiskey burning my mouth and throat on the way down.

"What do we need a director for?" Eli turned a shoulder to me.

"To get us back into the Web of Fate. Unless you picked up the knack?"

Eli's mouth opened, then shut with a snap.

"You're going off to get someone else?" Shauntelle's eyes narrowed.

"As soon as I have some names to pursue. To free Maksim, we have to get back into the Web of Fate."

"The Web." She closed her eyes and rubbed her face again. "I have a husband. He works at the Webmasters of Fate. I teach law at Temple."

Eli affirmed her returning memories, while I pulled out my phone in hopes Tanisha had sent her list. It didn't show at the top, so I skimmed through the threads while reading as little as possible of the actual messages. Only the few lines that showed in the list.

More from my mother, worried about me. Alas, I couldn't face them under the current circumstances.

Some from someone named Rick, yelling at me to call

home. When I checked the contacts, he popped up with a marker identifying him as one of my emergency contacts. My brother. I'd added a photo of him, and he resembled my youngest sister—my real sibling—except with a longer face and a carefully-shaped goatee.

The more I looked at him, the more every blink began to offer images of him at different ages.

A little boy only a year older, snatching away the truck I'd been playing with and sticking a pink tongue out at me when I wailed in protest.

A teenager rolling his eyes as our mother insisted he take me along with him to one party or another.

As a college student offering me a custom tour of the institution he attended. He smiled when our mother watched us, but when she turned away he muttered threats if I chose to go there too.

And as an eleven-year-old helping me puzzle through the directions on how to do an art project . . .

NO! I didn't remember him. I refused to remember him, especially at the same age as Eli.

All of which marked him as someone to avoid, not to reach out to. If I had to call on family for help, I'd go for my mother before him. At least she existed in both timelines. I hardly wanted to meet someone in this timeline who didn't exist in mine, and have to mourn him after.

Bad enough dealing with the losses I'd already faced.

At long last, a ding announced messages from Tanisha. She'd finally come through with not one list but two.

Glory be! Hope leapt in my heart—only to plummet as I actually read over them.

The first offered names of all the people in the Greater Philadelphia area who'd worked for Atropos or with Tanisha in the last year and were in the area now.

It had all of three names on it, one of them being mine.

The other two I'd never heard of. I could call them out of the blue and say . . . What? I might have one chance to reach them and help them realize they existed in a wrong timeline.

Then she added a second list containing people she hadn't worked with but other people on her team recommended. This had a whopping seven names, of which I recognized two.

Geneva and Neil.

I could call Geneva. She was my direct supervisor in the real world, but in this timeline? As the head of the Philly office, perhaps she'd know of me and what I supposedly did for the firm, which was more than I did. I could try to reach her. If she resembled her other self, she'd listen and consider my words.

But it would require time and energy.

I don't know how much time remained, but I lacked energy. It might be early evening here, but my internal clock considered it early tomorrow morning or later. I needed food and sleep, not necessarily in that order.

Which left Neil.

A whisper of air moving alerted me to Eli almost floating over the floor. Shauntelle lay on her side across the sofa, head buried in her hands.

"He'll help. You already know that." Eli pointed at Neil's name.

"Yeah, but I'll still have to convince him."

So now I had a task to fulfill, and added reason to leave them alone together.

"You'll be okay?" I nodded at him, rather than offering my hand. Though that was half out of not wanting to repeat the sensation of his hand passing through mine. Eli's form filled the same amount of space as before, but I could see the outlines of objects, and Shauntelle, through him.

"We be fine." A sharp nod, and a studied pose.

Though I suspected he'd retreat to his mother's side as soon as I was out of view.

I left my phone number for Shauntelle, in case Eli didn't remember it, and the promise to call first thing in the morning. Although I hadn't drunk much of the whiskey-laced coffee, I swayed my first few steps.

My feet marched me halfway down the alley. Then I ran out of steam, turning floppy. I limped over to a nearby post and leaned against it, just as Eli had a different one only an hour or so earlier.

The alley itself remained fairly quiet, apart from the hums of air conditioners or fans here and there. Beyond the narrow expanse, other sounds filtered in. People partying. Music playing at a pub. Cars with the bass set loud, mufflers roaring as they scooted up this street or down that.

A car with a ride-share placard stopped at the end of the alley. A tall Black woman in a short bright blue-and-gold dress with long dreadlocks pulled back with a sparkly gold band emerged. She gave me a measured glance, then headed past me. Her high heels clopped against the brick walk. No doubt if I turned around, I'd see her make a straight line for Shauntelle's house.

Instead I kept on, ready to hail the ride-share and arrange fare . . .

Only to stop in my tracks.

My phone worked in this world, but that didn't guarantee my credit card did as well.

And even if it did, I had no idea where the other me lived. Dipping into her memories—I wasn't about to risk that.

My fingers slipped over my phone and pulled up Neil in chat.

<<Need help.>>

Within a minute, he responded: <<Where are you? Are you safe?>>

Such a quick answer made me smile, a little, as I offered a crumb of reassurance: <<Safe yes. For now.>>

Paired with problems: <<Tired. Hungry. Could use a ride. Lost at Elfreth's Alley.>>

Neil leapt into action with a pledge: <<Don't move. I'll be right there.>>

15

I sheltered at a far corner of the alley, huddling against a brick wall, and waited. The foot traffic was almost all White people, apart from occasional families. Nobody bumped me, anymore than they had earlier. Nice for me, but . . . either they hadn't seen Eli earlier, or not cared about running roughshod over a young Black boy.

How different was this world when it came to questions of race?

So much easier to tally up the less important differences. The few taxis crawling the streets weren't yellow or white but red. Buses had SEPTA on them, but the logo seemed off, different lettering and coloring. The cars were also different, boxier in form than I was accustomed to. Most didn't have exhaust pipes. Were they electric? And then there were the odd lines embedded in every street except Elfreth's Alley. Not rails, but some other odd metallic substance that sparked occasionally as buses and cars crossed them.

Food smells hadn't changed much, still lots of things frying in oil—and a lot of pizza places.

Yet as I listened to music floating out of this house or

that establishment, I recognized maybe one thing among all the pieces. Distance contributed, but I should've known more.

Or not. After all this was *not* my world, at least not my timeline.

I didn't belong here. Eli might not exist.

Wrong. The timeline didn't belong.

Except memory shards insisted on sneaking into my mind and showing me belonging here. Walking along the mall, hand-in-hand with Neil. Listening to some of the tunes over internet radio at a party at a friend's home. The same songs playing, in full rock-and-roll style, between rounds as Neil and I joined friends in a pub for quiz night.

Shaking my head failed to dispel the fake recollections. Focusing on Eli and Shauntelle's faces kept me grounded. I owed them to remember the *real* timeline and help get it back.

The squeak of brakes grated on my ears, but centered my attention on a ride-share car pulling up along the curb a few feet away. Neil popped out, hanging on the door as it swung.

My body refused to move fast. Before I so much as pushed away from the wall, he'd spotted me and reached my side. He eased an arm around my waist as I drooped on him.

I even required help getting into the ride-share. Or maybe it wasn't a ride-share, because Neil addressed the driver by name and joked with them about how far out we lived.

Which had to be a joke, as we drove only as far as a hop, skip, and a jump up Chestnut. The traffic wasn't too bad, but if I weren't tired and hungry, walking would've been as good a bet to get there fast.

Then we were out of the car with Neil saying thanks and the driver no problem and hoping I'm better soon. Or something along those lines, though the words differed.

We took an elevator up lots of floors, but I retained no

memory of it. Just went where he guided me and wound up on a cushy green sofa in a comfy living room. Wall-to-wall carpet in pale green softened footsteps to almost nothing, a stark contrast to the plain, worn wood floors in my real place.

Nothing looked familiar, or rather I refused to admit familiarity in anything. It helped that this apartment was decidedly modern while my home, my *real* home in an old Victorian cut up into small studios, was furnished in late Goodwill and Salvation Army and Habitat ReStore, plus a couple of pieces my parents sacrificed from their respective attics.

None of that furniture met my eyes anywhere. Instead, I viewed an eclectic mix with some things newer such as the sofa Neil parked me on and the matching pair of armchairs, but a lot that were older or more worn. A single bookcase holding a selection of classics and children's books plus four different e-readers. Enlarged photos decorated the plain beige walls, some of scenes in Philly and others places I'd never been.

But they mattered less than the river visible through a long set of sliding glass doors and floor-to-ceiling windows. We'd scored a view. Not the best by any stretch of the imagination, as other high rises partially obscured the scene, but still a view. The skyline didn't match my memory of any part of the city. Based on the last glow of the sunset on the flowing water, I guessed this to be the Schuylkill.

A small kitchenette lay beyond a breakfast bar on one side of the room. Nearby stretched a small hall leading to a bathroom and two bedrooms, although the one I could see partly into had ample bookshelves and a printer. My home office or his?

Neil puttered around the kitchen, giving me space and preparing a meal. Savory scents of tomatoes and bread filled the air, making my stomach growl again.

He brought out a glass of something purple and . . . not bubbly but burpy, but I couldn't guess the ingredients. Without offering any information, he stood over me saying nothing and looking everything until I drank it.

It tasted . . . not half-bad, although way more fake-grape than I'd normally consume plus something that gave it a very thick texture. Yogurt? Within moments, the liquid perked me up, although it did nothing to stop my stomach rumbling.

Neil clearly heard the growls, for he smiled and brushed a finger along my cheek and chin to clear off a stray droplet.

"Thanks." For the drink which was magic whether or not he'd put sorcery in it, though he probably had considering how much better it made me feel, but also for everything else. For scooping me off the familiar-but-not street and bringing me somewhere I could relax, at least a bit. A wary section of my mind reminded me not to slip too far into this fantasy.

"That's nothing, and you know what happens when you thank me for nothing." He laughed, then bent and kissed me.

A long, deep kiss but with a sweet edge that didn't push for anything else. It was a kiss alone, an experience my bones considered very familiar.

"Think I'll ever break you of the habit?" he asked.

I frowned as I shook my head. No one had ever accused me of saying thank you too often. If anything, people were more likely to charge me with not saying it enough, though I brushed some of that off as sexism since it came mostly from great-aunts and uncles.

"Dinner will be ready soon. Our Sunday night special, a couple days early." He picked up the empty glass and headed back to the kitchen. The tomatoey scent increased with the unmistakable pops of liquid reaching a boiling point.

I slipped off to the bathroom to clean up—and check out the place.

Try and get some sense of Neil and the best way to approach him so he remembered and was willing to help out.

Unlike the living room, more familiar sights and scents reduced my sense of unfamiliarity. My favorite orange-rose soap rested in a blue porcelain dish next to the sink. A shelf in the shower supported an array of bottles and tubes, half of which resembled the brands I usually purchased.

Then again, Neil's stuff also lay around the room here and there: a worn leather razor case against the mirror, a tube of sandalwood-scented shaving cream, and a tiny blue bottle of soap water paired with a wand to blow bubbles. Definitely not things I was accustomed to seeing in my bathroom. I hadn't had a steady boyfriend since nearly two years earlier, and my subsequent flings failed to hang around long enough for either of us to leave stuff in each other's bathrooms.

On my way back to the living room, I paused for peeks into the bedrooms.

First the master bedroom, with a double bed nicely made up—and positioned so that people sitting in it could look out the long western windows. Two neat bureaus rested against one wall; a four-foot-high teak chest that I'd used for years in my childhood home, and a smaller affair with only three drawers instead of four in maple. The closet doors stood half-open, showing my clothes on one side, of which only a few pieces looked familiar. A part of my brain wanted to recognize other garments, but I squashed that and hot-footed out of the room.

The spare bedroom, something I definitely didn't have at home, where guests slept on the pull-out sofa, held two simple, matching computer tables and chairs set up with their backs to each other. Evidently we both had offices here and at Webmasters. A couple bookcases held a wide variety of materials, from thick reference books to thin non-fiction history works aimed at children to pamphlets and bound items intended for re-enactors or hobbyists. One of the desks, likely Neil's, had a sketch pad with a half-finished drawing of a Revolution-era winter camp.

I considered nabbing one or more history books to check over and see what differed from the real timeline, but what if that made things all the more familiar?

Reading might tip me further away from where I needed to be. Bad enough that this apartment struck me as comfortable. It might not be much familiar, I refused to let it be, but it was exactly the kind of place I could see sharing with a lover, a beloved.

Or, in this case, someone I'd barely met and who thought that was what we were.

Until I burst his bubble.

"Dinner's ready."

Turning my back on the books and bedrooms, I padded out to join Neil at a table covered with a white linen cloth and matching napkins at either setting. Unfamiliar edgy flatware rested near blue-and-white china very similar to the set my mother had given me as a house-warming present when I set up on my own.

Better to wait until Neil was well-fed, and me as well, before broaching tough topics.

Everything looked scrumptious, from the bowls of thick, red soup to the small plates with wedges of bagels toasted and slathered with butter, to the cups half-filled with water so cool that condensation dripped down the side to soak into the tablecloth.

Neil didn't press me over dinner.

Didn't demand I talk.

Didn't talk at me, either.

He glanced my way on several occasions that I noticed, and possibly more I missed, but otherwise we ate in silence.

As soon as I finished, I started to clear the dishes, but he waved me off.

"Why don't you go rest some more." He pointed at the sofa, and then turned around to clear the table without further comment.

"All right, but only if you join me soon. We need to talk." Since I was swaying on my feet, I followed his suggestion and curled up at one end of the couch.

When he came back from the kitchen and sat at the other end of the sofa, bringing a hint of citrus-scented dish detergent, he still didn't speak.

"You're not asking anything." I twiddled my thumbs, glancing sideways at him.

"Your job is more secret than mine. I knew that getting in. Complaining now would be . . ." He threw out his hands and offered a lopsided smile. "But anything you can share— that I want, when you're ready."

"It's not my job. What you think is, that is." I snapped my mouth shut, bit my tongue, and tried to figure out other ways to bring him to an awareness of his other, real, life.

"What isn't?" He blinked, scrunched up his nose, and looked at me sideways. "You were out there, tired and hungry, on your own choice?"

"I don't work for Atropos." A high-pitched laugh escaped me, with perhaps a manic edge. "I don't even know what that involves."

"O-kay." He nodded, stroking the taut fabric covering the arm of the sofa.

"I've been in Fate." At least Neil, unlike Shauntelle, worked for Webmasters, so he had to have some knowledge of the parent company's overall mission to keep Fate secure.

"No wonder you were hungry and tired. The couple times I've been . . ." He shuddered, fingers stretching and retracting as though imitating claws.

"Have you always come out to find the world the same?"

"Of course." A shrug.

I didn't say anything, so we both sat in silence for several minutes.

The silence spoke for me, but I shifted to set one foot flat on the floor. Back straight, I faced him and kept my gaze fixed on his face.

Comprehension dawned, bit by bit. He swung around on the sofa and knelt facing me. Leaned forward, staring as though trying to absorb every nuance of my appearance.

"You didn't find it the same."

"No." I swallowed hard, then reached out to grab and hold his hands. "This isn't just different, it's wrong. It's not how time should run. I have to go back and set things right."

"Okay." A thousand questions occurred to him. I could almost see them floating through his eyes. As he suppressed each and every one, his hands started to shake.

"And I need your help." I rubbed his fingers, but both of us had grown cold.

"Mine?" He pulled back and tucked his hands under his arms—to warm them, or as a defensive measure. "This is a matter for directors, for the webmasters themselves. I'm just—"

"There's a team on their way, but . . . they may not make it in time." I sat on my hands to warm them, and to keep from reaching for him again. "I have to find three directors or sorcerers willing to go into Fate with me and restore every-thing to the way it was."

Another pause. I lifted my eyebrows, head inclined his way. His lips twitched to the side.

"And you need me to be one of them." One of his feet tapped restlessly against the carpet.

"I'm running out of options, so yeah."

He pushed to his feet and paced around the room for

several minutes. Stopped to stand at the window and gaze out at the darkening sky and twinkling city lights, then paced again. At length, he removed his hands from under his arms, flexed his fingers, and leaned against the breakfast bar. "All right, what do we have to do?"

A bluff, perhaps, for he held his head high while his throat muscles stood taut.

"Well," I rose and marched over to face him, with only a few feet between us. "First you have to remember."

"Remember what?"

"The real world we need to restore."

"Which is . . . What?" he asked. "What's the point of divergence?"

"Atlantis."

"Hoo boy. Atlantis? It doesn't exist." He made a face and rolled his eyes. "Though I hear a good third of all failed sleazes try to create it."

I must've gaped, because my lips and tongue started to dry. Maybe I should've checked one of the history books after all. I snapped my mouth shut and retreated to the sofa. This time I kicked off my shoes and planted my feet on the cushion, wrapping my arms around my legs and resting my head on my knees.

Atlantis had been a point of divergence, but that had changed. What else had changed? Maksim, Eli, and I had destroyed the outer layer of sleaze with its connection to the Atlantis True Believers' website. The existence of Atlantis must've been tied to that. So we had succeeded in part.

"Rose?" The cushions around me shifted as Neil settled next to me. He wrapped an arm around my shoulder, gently as though ready to pull back should I shrink away. "Did I offend? If you want Atlantis to be real, then—"

"No, no I don't. That used to be the point of diversion. I guess we partly succeeded. Banishing the one sleaze kept that from changing, even though we failed to prevent the second sleaze from digging into the fate-line." Letting my feet slip off the sofa, I turned to face him. "I don't know what the points of diversion are, not all of them, but this timeline is different in several respects from the real one. Including . . . us."

"Us?" He touched my cheek, a single finger caress.

"In the real timeline, we're not together."

His throat grew taut again, and he swallowed several times.

"Not yet." I lifted his right hand from his lap and pressed it between mine. Our fingers again were cold to the touch. "In my timeline, you arrived in Philly at the start of the week. Didn't manage to ask me out until Friday, today. This afternoon. I said yes." Or sort-of yes, but better not to stress that part at the moment.

Neil dragged in a deep breath, head turned away so I only saw his profile. "I didn't ask you out until the end of the first week after I saw you, yeah, that's right. But that was over a year ago."

"For me, it was today. I'm an administrative assistant and receptionist at Webmasters' Philly office, but it's not a regional HQ. A backwater branch you called it. You're here on a six-week research jaunt, with a bunch of other guys, staying in a furnished house. I arranged that. Earlier today, you helped a spider find its way to Maksim's office—he's one of the directors, the junior one. Then you asked me out." My half-truth earlier itched at me, so I went on in hopes the accumulation of details might trigger memories in him. "I couldn't do tonight, because I was working overtime on the whole Fate-changing thing, but I said yes to tomorrow."

He stayed still, then pulled his hand away and rose, walking over to stand at the window. "You're saying this is all fake. The two of us together in Philly, my being based here, your job, everything I remember?"

"Maybe not everything."

"The important things." He shot a hard, hurt glance over his shoulder. "You want me to forget them, in favor of this other timeline. Forget us."

"We still might become an us." Something I found more enticing the longer I spent in this apartment, with him. He hadn't rejected my story outright, was considering it even if his attention, understandably, focused on what he might lose.

"But we aren't." He turned back to the window.

"Not yet." I got up, tottering more as my energy drained away. Too much, too many unexpected things in one day. I needed to rest. Grabbing hold of one of the dining chairs, I stayed upright.

"I have to think about this. I'm not going off angry. I'm .. . Pausing." He noticed my shakiness, and his eyes closed briefly. "Go ahead and take the bed. I'll sleep on the sofa. Won't be the first time." A deep, humorless chuckle escaped him, then he headed off into the office and shut the door—gentle until the last second when it slammed.

I drooped over the table. Mustering every ounce of remaining energy, I got myself up and off to bed with a brief pause in the bathroom. One look at my face in the mirror and I knew why he told me to sleep, because the streaks under my eyes seemed bigger than my eyes.

Slipping into the bedroom, I checked under both pillows. The one on the left had nothing beneath, the one on the right an oversized red Ohio State T-shirt. Too tired to search for anything else, I got undressed and pulled on the T-shirt.

I only had a twin bed in my real home, so the double seemed way too big, and smelled of Neil, but I had no strength left to do anything about either.

And too much sorrow.

I didn't remember anything of this timeline: living with

him or the job I had which was evidently several secrecy grades above admin assistant.

I refused to recall either.

But part of me already mourned the loss, or wanted to keep it. Given my druthers, I'd leap if some magic offered me the whole horrid day undone.

Maybe I slept some, but I dreamed and didn't want to remember any of them.

I woke while it was still deep night, both sure of where I was and unsure of it. Everything seeming familiar and strange simultaneously, and I started crying because I couldn't handle it. I lacked magic, had only my stubborn belief in what was real and what wasn't. Yet the very thing that Maksim wanted me as a witness for first and foremost, now shot around and hurt me and Neil.

A warm body curved around me. Arms pulled me close and nestled me back against Neil, the end of his boxer shorts rubbing against my thighs. He stroked my hair.

"It's okay. Everything's going to be okay. I'll help you." His voice hurt my ears with its depth and roughness. "But I warn you, I'm going to fight for this. Now or in the future."

We remained cuddled together and nothing more, but the warmth and comfort of his body enabled me to fall asleep and not dream.

❧ 16 ❧

A harsh buzzing sound wakened me from uneasy dreams that I was happy to escape.

Not so happy to be woken, though. I had no desire to move as I'd landed in a comfy situation. Half dozing, I snuggled under a thin sheet with a warm body at my back and an arm thrown across my waist. Some calculating portion of my brain identified this as Saturday morning. Maybe not so sacred a sleeping-in time as Sunday, but the same general principle applied. In short, a good time to stay in bed and not get up.

Especially since I hadn't slept well, and not because of my own nightmares, at least not after the one, but Neil's. He'd woken me twice with his thrashing, all the while muttering incoherent threats or maybe pleas. Only cuddling close eased his tremors so he slid back into sleep and I managed the same.

I pulled the cover higher, bunching it next to my ears to try and drown out the godawful sound.

Behind me, Neil stretched and pulled the sheet away briefly before returning to align himself against me.

"That's the doorbell." His gravelly just-woke-up voice made the little hairs around my ears dance as he grumbled. "Who's visiting so early?"

"Maybe they'll go away." I shifted myself, snuggling back against him. Surely for once neither of us had anything we *had* to do?

Only to sit bolt upright as the bell rang again, and my head near split with pain.

There was something I'd forgotten. No, something I didn't want to remember. Or both.

At any rate, the level of pain demanded I rise, stumbling and banging into a wall because the bathroom wasn't where I expected it to be. Competing apartment layouts conflicted in my mind. Go straight or left?

The bell rang a third time, louder than before if that was even possible.

"That volume takes magic. I'll get it." Rustling sounds and thumps came from the bed, then soft feet padded behind me and a warm hand brushed across my shoulders as he slipped by.

I didn't look, kept my eyes closed and leaned my head against a cool wall. Too many memories competed in my brain. Fumbling my way into the bathroom, I splashed cool water on my face. When I finally opened my eyes, there I was in the mirror. I hadn't changed, save for the bags under my eyes getting bigger—not enough sleep—but at least I'd reached Saturday morning so I'd caught up with myself.

Why did that matter?

Grabbing the mouthwash, I poured a cap and swallowed only to nearly spit it right back out rather than gargling. The taste was wrong, citrus instead of mint . . .

"Hey R.B." Neil knocked on the door, although I'd left it ajar. "Do you know someone named Shauntelle?"

My midsection jerked and my body hunched as though

someone had punched me. Harsh memories flooded through me. Shauntelle. Eli. Her holding onto him as he became intangible to the point he slipped through my fingers. The whole tangled web of yesterday flooded back, swamping me. I grabbed hold of the counter and refused to fall. Breath after breath, I worked through awakened memories and fears until the spate passed.

"Yeah, she . . ." I dragged in a deep breath to settle my trembling nerves. "She's part of this."

Turning, I yanked the door open. There he stood, half-naked and leaning against the wall, eyebrows raised.

Heat flushed through my face, as I tugged at the hem of my nightshirt—once his shirt. No matter how much I pulled, it only came down to my upper thighs. "Wait, how would you know about her?"

"Because she's here." He allowed himself a single once-over of me, then kept his eyes on my face.

"Here?"

"Downstairs, unless she's managed to get someone else to let her in." He gave me a level look. "Based on the determination in her voice, I wouldn't put it past her."

"Buzz her up. Is there anyone with her?" I cut off before a dozen conflicted hopes could pour out.

"Maybe you want to get dressed and ask her?" He turned to go. "I'll buzz her in, but when I get back, the bathroom's mine."

I finished up fast and darted into the bedroom. Although less familiar than before, when I'd just woken out of sleep, there were only so many places for clothes. Rather than fuss over anything, I grabbed the first reasonable, and clean, items I saw. New underthings, a plain green T-shirt, blue jeans, and light blue socks, but for shoes I went with my own sneakers. The tread had worn down a bit farther than I'd remembered.

Evidently, hiking in Fate wasn't good for the soles, but they were still decent and comfy.

After a couple minute's searching I located my phone, but alas, my bell earrings had gone missing. I'd taken them off and put them somewhere the night before, but where defied me. A pair of spider earrings on the top of the bureau caught my eye—copper and onyx—and it was insta-love so I put them on instead.

In turn, this brought to mind the spiders in my hair. Had they moved on or stayed with me?

I ran a comb very carefully through my disordered locks. Two spiders hopped onto the comb and clung to the shaft until I finished. When I held the comb close to my head, I missed any sensation of them climbing back in among my locks but they'd left the comb when I checked it.

Nothing appeared on my wrist. Nevertheless, when I ran my fingers along the skin they caught on the loop of spider silk. With fingers, not eyes, I traced the length that wrapped around and rediscovered the cord that drifted off into nowhere.

Neil got out of bathroom and headed into the bedroom as I left, right as someone thumped on the front door.

"I'll get that," I said.

He grunted agreement, closing the bedroom door behind him.

A second knock rattled the window panes. I hustled across the carpet to the door, drew in a big breath, then opened it.

Eli blew through first, whirling around to fix me with his eyes—half glare, half plea. "You see me, hear me, don't you?"

"Yeah." Blinking didn't change anything. He remained ever-so-slightly transparent, but most definitely in front of me. And audible at a level that made my ears ring.

"I don't have near half so much power as I ever did before, but I'm still here. You know that."

"You're here."

Footsteps up from the elevator, located far down the hall, presaged Shauntelle and her friend's arrival, but Eli had blasted ahead of them. Another set of steps closer by was the only warning that Neil had finished dressing lightning-fast. He'd cheated by leaving his feet bare, wearing only jeans and a green-and-black T-shirt advertising Webmasters's *What's Under Your Feet?* video game. A tiny spot of shaving cream remained on the far left of his face near his ear, but otherwise he appeared calm, cool, and in control.

"Who're you talking to?" Neil frowned at the open door.

"Eli." I nodded at the boy's form, vibrating with intensity.

Eli had both hands in fists pressed against his chest as he turned to glare at Neil. "You looking at me?"

"There's a haze." Neil squinted, then shook his head. "And a buzzing, but I don't see anyone."

"Thank you." The woman I'd seen leaving a ride-share the night before gave a heavy sigh. Her thick black dreadlocks, untouched by gray and now corralled by a leather tie, rippled along the back of her green-and-black Eagles T-shirt, the colors almost the same as Neil's T-shirt. In sneakers and jeans, she still topped me by a couple of inches. She gave Neil a half-wave as she swept through the door with Shauntelle in her wake. "See, I wasn't making not seeing or hearing him up. I get you got a son. You dragged me through the whole roundabout and I see you talking back and forth with fuzzy air, but I'm getting nothing else."

"I heard you the first seventeen times." Shauntelle knocked the door out of my hand so it shut behind her as she entered and aligned herself next to Eli. Red lines in her eyes, a droopy mouth, and a body vibrating in a too-much or too-little caffeine kind of way suggested she hadn't slept well. In place of yesterday's scrubs, she'd pulled on clothes basically similar to mine though her shirt was orange instead of green, her jeans and sneakers black, and her earrings trios of copper circles rather than spiders. A couple of enameled bracelets dangled around each wrist, and a set of yellow beads circled her neck.

"His name doesn't hurt, as I might not see or hear hair of his hide, but I sure as everything remember you always saying someday if you had a son you'd call him Elijah." The new arrival, presumably Shauntelle's friend Monique, shifted to give me a once-over. "You're this Rose she's been talking about being thick as thieves with Eli."

"R.B., not Rose." Neil stepped back and waved everyone out of the crowded entry hall into the living room.

"No it's Rose. Rosalind Celia Williams." I winced as a tic twitched in Neil's cheek. "The other me you knew might've been R.B., but not me."

"You couldn't tell me that last night?" His voice dropped to a whisper, but the kind that carried especially since Shauntelle and Monique, plus Eli, hadn't gone far.

"It didn't come up." I rolled my shoulders to keep from hunching them. "You never called me by any name, just talked to me."

"I guess." He wouldn't meet my gaze.

"Does it make a difference?"

"Just one more reminder you're not who you were yesterday." Head down, he scuffed at the rug with one foot.

"I'm still me, just a different version. And I guess introductions are warranted." I turned to Shauntelle first. "Shauntelle, this is Neil Brydall. He works at Webmasters of Fate, and he's agreed to help me restore the timeline. Neil, this is Shauntelle . . . Jackson." I took a moment to remember Maksim referring to Eli by his full name. "She's Eli's mother —he's the one you can't see."

"And this is Monique Dulaq." Shauntelle waved at her friend.

"Nice to meet you under strange circumstances." Monique nodded at me, then pointed a finger at Neil. "Now, how much'd she have to talk you into this? Shauntelle had to pour near three whiskey coffees in me while she was telling over the tale before I believed her."

"And even then it took a truth spell or three," Eli said, though only Shauntelle and I heard him.

"You going back on me?" Shauntelle's gaze flickered between her son and friend. She gave a huff, second-cousin to an outright laugh. She braced her hands over her belly. Although her body remained the same as yesterday, it was a sign she might have started remembering being pregnant.

"Not me. I make a promise I'm good for it." Monique took over one end of the sofa, stretching her legs out.

"Likewise." Neil waved at the sofa and chairs, and the kitchen beyond. "Anyone want coffee and some breakfast, cereal or toast at least, before we get about heading into Fate?"

He headed into the kitchen, where distance offered an illusion of privacy although he would hear well enough from there.

Shauntelle settled gingerly onto the other end of the sofa so I sat on an armchair facing her and Monique. An instant later, Shauntelle popped up and paced around the room.

"When we go in and free . . . Maksim, my husband . . . will that also bring Eli back to being able to touch and be touched and seen and heard?"

Eli nodded, sinking cross-legged onto the floor by the window.

"I would think so." I craned my neck, trying to follow her winding route. "I mean, he's intangible *here*." I tangled my fingers together, pressing the heels of my hands against my chest. "But if we can restore the original timeline he should be *there* as himself."

"Think. Should." She whirled, hands on her hips. "You don't know?"

"I'm guessing. The only experts I know to trust are in Fate right now, or on a plane to Bermuda. If they arrive in time. Unless . . ." I turned toward the kitchen. "Neil?"

The smell of fresh coffee started to fill the apartment as the coffee maker hissed and bubbled.

"You called?" Neil positioned himself in the passage from living room to kitchen, glancing back and forth between us and the coffee.

"If someone accidentally wound up in Fate and came out into a timeline in which they didn't exist, and went . . . hazy . . . if the original timeline is restored, are they there?" I was getting better at summing things up, though that gave me little ease.

"Let me think on it a second, though I'm not an expert. Keep that in mind." He vanished from sight, but returned shortly after with mugs of coffee that he handed around before perching on the other armchair.

Shauntelle managed to settle back onto the sofa near Monique and stay seated as she drank coffee, though one foot tapped restlessly against the floor.

Neil drained his mug, then set it on the coffee table. Both Shauntelle and I paused, cups half-empty, and waited with bated breath.

"No pressure," Neil said in a low tone, then blew out a breath. "All right, here goes. Fate does not permit paradox. People cannot interact with the past or change what happened unless they introduce an artificial difference and force Fate to accept it. Fate doesn't want to change, and will resist it and try to get back to previous conditions as completely as possible."

"You saying what?" Eli rolled his eyes.

"What does that mean for Eli?" I asked, as I worked through the ramifications of Fate being stubborn, or set in its ways, or just understandably resistant to externally provoked change.

Shauntelle appeared equally taken aback, although her eyes narrowed rather than crossed. Maybe familiarity with magic made a difference.

"Eli being the person in question who isn't wholly here?" Neil glanced around.

He showed no signs he'd started to see or hear Eli—who waved his hands and called out "Over here, man."

"Yes," Shauntelle said in a hoarse voice.

"He should be restored if—when—the original timeline is reinstituted." Neil raised a finger. "That's contingent on how he left this timeline—if he went hazy because he wasn't born, didn't exist here. If he was killed in this timeline and then the original timeline is restored, that's a different matter. Authorities differ over the matter. Some say the dead will be returned to life, unless they were also killed in the original timeline. Others say death applies regardless of timeline reestablishment. Nobody's come to any final conclusion I know of."

"Nobody killed me." Eli made a disgusted noise.

Shauntelle wrapped her fingers tight around her coffee mug.

"He went hazy because he wasn't born here." I slumped back against the chair cushions. "So if we bring that timeline back, he might exist again."

"Might, yes." Neil went off to top up his mug, and brought the whole pot of coffee back with him.

"That's one reason to go into Fate and set things straight." The coffee sent streams of caffeine through my body, waking up any and all sleeping cells.

"Good enough." Shauntelle took herself, and coffee, over to kneel on the rug next to Eli. She wrapped one arm around his shoulder. Both Neil and Monique gave her curious glances, but said nothing.

"What are the others?" Monique asked, sipping more cautiously than I.

"The sleaze was set by a group of White supremacists. Extremists, the kind who think being White is the end-all be-all. They attacked us—Eli and Maksim and me, in Fate. There might be some here, who knows." I threw the possibility out, then followed it through to the bitter end. "If so, they may remember what their other timeline selves were trying. Maybe they'll organize to try and protect the changes as much as they can."

"Extremists again?" Neil rubbed his temples. "My cousin swears every time he turns around there's a new plot to turn Fate upside down."

"You believe him?" Monique crossed her arms.

"About his work? Yeah. He doesn't share much, but when he does he's on the level."

"And how do we know you're not part of this . . . group?" she asked.

"According to their website, they're the Atlantis True Believers." I said.

"Never heard of them." Neil shook his head, nodding at Monique. "But I get you don't know me, don't have any reason to trust me."

"Rose could've gone off without me yesterday. Left me, and maybe I'd have found you," Eli grabbed hold of his mother's hand, "maybe not. I trust her for this."

Shauntelle repeated his words for Monique, staring at me. "You sure of him?"

Swallowing hard, I nodded and shrugged. "I got his name from Tanisha as a possible. At this point, I can't be sure of anyone in this timeline because I don't remember it. I refuse to let any memories in. I'm trusting Tanisha because Maksim did."

Shauntelle and Monique exchanged glances, neither speaking, then Monique waved a hand at her friend. "Your call."

"For you," Shauntelle gripped her son's hand, then nodded at me. "Go on."

"Once in Fate, we managed to undo half of the sleaze, but the rest sank in. That's what Maksim's fighting to keep from fully manifesting. If he fails, even this timeline will probably change more. If you don't help us,"—I glanced back and forth between them—"our lives might change even more for the worse."

"This doesn't count as worse for me." Neil swirled the coffee remaining in his mug, avoiding my gaze.

"No reason it would." Monique gave him a once-over. "You're a White man. Odds are, any changes that favor White men generally will help you even if you're not involved. But what you're saying,"—she pointed a finger at me —"is that this, the timeline we're living in now, isn't stable or guaranteed to stay as it is."

"Pretty much. Probably." I threw in the qualification as a hedge, in case. Setting down my mug, I faced Monique, back straight. "We need three directors or sorcerers to banish the last of the sleaze and rescue Maksim and restore Eli. You, Shauntelle, and Neil."

"Not you?" Monique asked.

"I'm not a sorcerer. I turned but got stuck halfway." I drank, unable to avoid the pity or condolence in her face.

"Ah, I've a brother-in-law by that description. Believes my sister and whole family's magic, but can't bring himself to make that last leap," Monique said, nodding.

A thread of tension in my shoulders eased, only to

multiply as Neil coughed. "There's a problem. I'm not, none of us, are Web-qualified."

"But you're a webmaster!"

"No." He reached over and grabbed my hand, fingers warm to the touch. "I work for the Webmasters. I'm researcher and art designer. Half of my cousins work for the magical side of the firm, but not me."

"You mean we'll need someone else?" Shauntelle and Eli rose from the floor to tower over those of us still seated. "Where you going to find one?"

"That's . . . a good question. I have the list from Tanisha—"

"You said that name before. Who're you talking about?" Monique asked.

"Tanisha Aponsu, she's with Atropos—that's the part of Webmasters, of Lachesis, that . . . that . . ."

"The thread-cutters." Neil stepped in. "The spider-train-ers. The Fate equivalent of Internal Affairs. In short, the staff members who keep the rest of us honest."

"She's part of the team flying up from Uruguay because she couldn't find anyone closer she trusted to deal with this. Apparently the sleaze is really strong, and blanketed the Eastern Seaboard, most of the hemisphere even." I shuddered as I slipped my free hand into my pocket and retrieved my phone. "She gave me some names of people around here to approach for help. Neil's was on it."

I swiped into my phone. No new updates from Tanisha, which meant all might be well or they'd fallen into this time-line. Everything else was ignorable, being only more texts from my mother and from names I didn't recognize, such as the man who supposedly was my older brother and whom I refused to admit existed.

Scrolling to the lists of possible enlistees, I passed the phone over to Neil.

Monique stood. Along with Shauntelle and Eli, she walked around to where she could look over his shoulder. Apart from one glance up, Neil shrugged.

"They're out of town, in the mountains, or they'd help in an instant." Neil pointed to a couple of the names, then pursed his lips. "I think most of the rest would, too—Andrew, Mei, Alejandro, even Geneva—if we can convince them."

"You agreed."

"I had you giving me an alternate view of the past—one I dreamed about last night. I doubt you'll have the same kind of details to offer anyone else, or the patience to wait to see if they dream of different pasts as well." He tapped the phone. "How about a shortcut?"

"What?" I asked.

"Magic." He cupped the phone in his hands. "It'll take us some time to get to the office. Let's say a half-hour. Whoever's on the list and can get there fastest will feel an urge to go there in time to meet us."

I didn't see anything, but Shauntelle, Monique, and Eli all stepped back and watched closely.

Monique raised her eyebrows. "Nice spell, though I'd've used different conditions. Something more flexible."

"What, best match?" Neil asked. "I prefer not to leave too much to the universe."

"Guess not." Her lips twisted to one side and she took a step back.

Turning to me, Neil set the phone aside and grabbed both my hands. "I'm doing this for you. Remember that when we get to the other timeline and haven't gone on our first date. Yet."

§ 17 §

The apartment turned out to be entirely too close to the Webmasters offices for my comfort, and yet not close enough.

Neil led the way along the couple of blocks, twisting his head around now and then to confirm the rest of us followed behind. Which we did without much trouble, since Saturday morning ranked low on foot traffic other than folks headed to or from the farmer's market on Rittenhouse Square. They stuck out against the black, gray, and brown corporate towers, especially with their arms filled with reusable bags in all colors.

We'd all dressed appropriately for the weather—overcast skies and a hint of sultriness suggested rain later. Perfect T-shirt and jeans days. At least half of everyone else dressed likewise.

But almost everyone else was White.

Many young.

A stupid memory from this timeline inserted itself into my head, my older brother whining about not-all-White-men being this, that, or the other, namely racists or sexists. I pushed every detail away—his image, voice, the words.

Of course not all White men, just way too many of them.

Given the ones who'd tried to swarm Maksim, Eli, and me in the coffee house—and then attacked us in Fate—no wonder I'd got more sensitive.

No one here appeared familiar.

Shauntelle marched right behind Neil, hand-in-hand with Eli, but she noticed the shifting crowds and gazes as well.

Before she could do anything, Monique made a motion and sparkles dotted the air around us. Faint to the eye, seen more out of the corners than straight on. Each sparkle flared with a soft crackle, so we walked through an almost-invisible field of popcorn stars.

Instantly viewers' eyes skimmed over us, and no one came too close. One farmer's-market-bound woman fast-walked past me while swinging empty bags to and fro, creating a miniature wind. She veered no more than five inches away, while her bags remained a good three inches off from me.

From five paces ahead, Neil glanced back. His eyebrows rose, but whatever he saw reassured him. He continued on, dodging around a kiosk selling fresh fruit—oranges, apples, pineapples—alongside candy bars, magazines, and newspapers.

"You said White supremacists were behind this. Making the world better for them." Monique wrinkled her nose. "So are things better in your version of the world?"

She must've protected our voices from being heard, as well as our bodies from being seen. Her lips moved but, as with Eli's spell, her words resounded in my ears as though the tinny sounds had been inserted there alone.

"I don't know how things are here. I've been focusing on not learning about this timeline because I've got to stay remembering the real one." Head down, I focused on navigating the intersection and crossing before the traffic could start up—in case drivers couldn't see us. The hum of motors swallowed my voice, except the reverberations in my ears.

But she heard me, and even I couldn't miss the weakness in my words.

"That's not an answer."

"It's also the truth. I don't know what life is like for you here, any more than I can know exactly what it's like for you in the real timeline. That said,"—my shoulders slumped and my head turned down further—"it's not good for a lot of people. There's racism and sexism endemic in the system."

"Either timeline stinks?" Even with the mouth-to-ear delivery, there was no mistaking the sound of teeth grinding.

True enough. Truer than it should be, actually. Things seemed enough the same that Maksim must've kept most of the sleaze from leaking into Fate, unless it wasn't meant to change a lot. "Eli'll be fully alive there."

"So we hope. I'll look forward to meeting him proper. But why are you all up-and-doing,"—she waved a hand at the kiosk—"trying to restore a world that's no better than this?"

"Because it's the original, or at least it's closer than what we're walking in. There might've been changes in the past, probably were. Nothing I can do about that, but I can hold the line here." I stamped a foot against a curb, before making a sharp left turn to follow Neil. "Besides, it's partly my fault."

I slapped a hand across my mouth.

"How's that." Monique gave me a hard look.

"When we got to the sleaze, it was connected to the internet. Let a group of White men go straight to us and attack." I snapped my head around, spotting for them even though her spell protected us. "Maksim wanted to shut it down, but he needed three directors or sorcerers. We didn't have three, just him and Eli. But I suggested trying anyway, with me as a third even though I can't do magic. It worked."

The fragments of the frozen outer sleaze falling away flashed through my mind. "But only halfway. There was a second sleaze underneath that started working faster. I should've kept my mouth closed."

She paused, then shrugged and headed on. "Maybe you should've. Too late now."

I hurried after, lungs working harder and stuttering as I exhaled.

Yet when I caught up, she merely lifted an eyebrow at me. "Who says you can't do magic here?"

"I can't there." Despite the warm humidity, a cold finger ran along my spine.

"So?" At the Webmasters building, she slipped through the door Neil held open only to turn and give me a tight glare. "You tried?"

Could I do magic here? I froze in place, in the middle of the doorway. Why hadn't I considered the possibility?

"You okay?" Neil laid a warm hand against the small of my back.

If I could do magic surely Neil would've mentioned it sometime. So I had my answer, or at least I'd take that as an answer. Surely I was as magic-less here as in the other timeline.

Anyway I didn't need any reason to want to stay in this timeline. I had to hold onto the old. The real. The one I knew, even though it stank in so many ways. How had Maksim put it? Draw a line somewhere and make everyone play by the rules?

"Yeah. Just . . . nervy," I said.

"Hold on. Help is on the way." He smiled and bent to brush a kiss over my lips, one hand still bracing the door.

"Help would arrive faster if you two would keep moving." The astringent tone was unfamiliar, but I recognized the breathy alto.

"Hi Geneva," Neil said as his hand on my back eased me through the doorway. "Fancy seeing you here."

"Don't try to play innocent, it doesn't suit you." The low heels of Geneva's black pumps clattered against the hard floor as she breezed through behind us. Her pale pink blouse and neat black slacks suggested plans for a day of shopping or lunching with friends. Her hair brushed her shoulders, slightly longer than the cut I was familiar with, but that was the only visible change. Apart from a pointed glance our way—timed with the word "innocent,"—she made a beeline for the elevators.

The atrium inside the doors was empty except for the four of us. No guards, no other employees of any firm hanging around. Little in the way of anything soft, either, just tile floors, stone columns, and glass walls. Softer sounds were nearly swallowed, while louder—such as Geneva's heels—echoed in the vastness.

Geneva nodded at Shauntelle and Monique, but not Eli, as she swept by and punched the up arrow. An immediate ding accompanied the closest set of doors swishing open. She didn't wait for the rest to enter, but the doors remained open as Neil and I crowded in after Shauntelle.

The light for the Webmasters floor glowed without anyone touching it. The doors closed and the car started upward with a soft snap. It knocked me off balance, but Neil's hand around my waist steadied me. He and I stood to one side, Geneva at the back, and Shauntelle on the other.

"Um, Shauntelle and Monique, this is Geneva Harperton, head of the Webmasters' Philly office?" Although Neil had said as much, a hint of doubt crept in.

"You should know." Geneva leveled another pointed glance, this one more at me than Neil, then smiled at Shauntelle. "I am most definitely the head, for I get all the headaches."

"This is Shauntelle Jackson and Monique Dulaq. They're with us."

"Part of the emergency that requires my presence here, I take it." Another glance at Neil as the car came to a stop and the doors parted. "Welcome to Webmasters."

"You noticed the spell?" Neil gave a huff. "It's just supposed to encourage people to be here if they can be helpful, not mandate anything."

"Of course I noticed. I am not in the habit of spontaneously deciding to head into work at eight in the morning on a Saturday. Eleven, on occasion. As needed. But not eight, unless I'd made plans the night before to do so, and I most assuredly did not." Geneva strode down the corridor, her shoes silenced while crossing the webbed carpet and only clacking again when she reached the tiled break room.

Unlike the neutral blues elsewhere in the suite, this was done in green and yellow. All the decor—tables, chairs, cabinets—matched. Only the appliances—immense refrigerator, two microwaves, and three coffeemakers—offered touches of other shades, white and black. A door in a corner lay ajar, open just enough to show a large room beyond stocked with food and water. One of the three tables still had a foosball setup atop it, and all of the plastic chairs ringed it. The area had a strong smell of day-old pizza, thanks to the numerous rectangular boxes squashed into a trash bin.

A young White man sat atop one of the tables, texting away. He bore a surface resemblance to Neil: same kinds of clothes and body language. When he tucked away his phone and deigned look at us, the differences became clear. Blond-brown hair sun-streaked lighter than Neil, and a face with sharper, more distinct lines.

"Bout time you got here." He nodded at Neil, but frowned at the rest of us. "Must be something big if you're calling in this many reinforcements. So what's up?"

"Wait, you got an encouragement to come in, too? Andrew and Geneva?" Neil studied his left palm, his right index finger tracing lines on it. "I'd have sworn I set it to ensure we had one Web-qualified person to help, not two."

"Well the best way to be sure you've got one is to have more." Andrew hopped off the table—and with that the nagging sense of familiarity resolved. He was this timeline's equivalent of one of the other researchers who'd tromped around Philly with Neil in a group.

Everything could be right and proper, Neil having just summoned twice as much help as he'd planned.

Or something else might be at work. We were bent on undoing a White supremacist plot, after all—and four of the seven of us were White including both new arrivals.

None of whom I knew well, not Andrew or Neil or this version of Geneva. For that matter, I didn't know that much about my other self, apart from her having done better than me with respect to position, apartment, and love life.

I pulled my arms in tight against my side and shook my head. Too easy to slide into conspiracy theories. I'd just have to take them on trust—but keep my eyes open.

Popping open the refrigerator, Geneva retrieved a bottle of orange juice. She glanced at the rest of us, then waved a hand. "Help yourself." Then, settling one hip on a table, she turned to Neil. "But you haven't answered my question, or Andrew's for that matter. What is the urgency?"

Neil's brow wrinkled, as though he were working something through or coming up with the right words . . . but he didn't say anything.

No sense making Shauntelle or Monique do so. I stepped up, drawing Geneva and Andrew's attention. "There's a sleaze in Fate. Maksim's trying to keep it from changing time more than it already has, but he needs help to blast it out of the Web."

"Maksim?" Geneva blinked once, twice.

Andrew waggled his head as though a dog with a flea in its ear.

Or a spider.

Why hadn't I thought of the spiders in my hair before—surely Geneva or Andrew or Neil, one of them at least, could speak to them. Neil had in the other timeline.

"Spiders?" I lifted a hand to rest atop my ear. "Would one of you be willing to help explain?"

Nothing for a long moment, then soft, light taps on my hand suggested one was climbing out of my hair and onto my hand.

Shifting around, I offered the spider to Geneva first. She let the small, long-legged arachnid clamber onto her hand, and brought it to her ear. Andrew stayed a respectful distance, but craned his head ear-ward-in.

Neither Shauntelle nor Eli had any particular reaction, splitting their attention between glancing around the room and narrow-eyed checks on the rest of us.

Monique had stood nearby, but she took several steps away until her back rested against a wall. Her eyes had gone big, flickering between me and Geneva's hand. "You were carrying *that* in your hair? The whole time?"

I nodded, a whole-body shiver rippling through me though the spiders had been perfect companions. Given her reaction, it was only fair to let her know. "There's one left."

"Fine, you just keep it there." She scooted several steps further away. "I didn't think you folk took the whole Webmasters thing quite so seriously."

"Neither did I, until yesterday when I first saw spiders boiling out of the carpet." I touched my hair lightly, careful not to press down anywhere. "Seems like that was ages ago."

"You didn't bring one out to talk to me." Neil nabbed a couple of waters and offered them around.

"Would it have made a difference?" I accepted one as well, though I didn't open it yet. A hint of the coffee earlier lingered in my mouth, and I had no desire to wash it away.

"Not necessarily," he said, "I don't speak with them much. Don't need to, since I'm not a director. But it might have made things easier. Faster."

We shut up as Geneva's shoes clicked against the tile. She stormed across the floor to the carpeted hallway—all the way to the blank wall facing the break room. There she laid her hands against cream-colored surface.

An intricate, 3-D model of the globe shot out from the wall. Thick layers of webbing covered it, although transparent so as to show the world itself beneath. The continents and seas were rudimentary and rendered in muted shades of gray. All the colors and vibrancy lay in the layers of web, which glittered in every shade of the rainbow. As a model of the Web of Fate, it offered only the merest hint of what it was like to hike into Fate. It was nowhere near as complex—or beautiful—as the real thing.

Various colored nodes glowed particularly bright in different places, mostly in greens and blues, a few yellows and oranges.

And one big, fat red spot out in the ocean off the southeastern coast of the United States. Around about the Bermuda triangle.

Geneva tapped the node, and a box manifested above filled with text in three languages or alphabets or syllabaries. I drew close with the others, Monique carefully placing herself as far from me and Geneva as possible.

Unfortunately proximity didn't help me at all. One of the languages appeared to be Greek. Another might be Chinese, but the third . . . The best guess I had, which could easily be wrong, was Sanskrit.

"Tanisha Aponsu initiated an incident of concern

yesterday morning." Geneva flicked her fingers to expand the box, allowing more text to fill it. "It was upgraded to in-process sleaze at noon. Blurry initials, can't see who, and that's shoddy work deserving a reprimand if I ever catch up with the person." She leaned in and squinted, then made a disgusted noise. "Someone upgraded the incident late yesterday afternoon. Marked it as accelerating, shifting to crisis mode. The last note is from Tanisha, a report of partial banishment and further acceleration, confirmation of a team on the way with an estimated time of arrival twenty to twenty-four hours, dated twenty hours ago."

Whirling around, Geneva pointed a finger at me. "Do you have any reason to think Tanisha won't make it in time to destroy the sleaze?"

"Only that she hasn't done it yet?" I threw out my hands. She was the expert, after all. "Last I saw him, Maksim was lying on a fate-line with his arm shoulder-deep, and . . . I think we should make sure people show up to destroy the sleaze. Better to send two teams in than count on one, espe-cially when they haven't been heard from in nearly a day. I mean, I can't do magic, but they can. Why hasn't anyone updated even if they are in a plane?"

"Good question." She turned her attention back to the box, rubbing her chin with one hand. Then tossed a side-glance at me. "I'm not clear on why you were involved in the first place."

"Maksim wanted a witness, as a safeguard of some sort. And he picked me because I didn't believe in the alternate timeline changes that were happening, and I have no magic, and he thought I'd be a good witness." It had seemed so simple back then. "Except his stepson got roped in too, when we nearly were ganged up on by a group of White suprema-cists at a coffee house. We made it to the sleaze, which was tied to a website, but when we tried to banish it we only managed to do the outer layer." I ran to a halt, having told the story too many times.

"That's what the spider said." Geneva scanned the three of us, lips pursing. She nodded at Neil. "You're willing to go in. Have you participated in any banishments before?"

"No, but my cousin has so I know a little about them." He drew a deep breath, chest rising high, and his back straightened. "I'm here. I'm willing."

"Count me in, too." Andrew's stance mirrored Neil's. "Sounds like something worth doing."

"Very well." Geneva inclined her head, then glanced at Shauntelle and Monique. "You're not part of Webmasters or Lachesis, but you're willing to help?"

"Yes." Shauntelle had her hands braced on Eli's shoulders. A fine picture to me, though no doubt odd to those who couldn't see Eli. He didn't look too good, head and shoulders slumping and a hair more transparency to his body.

Monique chewed on her lip for a few moments, hands flexed and clenched. At length she gave me a side-eye, then nodded. "Yes."

"I suppose you want to come too?" Geneva turned to me last.

"Yeah."

"Very well. Let's get some supplies and be on our way." Geneva clapped her hands together.

A sudden flood of relief nearly made my legs crumple under me. I'd have sunk down except Neil grabbed me and held me up. "You mean you'll help us?"

"It is the duty of every webmaster, every Lachesis director, every Lachesis employee, to protect, preserve, and safeguard Fate for the betterment of the human race and all who depend upon us." Geneva waved a hand at the model of Fate and it slipped back into the wall with a soft thud. "Let's get going."

$$\text{❧ } 18 \text{ ☙}$$

The first time I entered Fate, I had no idea what I was doing. Going there deliberately and with full intent made all the difference.

For starters, Geneva made us walk through all the preliminary steps that Maksim had done without me, or Eli since the boy's presence with us was so unexpected.

"Clothing check," she said, walking around each of us and examining us up and down. "Comfy attire only, things that will stand up to extended wear. Most especially your shoes."

My sneakers received a second and third glance before she accepted them. In the end, we all passed muster.

It all took so much time, but when I said as much she gave me a sharp glare. "Fate is not a place to run into."

Or rush.

Or move fast.

After clearing our clothes, she opened the door in the corner of the break room. It led into a space twice as big—and three times as full of supplies. Bright overhead lights revealed plain concrete flooring and gray industrial shelving lining three of the four walls. One held flat after flat of bottled water. Another contained a variety of clothes from shirts down to sneakers, just in case we hadn't been acceptably accoutered. The third featured an assortment of nutrition bars and grab-n-go snack foods, plus varying sized first-aid kits and other pre-packed boxes of . . . tools? I itched to explore, but this wasn't the time.

Backpacks in all styles, shapes, and conditions hung from a rack in the center of the room. And such a miscellany! Big and small. Made of fabric only or attached to an aluminum frame suitable for hiking the Appalachian Trail. Not to mention every color under the sun and then some.

"Where do they come from?" I picked up a lightweight one in yellow. Someone had drawn all over it in pen—a zoo theme featuring all manner of animals from baby ducks up to long-necked giraffes and a black-and-yellow zebra. This had to be custom drawn, especially as the top bore initials: N.G.

"The Museum of All Things Lost and Forgotten keeps us supplied. They don't say what criteria they use to determine what we can have,"—Geneva tapped her fingertips together—"and we don't ask. At least, I never have."

She picked a dark blue bag similar to mine in basic—generic—style, and began stuffing it with supplies.

First up: two flats of water. With each one she slipped the backpack over one corner and then somehow managed to navigate the whole thing inside. Despite all she added, it seemed no heavier. Not even when she added several fistfuls of different snacks.

I had lesser ambitions. A few loose bottles had rolled to the side. When I snagged them up, plastic cool and smooth against my skin, I popped them into my bag and immediately felt the added weight.

The Museum might supply bags, but they were everyday ones rather than magic like my pocket.

No way would I even consider trying to stuff in a flat.

"That's not necessary, Rose. The rest of us can carry extra for you." Geneva tapped my hand holding the middling-heavy bag.

She swung around and exchanged nods with Neil and Andrew, who were filling bags and suggesting things for Shauntelle and Monique. Eli stuck close to his mother, but kept out of the way. The one time he didn't move fast enough and Neil passed through him, Neil only shivered as though touched by a cold breeze but Eli arched and quivered.

"I can carry a bag for myself." I wrapped my fingers tighter around the strap at the top. The last thing I wanted was to be a burden, someone others had to make up for.

"But you'll have to actually carry the weight." Geneva blinked at me. "We can't condense and virtualize the contents since you'll have no way of retrieving them."

"Then I'll just carry a couple of bottles of water and some granola bars. They won't weigh too much." If she took it from me, so be it. I wouldn't fight over it, but I didn't draw the line at a minor fuss.

"That's not—" Geneva's lips tightened, then she tossed up her hands. "Oh, very well, but as long as you're carrying food and water, don't forget other necessities." She grabbed the smallest of the first-aid kits and slapped it against my palm.

Skin smarting, I tucked the lightweight plastic rectangle alongside four bottles of water and a matching set of granola bars.

"No soda or coffee or anything flavored?" I glanced through the doorway at the variety of drinks filling the break room shelves as I swung my backpack on, slipping my arms through the straps. A solid weight rested against the small of my back.

"It's safest that way." Geneva shifted the door to block the view. "You can take those, but I'd advise against it. Sometimes the winds of Fate blow along the lines, and any food or drink that doesn't have an equivalent in the time over which we're walking turns into whatever Fate considers the closest temporal equivalent."

True, Maksim hadn't brought any flavored drinks, although he'd provided my favorite ginger beer in the coffee house. Yet if the drinks were at risk of getting changed . . . "What about the plastic bottles?"

"Oh, we pre-treat those to make them Fate-safe." She plucked various boxes and kits from the wall to shove into her pack, only one of which I recognized. "It's good for the environment, too, as it makes them break down faster when they're recycled."

With a wave of a hand for me to wait, she pivoted on one foot—sole squeaking against the floor—and reviewed everyone else's selections.

I slipped over to Shauntelle in the meanwhile. She had a tight grip on Eli, who leaned against her. His energy and bounce had caved in, likely due to the press of surviving in a world where he didn't technically exist.

"How're you doing?" I asked.

He barely showed he'd heard me.

How would he handle going into Fate?

Worry shone on Shauntelle's face, but her chin was up and shoulders back and straight.

"Will you be okay going into Fate?" I jerked my chin at Eli as much or more than her. "Maybe it would be better if Monique goes with Neil and Geneva and Andrew, since we have more than three."

"No, I'm going, and Eli'll be with me." She stroked his hair. "I'll keep him safe in my heart."

A loud whack made me jump and whirl around. Geneva had finished reviewing our packs.

"You're Fate-qualified, I already know," she pointed at

Andrew, then raised an eyebrow at Neil. "How many times have you been in Fate?"

"Three. Training runs." Neil shifted to stand next to me, squeezing my hand.

"Right, then the three of us will swap lead and rear guard." She rubbed her hands together. "Everything ready? Then get your last pit stop in and reassemble here."

Within a matter of minutes, she told us to line up on the webbed carpeting outside the break room. There were no spiders anywhere in sight.

Nerves up and down my limbs jangled. I both wished I could mainline coffee and was glad I couldn't. The morning's cup sat heavy inside me.

Monique shivered next to me, probably way past second thoughts given her light, choppy breathing. "Why'm I doing this?" Perhaps she didn't realize she'd spoken, but her soft whisper tickled my ear.

"For Shauntelle and Eli." I said, equally quiet, offering a hand.

She stared at my fingers. She huffed and shrugged, but slipped a cold hand into mine all the same. "That girl can talk me into about anything."

"Same with you." Shauntelle lined up next to us, Eli hovering behind her with a hand on her shoulder.

"And if you're worried about going into Fate . . . it's beautiful." I said.

"What is?" Monique's fingers twitched against mine, and she started to breathe deeper.

"Fate. It's like walking through stars and the aurora borealis and . . ." My mouth opened and shut as I lacked the words to explain.

"Even on a bad day, it's glorious." Neil settled into place beside me and smiled over my head at the others.

Monique's fingers gave one last twitch, then began to

warm. A few more breaths, and she held on as tight as I clung to her and Neil.

Geneva glanced down the line, lips pursed, then took a place between Shauntelle and Andrew.

The transition took place in an instant, without any stop in a webpage. I inhaled in the real world, albeit the alternate timeline, and exhaled in Fate.

Once again, it was glorious—but not so welcoming as before.

In all the packing fuss, I skipped over Geneva's comment about winds of Fate.

Instead, I should've taken it literally.

Maksim, Eli, and I had walked through relatively still weather during our trip through Fate. So still I hadn't realized Fate *had* weather.

Yet the instant we arrived, a hard gust slapped against my face. My eyes reflexively closed against the lash of air with a hint of moisture. A wind ebbed and flowed around me, mild one moment and chill-to-the-bone the next.

A drop of cold water slipped under my collar and rolled down my back.

When I opened my eyes, Fate surrounded me as glorious as ever. Stars hung overhead so close I could dream of touching them. But the clouds of gas and colored light had increased. They fluxed and shrank, and shifted shape as the winds blew through and around them.

The fate-line beneath our feet had a faint green cast. Perhaps it was the sleaze trickling through to taint this present.

The air remained neither warm nor cold, but the celestial aroma had developed an astringent note.

Worst of all: the fate-line stretched before us as a long and narrow trail. Maybe two people could walk abreast, but they'd be at risk of slipping sideways and falling off. We'd have to go single file. Only the spot where we stood, over the present, extended far enough to the sides for the lot of us to stand alongside each other.

Shauntelle and Monique stayed still beside me, mouth open as they gazed at the stars. Tears glinted in their eyes. Monique circled, much slower than Geneva, and stopped halfway with a sharp, indrawn breath.

Mirroring her turn and stance, I didn't have to wonder what caught her attention.

Behind us, the fate-line led to an approaching sunrise. The array of purples, oranges, and reds beat any real sunrise all hollow.

I started to take a step forward, and she might've too—

But fingernails dug into my elbow and a hard hand yanked me back a couple of steps. Nearly sent me reeling, and the same with Monique.

Geneva stretched her arms wide and positioned herself between us and the sunrise. "That's the future. We don't go there. Only webmasters with specialized training venture forward. We're going that way." She pointed the opposite direction, from whence the winds blew.

Unlike the future, the colors in the distant past had a taint to them. No pure colors, only those with a tinge of the kind of gray light that on earth would be a sign of a nasty blow of a storm.

The lot of us minus one.

No Eli anywhere to be seen. Even with how he'd faded, he should be visible to me.

But Shauntelle didn't seem concerned.

"Where's Eli?" I asked, careful to keep my voice low.

"He's here." She patted her chest. A pendant hung about her neck, a thick chunk of amber with a faint human-shaped shadow inside. Rather similar to the water bottles in which Maksim had imprisoned our attackers, but far more elegant.

"I'm not taking the chance of losing him going into this strangeness."

"At least he's okay." I said.

Monique seemed the only one close enough to hear. She took a closer gander at the necklace and gave Shauntelle a high-five. "Good craft there."

We'd gotten away with our whispers in no small part because the others were busy frowning over the condition of the fate-line. Andrew crouched down and ran finger along it. Bits of green dust clung to his skin as he turned his hand over.

Geneva turned around and around, her head snapping this way and that.

The spider silk bracelet began to tighten around my wrist. The cord running off from it grew taut.

Then something tugged, hard. Not enough to make me stumble forward, but impossible to ignore. A second followed.

Then more and more, some short and some long . . .

"Anyone know Morse code?"

"Yeah, why?" Andrew asked.

Geneva showed equal surprise. Shauntelle's mouth twitched, but she kept shifting around to watch the celestial colors. Monique and Neil just shrugged.

"I think Maksim's trying to send a message." I showed them the spider silk bracelet.

Geneva tucked two fingers under, pulling it sharply against my skin until I grimaced at the sudden burst of pain. "Sorry." Moving her hand, she wrapped her fingers around the cord and yanked several times in succession. "Report."

Tug after tug, Geneva spelled out letters for Andrew to shape into words as he scribbled Maksim's message. The tugs stopped at her hand, protecting me from being yanked this way and that.

"Anyone there? Holding fast. Need help."

Flexing her fingers, Geneva let go and winced. "You send a message back." She gave Andrew the exact words, watching as he jerked on the thread to tell Maksim: "Relief on the way. Leaving Philly. ETA unknown."

"He says roger." Andrew gave a sharp nod, likewise grimacing and massaging his fingers after he let go.

"Right, then let's head out."

Geneva set the order: herself first, then me, Shauntelle, Monique, Neil, and Andrew bringing up the tail. Then she turned to face the past, and frowned. Maybe we shouldn't have waited through the exchange of messages. The bursts of green and purple gasses encroached upon the fate-line. If we didn't take the first cross-line, we'd have to march right through them.

Likewise, the winds picked up. My shoulder-length hair whipped around and scourged my face as I strode forward, despite Geneva's form offering a little protection. She had none, and her hair danced around her, one minute forming an immense aura and the next slapping against her ears and face. Monique's locks flew about, but the thick tie held them back from her face. Andrew, Neil, and Shauntelle's shorter hair meant they didn't face the same peril, but Shauntelle's thick, short curls got flattened and would likely need to be fluffed out when we got back out to the real world—and real timeline.

None of us were safe from the invisible bits of ice in the wind. Worse than any snowball, they stung and left red welts along my arms and other exposed skin. Even my jeans didn't completely protect my legs from the minuscule darts. More pellets made the fate-line below as slick as a freshly washed-and-waxed linoleum floor.

"This isn't normal!" So many welts marred Geneva's face she looked to have a case of the measles. She shouted, and even so the wind whipped her words by me so fast they slurred together.

"Is it the sleaze?" I cupped my hands around my mouth to try and be heard.

"Possibly. Or Fate trying to reject the changes." She stopped so abruptly I nearly slammed into her back, and ditto the others behind me. "Watch out!"

She pointed here and there. Everywhere around us, the air started spinning. Several mini-tornadoes started to form.

But I shouldn't have let my attention get distracted by them, because it was a plain old wind gust—albeit big and nasty—that pushed me toward the edge of the fate-line. My feet skidded under me. I scrambled for purchase. Geneva and Shauntelle both grabbed for me, the one slamming a hand into my shoulder before latching onto the collar of my shirt and the other getting a fistful of my shirt side and hold of one arm.

Neil wrapped his arms around my waist and anchored me.

"Thanks. All of you. That was close." I bent over breathing hard. Shauntelle patted me on the back.

Geneva did the same, but on the top of my head and took a step back. "Keep close. We'll go slow. Back into line."

With a quick kiss to one cheek, Neil backed up to allow us to reorder. I missed the warmth of his arms and body within moments. Geneva started off at a glacial pace, but I took a moment to glance back and smile or do something to show my gratitude for the comfort as well as the partial rescue—in time to witness another gust of wind whipping around.

It lashed out at me, pulling at my legs and feet. I dug my heels in and refused to move. Hah, I skidded, but kept it to a minimum.

Only to watch as the same gust slammed hardest against Shauntelle. Her legs parted. One mostly stayed put while the other inched ever further toward the danger zone. Her torso wavered.

"Don't fall!" I yelled, only a beat after Neil and Geneva saying the same thing.

Andrew and Monique grabbed for her, each getting hold of one arm as they dragged her up closer to the center.

Without a shriek of warning, another wind gust knocked me off.

$\maltese$ 19 $\maltese$

Falling.

Grayness everywhere. Flashes of light.

Cold. Ice arrows stung my arms and legs. Pulled one arm up to protect my face. A little warmth in the curve of my elbow.

Nothing visible.

Throat hoarse.

Someone screamed—me?

The winds battered without ceasing, but never the same way twice. Pulling one moment, pushing the next. Turning me upside-up or upside-down or sideways. No telling where anything was. I swirled around. Even with my eyes closed, my head whirled outside and inside.

The spider silk bracelet went limp and loose around my wrist.

Only the winds seemed real.

Nothing else but air around.

Two sets of forces wrenched me this way and that. The winds wanted to play or blast or whatever, while gravity sped my descent. I stopped screaming, throat too raw to sustain any noise. Dragging in any breath hurt, even when the chill began to dissipate.

The winds shrieked for me.

As I kept dropping, twirling until I lost all sense of what direction was what except . . .

Down.

Air warmer, humid, easier to breathe and carrying a hint of brine.

The wind pulled the straps of my backpack taut against my back, and one snapped. The whole thing tore away, leaving my back cold and vulnerable to the wind's blast. Wriggling my body, I tried to get control of the whirl. Was it better to fall face forward or backward?

I hit ground face-down, body first. My head ricocheted forward and knocked against something hard.

I didn't know how long I lay unconscious, only that I woke to a world of pain.

Everything hurt, from my toes to my hair. Impossible to rank one agony above another, but on the other hand a couple throbbed and spiked above the rest. My hands and knees had impacted against something hard and uneven yet rather smooth. Stone, perhaps. Certainly my palms had two or three dozen pebbles or bits of bracken embedded in them. My wrists and knees quaked as though they'd absorbed far more stress than built to handle.

All this in addition to the goose-egg no doubt grown big and red at the top of my forehead.

The only grace amidst the agony: nothing seemed to be bleeding.

At the moment, at least.

No prickling of my skin as fluid trickled over, though parts of my hands and knees and the side of my face had a tacky stiffness suggesting something had flowed and started to dry.

But there wasn't any hint of iron in the air.

Then again, would I even notice amid all the other smells: urine, manure, wood smoke, tar . . . and the brine of the ocean.

A light breeze danced over me, tugging at strands of my tangled hair. A stark contrast to the blasting winds of Fate that had dropped me here.

Wherever *here* was. The warm, moist air had a hint of chill. It was the kind of temperature I associated with spring.

Gulls cried and squawked overhead, bringing the stench of decaying fish with them.

Bangs and thumps and laughter rang out. Feet tromped around me, though no one stopped to check and see if I was alive. Not very nice of them, especially since there were so many people talking here and there. Men and women, all speaking an incomprehensible language. Now and then I caught a word I recognized—one word, at least: I. Everything else hit my ears wrong.

Creaking and in need of a good oiling, wheels rolled right near me. Must've been no more than a foot away. Followed by the clop of horse hooves, though I'd have expected it the other way around—if I were going to expect anything.

Bits of crust clumped in my eyelashes when I first opened my sore, dry eyes. Several blinks dampened my eyes enough to let me see more than a gray blur.

I lay sprawled across uneven, semi-square stones placed in a relatively straight array.

Pulling up one hand then the other, I checked them. Palms definitely red and stinging, with numerous scrape marks over hands and wrists, but no bleeding. Grimacing and hissing as new aches shot through me, I pushed back onto my haunches. An instant later, shooting pain in my knees made me slip sideways and sit on my bottom with my legs canted to the side.

Unable to move due to the pain—and startlement over my surroundings.

A warm, yellow sun shone overhead, about a quarter above the horizon. Clear light filled the air save for a tinge of smoke here and there. When the breeze shifted, it wakened my appetite—just a little—with the scent of fresh bread baking.

Cobblestone streets stretched out in four directions. I'd landed almost in the center of an intersection where the two met. Wooden buildings, painted in bright reds and yellows, blues and greens, lined the streets. Some set far enough back to have small gardens, penned off with picket fences or simple wood slats, but most came right up to the crude side-walks lining the streets.

It resembled Elfreth's Alley, only wider and with bigger buildings that weren't all houses.

Except also, more wood and less brick.

Not to mention the addition of horses and wagons—and people, none of whom were dressed in modern clothing. The men wore pants or breeches of all sorts of fabric and colors, plus shirts and vests and long coats. The best dressed had hats on their heads, but even those in the raggedest attire had sloppy or sloped caps. As for the women, they mostly wore narrow dresses that gathered under their bosoms, though some had wider skirts. Nearly all, rich or poor or in between, had some kind of bonnet or cap over their hair and an apron to protect the front of their dress as well. Though there weren't many women compared to men. Likewise, there was a mix of Whites and Blacks.

At a guess, I'd dropped somewhere along the Eastern Seaboard in the early years of the United States. But where and when?

Did it even matter, especially since I couldn't understand

what they said? They spoke enough, I should have caught something.

Plus, no one noticed me.

So perhaps I shouldn't have been surprised when someone walked toward me without stopping. A tall, barefoot older White man dressed in muddy brown breeches and a stained yellowish shirt, with a light green coat, much patched in any fabric handy, hanging open. The heavy bundle atop his back, wrapped and strapped up in burlap, made him tilt forward.

Nor surprised that he passed through me, though I was.

But I had extra reason for shock because he walked *backward*.

Lurching to my feet, despite the bursts of pain rocketing through me, I turned around and took a second—better—look at everything.

The world rolled in reverse. People moved back, unloaded baskets and wagons, bowed and curtsied and everything as though I stood in the middle of a virtual reality movie and someone had hit the rewind button.

Even the white-and-gray gulls overhead moved tail-first toward wherever they'd come from rather than winging forward and away.

No wonder I couldn't understand anything anyone said. They spoke backward.

Anything and everything passed through me. Quite an unnerving sensation to realize one was so thoroughly non-existant to people, though the whole backward thing actually made it a bit easier.

And trickier.

Where the hell was I and, of equal or more importance, where had Shauntelle and Neil and Geneva wound up? I could only hope we'd landed somewhere near each other.

In space—and in time.

I tugged on the thread leading off from the spider silk

bracelet, but got no response. Just as well, since I didn't know Morse code to tell Maksim he'd need to wait longer on reinforcements.

As I spun around, trying to make sense of my surroundings, a lump partway down the street caught my attention. Unlike the piles of horse manure, complete with bits of straw, dropped here and there, not to mention the streams of bright, stinking urine, this lump had a bright, yellowish appearance.

Could it be . . .

I hobbled over. My backpack had landed near me, though for all I knew it had arrived minutes or hours before me. Either way, I pounced on it with joy despite the pangs ripping through my bruised body.

Water.

Food.

Medicine!

I clutched the straps, whole and broken, in my hands as I sought a place to sit. Even knowing it didn't matter where, I inched my way down one of the streets to a square surrounded by a tidy picket fence that had grayed since its last coat of whitewash. Likewise the nearby clapboard church had once been white and turned a soft gray. Several tall gravestones stuck out of the grass in clumps—three here, two there, but at least there were no open graves.

Better to rest and recoup in a graveyard than out in the street. It smelt moderately nice, of grass and brine and wood, and there I could ignore how time around me ran backward. I sat on a section of rough grass near the church, legs straight out and back against the cool stone. The leaf-filled branches of an oak tree in one corner offered shade and a quiet rustling in between bursts of activity from the street.

My hands shook and ached so much it took three tries, the last with my hands wrapped in the hem of my shirt, to open a water bottle. Prying apart the clasp of the first-aid kit and ripping open a packet of pain pills was almost as tricky. After chasing the pills down with the whole of the bottle, I rolled up my pants to check my knees—and applied a couple of plain beige bandages over clotted scrapes.

Then leaned back and discovered with pleasure that I did *not* pass through the church wall.

What could I do? No wonder Maksim had warned Eli not to fall off the edge of Fate. But surely, Maksim had also said something suggesting he could retrieve the boy if he did.

Watching time roll backward surprised at the start, turned faintly amusing for a moment or two—but otherwise grew old really quick. I just wanted to go home, back to my own time, and crawl into bed. If I got under my covers there now, I might never emerge.

But I was so far away.

Still without magic. Or was I? Monique's suggestion that perhaps I could do spells had stuck in my brain and popped out no matter how unwelcome.

Except, if I tried and succeeded, I could get found faster.

Yet what might happen to the spider silk bracelet and Maksim then? Doing magic, assuming I could in the altered timeline, might cause me to forget the real one.

And even if I could do magic, I had no idea what spell might help. I'd still be left alone.

If I was alone.

"Spider? Are you there?" I lifted a hand to my head. The winds had torn the backpack from me, and whipped my hair around, but maybe the spider had held on.

Light taps against the back of my hand suggested it had. Lowering my hand gingerly, I found the small gold-and-black body sitting atop my skin. It clambered over as I rotated reflexively to offer my palm.

Once there, it started dancing and spinning.

Strands of silk floated in the breeze, slowly cohering into an array of connections. Line by line, an immense irregular web formed around me. How could one spider weave so much so fast? With help. Squinting at the ground, I turned around to find two or three dozen spiders adding strands to the mix.

They spun enough for not one web, but two. They lay so close together, one upon the other, to seem as one save for their colors. The strands of one shone gray with a silver tinge, the other limned in gold.

It all whirled into existence so fast I barely moved before I was surrounded. At first the webs floated around. Any stray gust of wind should have carried them away.

Instead they began to contract. A millimeter here, an inch there, but the amount of space between me and the webs reduced. I circled, seeking a gap and finding none. The mixture of gray, silver, and gold continued to shrink.

A strand brushed my elbow and clung.

Memory burst through me, familiar and strange. I stood next to the door into a white-washed room covered with posters in brilliant, blinding colors to the point only tiny patches of the walls showed in stray spots. A dozen people sprawled on well-used chairs and couches—a couple White, most Black. The smell of pizza, fresher than in the break room, filled the air. A couple of boxes and layers of paper plates and napkins filled a trash can in one corner. A single box remained on a low table in the center of the room.

A young Black woman in a ripped gold T-shirt and jeans refused me entry. Blocked the way and called me out. I'd made decisions that weren't mine, led where I should follow. So she'd put it to a show of hands.

Nothing more of the context came through, but it didn't have to. The day lived in my brain along with others—toward the end of my senior year in college, when the students with whom I'd occupied the admin building to protest the college's lack of response to racist incidents decided afterward that I'd taken too much on myself after negotiating with a vice-president.

They voted me out. No appeal.

An instant later the other web attached to my elbow as well. A similar scene rolled by, but this time I was one of the students on the couches. Keeping my mouth shut, except when asked, and being a support.

The web continued to contract around me. More strands of silk adhered to my skin.

I relived—twice—the moment when I believed in magic. First standing on cold, damp hillside searching for my younger sisters who'd gone off, giggling, without me. Mere weeks after the earlier scene, with my pride and confidence sorely bruised, I'd followed in time to see my middle sister transform into a swan and back. Twice! With my youngest sister offering commentary.

Then a second, alternate scene. I had no sisters, only a brother. A much older brother who often escaped when I tried to follow. I was younger in this memory, much younger, barely in my teens. Hot on my brother's gangly heels, typical kid sister not wanting to be left behind, I fell back onto my bottom when he leapt over a six-foot fence in a single bound.

Other recollections flooded through me, always in twos. One from my life, one from the alternate me.

I'd grown up an older sister, sure of my importance and purpose in the world. *She*'d been more tentative and diffident, though determined to make a place for herself.

I stumbled and fell, then flailed around. Mourned the loss of my dreams when I dropped out of law school unable to hack it. Took a dead-end job at Webmasters to pay the bills, lost without my goal and unable to make new ones. Not even able to realize just how lucky and privileged I was to have the time and space to reinvent myself.

She grew from weakness to strength, finding purpose in service and support functions—and earning a trusted role, interesting work, and happiness in love.

I wanted to be *her.*

What would it mean if I gave into the longing? I was lost in time anyway. Fallen from Fate as far as I'd fallen in myself. What harm luxuriating in remembering the life *I* hadn't lived, but now wanted to. It wouldn't make any difference. Shauntelle and Monique, Neil and Andrew and Geneva, they all remained in Fate to head off and cleanse the sleaze and free Maksim. My falling shouldn't stop that.

One of the webs began to gleam brighter than the other.

Except.

It wasn't right.

I'd helped encourage Eli to wake Shauntelle from the dream of her other life. She'd faced a similar duality. Struggled. Emerged strong enough to keep Eli from disappearing.

Could I ask any less of myself than we had of her?

I'd been standing still as a statue, as the webs closed in around me, but I burst into motion. Flailed. Threw out arms. Kicked forward and back. Refused to let any more of the strands touch me. Burn me. Make me doubt.

Until a sharp sting on my palm stilled me. My chest heaved. Sweat covered my body, and a sour taste filled my mouth.

The webs had vanished. The spider remained on my palm, having managed to cling tight despite my exertions. A red mark glowered on my skin below it.

Then it brushed the bite with a leg, and a healing coolness spread through me.

Tossing out a length of silk, it scrambled up to my head. Instead of hiding in my hair, it leapt here and there across my scalp. Light began to glow where it passed, clear in the fading sunlight as it cast purple shadows all around.

The spider spun a beacon of light and warmth atop my head.

The rest of me remained chilled. I'd chosen the life and memories where I'd stumbled and gotten stuck in mud. But I was still young and strong, I could do better.

I would do better.

If I ever got out of here.

❧ 20 ❧

No one arrived to retrieve me before the sun went down. The reverse sunrise painted the sky in glorious pinks and purples, almost as lovely as that in the future of Fate before I'd been knocked out by the winds. Morning in reverse resembled twilight, but in all the wrong ways. Same shifts in light quality and array of glorious colors across the sky. The air cooled far more quickly than with nightfall. Well before the sun vanished, I started shivering.

Deep in my bag lay a thermal blanket. Wrong name, it wasn't much more than a throw. Dark blue on one side and bright aluminum on the other, it covered only part of me— my bare arms at least. I sat in the churchyard and leaned back against a tree and made-do. The spring weather managed a starker drop in temperature than I'd anticipated.

More smoke on the breeze, and the first breads starting to bake.

Off and on over the hours as I sat and waited, the spider danced around the top of my head. Occasionally it touched skin, but mostly its legs brushed against my hair as though imitating a small, localized breeze.

My first intimation that it wasn't actually air flowing around my head came when I slipped an arm out from under the blanket and went to finger-comb my hair.

No sooner had my index finger started to part strands, than the spider bit me. A quick sharp pain ran up my arm. I pulled back instinctively. The sun hadn't quite un-risen at that point, offering a bare minimum of light but enough to see a small welt similar to a bee sting.

Yet once the sun went back down, the light blaring from the top of my hair increased. Although I couldn't see it myself, it cast sharp shadows all around.

Fortunately, no human gave any evidence of noticing the glare. I sat on the cliff-top, a human lighthouse waiting for someone outside of time to notice.

One thing I had in consolation: a gorgeous, clear sky for star-gazing. Better in the distance, farther from the spider's corona. Still, even so I saw notable arrays of stars.

A brilliant, super-bright star blazed across the sky. Tinted blue-white, it traced an arc toward us.

A shooting star.

A comet. Meteor.

A sorcerer searching for me.

Or rather, two, for a second shooting star bearing a faint reddish tinge manifested in the wake of the first. Their speeds altered as their trails crossed and recrossed—the first sign this wasn't a true celestial phenomenon. I'd never heard of real shooting stars shifting their trajectories, much less in a way visible to the naked eye.

The stars slowed and dimmed as they arced toward me.

The first resolved into Neil jolting forward. Monique, the second star, a beat behind him.

Tossing off the blanket, I ran to meet them.

Neil headed straight for me. "Are you all right?"

He waited no longer than a breath, only time enough for me to nod, before grabbing me in a tight—and warm—embrace. Tucking my head into his neck at least meant I didn't have to look him in the face just yet.

They'd come for me. Muscle after muscle unknotted and relaxed in the warmth of Neil's body pressed tight against me. Some tension released, but worry remained. Had I fallen, or been pushed? I wasn't important, except . . . other than the spiders, I was the remaining visible, audible link to Maksim and the partly banished sleaze. Without me, Geneva or Andrew might rethink heading further in. Or maybe they'd wasted valuable time retrieving me that might cost us, especially Maksim, in the end.

"How'd you find me?" I asked.

"It took way-the-hey longer than it should've." Neil's hold loosened and I stepped to the side, with one of his arms curving around my waist to rest on my hip. His lips stiff, he made a disgusted noise. "We knew you'd fallen far, based on the clear rents between the fate-lines. We should've done a chronological scan right off the bat, to pinpoint the year and date you'd dropped into."

"Geneva spouted off something about a geological spectrum base analysis?" Monique raised an eyebrow as she retrieved the blanket and folded it into a small, compact square.

"Yes, but it meant we overshot on our first extraction attempt." He lifted his arm from my waist, leaving a cool spot behind, as he brought both hands to my head and removed the web from atop my hair. The spider silk resisted in a few places, then came away. "Andrew and Geneva are on a second try a couple few decades further down the road, but Monique came with me when I spotted the flare. Good thinking to set the spectral light in your hair. We might've gone past without it."

The web's light had faded to a pale, violet glow. Yet the trickle of luminescence along the strands and nodes turned it into miniature night sky with ample constellations.

Reaching up a hand, and the same finger still bearing a red bite mark, I patted the side of my head gently. "Thanks."

A tiny tap acknowledged me.

A darting breeze snatched the web from Neil's hands and sailed it out far over the waters. I watched until it vanished from sight.

"Did anyone else fall?" I asked.

"No." Neil rubbed my back, eyes narrowing.

"Shauntelle nearly did, but I nabbed her back." Monique crossed her arms over her chest. "We kept to the center of the line after that. You were the only one tossed off."

"Or pushed." The words slipped out before I could keep them back.

"That would explain, except . . ." Neil drew in a hissing breath, expression troubled and gaze distant. "I think, I might've seen, might know . . . but it's blurred together."

"You saw me getting pushed?" I pulled back to study his face.

"No, I don't think so. But my memory's getting foggy." He ran a hand through his hair, rubbing the side of his head. "I'm starting to remember two timelines, I think. Maybe. Something's wrong."

I bumped his shoulder with my head, glancing over at Monique. "You don't seem surprised."

"I don't know any of you well enough to trust you farther than I can throw you. Shauntelle and I have our own safeguard that should work from anywhere, though she doesn't want to pull the plug yet. Still bent on tracking down her husband and getting her son back safe." Monique rapped her fingers against her arms. "Any false moves, though, and I'm getting both of us back where we belong."

"Wish I could do that." I shivered in the night breeze. "Let's get out of here and back underway."

Neil wrapped a hand around my waist and we started back up.

Rising proved a very different experience from falling. It wasn't a straight movement, for we lifted up but also away. Everything about the real world grew distant and faded in increments. The regular night shifted to the night-skies-and-colored-gasses of Fate.

The actual transition between the two proved unsubtle. We hit some kind of film that clung to our bodies. It stretched and pressed taut against me as Neil pushed us— forward? Sideways?

Something ripped, and then we were back in Fate.

Gusty winds still blew along the fate-lines, but this time the main line had widened. Two might walk alongside each other without verging close on the rounded edges.

I didn't plan on testing that anytime soon. Thick rents marred the substance on one side of the fate-line, where we'd passed through.

To think I'd watched Eli surf along this only a day or so earlier in my lived time. A shudder ripped through me.

"You okay?" Neil rubbed my back, peering at me.

He'd been *right there* when Eli and I emerged from Fate. Same thing earlier in the day before I went into Fate the first time, after Maksim drew out the swarm of spiders and sent them questing. Coincidence? Maybe. Perhaps the other me in the altered timeline loved him, but I still didn't know him well enough to be sure of anything.

All the same, easier to be suspicious of the others, the newest additions.

Andrew seemed bland as white bread toast but there had

to be something behind the smooth facade. In the real time-line, he'd been a research geek along with Neil—and a handful of other young White men. This version had more cool, less geekiness, but he might be a case of still waters running deep.

Likewise Geneva. A good boss, and one I could see over-seeing the Philly office I'd worked in and doing a better job than Bob. But in the altered timeline she'd hardly changed. Surely someone in charge of such a bigger office should be ramped up in competence and efficiency. Then again, I might be projecting onto her.

And/or him.

They had found me, before more than seven or eight hours passed.

But the very air in Fate seemed more charged than before.

"This time,"—Geneva dusted off her hands and settled her backpack firmly over her shoulders—"let's stay together."

"Sounds good to me." Shauntelle hung close to Monique and me. In the time I'd been gone, her body had shifted to show a slight but likely baby bump. A promising sign, or at least I could hope.

"Ditto," I said.

"Then let's go." Neil gestured for Geneva to take lead again.

"Where's the spider?" She turned around, whirling a second time before stopping with her face to Andrew.

"What spider?" he asked.

"The one that knows where Maksim is." Geneva held out both hands, showing them as empty. "You had it when we checked for them in the eighteenth century."

"No, I never had it." He drew back, eyes darting at me rather than Geneva.

The two of them broke into a squabble, all fractured half-sentences and vagueness as they tried to retrace their steps with respect to the spider.

Shauntelle didn't say anything, but her look conveyed doubt and fear.

And weariness.

I had another spider. Neil or Monique might know, since they saw the result, the spectral web in my hair. Shauntelle and Monique had also both seen the two spiders in my hair in the first place.

But we didn't need the spider to lead us. The bracelet had gone taut around my wrist, the thread leading off in a clear direction. The same light that had shone from my hair now vested the bracelet and thread with a faint violet luminescence distinct from the celestial pinks and greens billowing around us.

"I'll lead the way." I slipped around Shauntelle, gesturing for her to come along. "You all follow."

"How—oh." Neil's gaze slipped to the bracelet. He gave a thumbs-up. "That works for me."

"All right." Geneva clapped her hands again. "Rose first, then Shauntelle. Andrew, Neil, and I will take the hindmost, taking turns."

The thread led in a straight line as a crow might fly. I had to pick the equivalent in fate-lines and choose which cross-lines to switch to since no single fate-line headed the right way. At least Fate offered clear vantages along the cross-lines —some of the time—to see which curved or bent versus heading straight.

I tried to recall the cross-hops Maksim had made, but the lines might've changed. This meant we spent more time than I liked standing on cross-points figuring out which line to take that would keep us headed in the right direction. Some of them were narrow, to the point we held hands and inched along trying not to fall.

In the end, we made an even more zigzag progression than the first time around, though no one knew but me.

All that apart from the wretched pulses of other travelers in Fate headed this way or that. The first one nearly knocked me off balance. It did sweep Shauntelle's feet from under her, but Neil caught and braced her. The worst thing about the pulses was their unpredictability. And they went either direction too.

Maybe one of them was Maksim and Eli and me making our merry way forward, or Eli and myself traveling back.

No time to wonder and explore.

The billowing clouds of gasses came closer, grew thicker. A smog blurred the lines around us, reducing visibility, bringing the stench of ineradicable dampness and mold and decay. Although the fate-lines grew broader—so we had more space to move, the difficulty of seeing where we went more than balanced out. I'd have rather been able to see, even knowing one misstep would send me plummeting again.

Especially when we stepped off a cross-line and a gust of air showed a lump a few leagues in the distance—a Maksim-sized lump—then the smog closed in around us twice as thick. The fate-line turned slightly spongy beneath my feet, and the rank mold increased.

I paused and coughed. Shauntelle ran into me, or her head did.

"Agh!"

Her cry carried and echoed all around as I turned and squinted. Her blurry form bent over, hands grasping at her belly. Her body bulged and shifted around her, moving from not-pregnant or at least not-showing to a characteristic bump.

How long had Maksim and Eli said she was? Seven or eight months—and supposed to stay at home, which meant she shouldn't be hiking in Fate.

"Are you okay? Do you need water?" Please let her not be going into labor.

"No, no." Her voice grew thick with tears. She panted, gritting and grinding her teeth. "Give me something to hold."

I put my hand in hers, and she squeezed tight. Tighter. My mouth gaped open, gulping in air against the ache.

Geneva elbowed in next to me, a first-aid kit in her hand. "What do you need, aspirin? Ibuprofen? Something stronger?"

"No, just give me a minute or two. You go on ahead. I'll follow. I'm remembering." Her grasp on my hand eased as her back arched and her head tilted up toward me. Elation and agony showed clear on her face. "Get things ready to free my husband."

"We can wait." Geneva tucked the kit under one arm and patted Shauntelle's shoulder.

"He can't." Shauntelle glared at her, pointing behind me.

Geneva gave me a sharp glance and jerked her head in Maksim's direction.

"Got it," I said. Shauntelle was remembering what—Maksim? Eli? Both people or both lives? Shading my hand, I squinted as I jogged down the fate-line.

Each step sent tremors through the line. Instead of firm, this more closely resembled running across a sandy beach. The closer I drew, the more small clouds of poison green dust puffed around my shoes. The few motes that reached me retained a tang of mold with an additional layer of the spoiled spinach taste familiar from my last time here.

Despite the vibrations in the line, the sprawled figure barely moved.

"Maksim?" I dropped down next to him. His body had curled up, knees and chin close to his chest. One arm remained trapped in the fate-line. The other lay loose along his body, hand open. His chest barely moved, though he still breathed. Each exhale contributed to keep an arc near his mouth free of dust.

He'd pulled his bag close. The gaping top revealed a sizable pile of protein bar wrappers and empty water bottles. The closed bottles with human markings—imprisoning our attackers—stood just far enough away he wouldn't accidentally grab one instead. All the same, he'd lost weight in the short time we'd been gone. His shirt and pants hung loose around his torso.

The fate-line quivered beneath me as Geneva helped Shauntelle ease her way over.

"Maksim? Shauntelle's here." Reluctant to touch him without permission, especially since he might burst into defensive action, I inched around the piles of bottles.

"Shauntelle?" The word barely scattered any more motes of dust than his soft exhales, but he lifted his head, eyes still closed.

Both hands wrapped over Shauntelle's baby bump, clothes straining and pulling at the seams. Geneva had one arm around her waist to support her. I jumped up and hurried over to help ease Shauntelle down next to her husband.

His eyes didn't open, but the instant she was near, his free hand clawed empty air seeking her. She grabbed it and pressed it against her heart.

"Oh, Maksim."

At the unshed tears in her voice, I leapt several feet away and turned my back. Geneva joined me after a moment, both of us giving them privacy for their reunion.

Three sets of footsteps overlaying each other marked the dust covering the fate-line from where we stood to a couple of yards out from the cross-line. The winds still blew, but soft and high, teasing at my tousled hair. The breezes carried away the smog—and smoothed all differences between consonants and vowels behind us, sharing only the soft murmur of voices.

Other than that, the usual array of stars and colored gasses surrounded us. Nothing else.

It took me precious seconds to realize that the smog had cleared as far as the cross-line.

And that Neil had vanished.

21

Neil missing.

Gone.

I whirled about, searching for any sign of Neil. Called his name, ever louder but the distance and vast celestial night sky around us swallowed it. The winds continued to die around us, letting the last motes of dust fall to the fate-line. Even with the murmur of Maksim and Shauntelle's voices, plus Andrew and Geneva and Monique's, a hush filled the air around me—so quiet that a distant ringing resounded in my ears as I strained to hear Neil acknowledging my call.

Hurrying across the dusty fate-line, my backpack bouncing against my side, I peered over the edges. No rents manifested in my view, no sign of his having fallen through into time.

A variety of footprints marred the surface, except for the yards closest to the cross-line. The fate-line remained spongy beneath my feet, but not enough to retain even heel marks to show he'd been here or what might have happened.

Perhaps he'd missed the turn off the cross-line and gone on instead?

Throat tight and heartbeat so fast as to make swallowing tough, I hurried to the cross-line.

"Neil?"

No sign of him. The winds blew more around the cross-line than where I'd left the others, now bringing a hint of brine to mix with mold. It made for an astringent mixture. My eyes watered. A pulse rippled by beneath me, roiling the line and moving me up and down.

My breath caught in my throat, moisture dampening my eyes.

"Neil?"

No answer. Nothing anywhere, ahead or behind.

As though he never existed.

But he had. He did. In both timelines.

I'd liked him. Not as much as the other me had, but . . .

Maybe the alternate timeline Neil had been a good guy, and not part of any conspiracy, but the one from the real timeline was.

Yet why run off? Why not pretend?

Unless he couldn't manage that much.

Or planned something else?

Worse and likelier—someone had realized Neil suspected their involvement. But which, Geneva or Andrew?

Again and again I whirled about checking past and future, future and past.

A bunch of pulses headed along the way, so big and thick they made sizable ripples in the line—enough to be mistaken for waves in the real world.

Still no sign of Neil, but I shifted backward off the cross-line to let the big pulses go on by. A breeze lapped me, tugging at my bracelet and tossing tangled strands of my hair about before heading forward to the future.

Tossed my hair—but I had more than hair on my head.

"Spider?" I lifted a hand to my hair.

Dainty taps on my hand signaled the arachnid had stepped onto my palm. With a curving motion, I brought my hand around to gaze at the long-legged gold-and-black body through tear-blurred eyes.

"Neil's missing. Can you find him?"

The front legs tapped my palm. Anchoring a bit of silk around my thumb, it swung down to the fate-line and scurried off.

"Rose, are you all right?"

A hand on my shoulder made me jump. I nearly slipped toward the edge of the fate-line, but the taut thread of the bracelet, still connecting me to Maksim, helped brace me. I grabbed hold of Andrew's hand and held on.

"We're looking for Neil as a third to banish the sleaze rather than draft in someone who's never worked with Fate before." He peered around me. "Where is he? He was right behind us when we turned off the cross-line, last in line. I heard a thud or a grunt or two, but nothing more than any of us've given."

"He's gone." I swallowed the sob that wanted to follow the words. My fingers grew cold despite proximity to Andrew's warmth, and I pulled back to cradle them against my chest. I refused to believe Neil had betrayed us and scampered off somewhere else. Which meant Andrew or Geneva had done something—unless we weren't alone and someone else lurked out there.

"Gone where? Further back?" He circled me and stepped onto the cross-line.

I followed in his wake, hoping this time would be different. Maybe Andrew's magic would show where Neil had gone.

All the same, I kept a weather eye back on the others and stayed in the center of the line.

"I've called for him, but he's not answering." A thick boom resounded deep below, rumbling up from my soles to rattle my teeth. The big pulses inching down the cross-line had grown in size to the point they could hold a human being. Or two.

"Neil! Get back here now!" Andrew shifted back, bumping into me. His breath whistled through his teeth as he stared down the line. "I don't like the look of those pulses. Let's get off this line."

He practically pushed me onto the other fate-line. One hand around my wrist, he dragged me toward Maksim and Shauntelle, Monique and Geneva.

The pulses took the same turn we did, shifting onto the fate-line.

One biggest ahead. Then, further behind, several more.

Another deep rumble passed beneath our feet as the pulses doubled in size.

"Hurry!"

Geneva's encouragement, waving from ahead, wasn't necessary. I raced alongside Andrew back toward the others. My backpack slipped from my shoulder, but the strap held against my elbow. Fortunately, I'd drunk all the water so it didn't hang too heavy and pull me off balance much.

The spider hadn't come back. Could it survive the passage of those immense bubbles?

I wasn't any too sure about us. The immense pulses didn't curl as waves did, or even flow under the fate-line as though swells on a wave. They erupted from the surface like mobile . . . pustules.

As if the universe had heard my internal descriptor, the material covering the first began to thin and show vague human forms within. Did it contain Neil? Except, it held more than one person inside.

The fate-line started to twist and lurch beneath us, almost bumping us off. Maksim and Shauntelle were slightly better off, lying and sitting respectively. They flowed up and down with the line. Shauntelle was trying to help Maksim drink, but most of the water wound up spilling over him. Monique had opened a first-aid kit and was dissolving tablets in another bottle.

"We have to get him out of here." Geneva's eyes narrowed as she glanced back and forth between us. "Where's Neil?"

I tripped and nearly fell on top of them, but managed to twist and drop to the line nearby. Rolling off to the side, I sat, wrapped my arms around my body, and rocked.

"He's gone." Andrew crouched next to Maksim, inspecting where his arm sank into the line. "Where's the sleaze you're holding? At an angle or straight below?"

"Straight down." He grimaced and hissed as he drew in a breath. "No way . . . for me to serve . . . as a banisher."

"Shit. We can't wait to find Neil." Geneva glanced back at the pulses.

The front one had slowed to a crawl only a few yards away.

"We'll have to use Monique as the third."

"Show me what to do." Monique stood tall, hands fisted at her sides.

"Follow Andrew's and my lead and . . . Hell—" At a creak and subdued roar from the pulse, Geneva stood up. Slinging down her backpack, she opened it up and piled several empty water bottles next to it. "Give over yours,"—she stabbed a finger at Shauntelle, Monique, then me—"all of yours, any empty bottles. Now."

Maksim waved a finger and half of his empty bottles rolled over to Geneva's growing pile.

I emptied my bag and shoved my bottles over with my hand. Andrew gathered them, forming two piles, one close to Geneva and one for him.

"What do you mean?" Shauntelle mirrored Maksim's spell, inching closer to him.

Whatever covered the pulse—Fate or goo or soap-and-water—thinned to show it held a half dozen people at a minimum. All nearly of a size, forming ranks two wide and three or more deep.

"We're about to be under attack." Geneva grabbed several bottles. Sucking in a breath, she stuffed them top-down through the waistband of her slacks. Had to be magic that let her stick several there at a time. She kept one in each hand, hefting them as though they were clubs. "Defend yourselves however you can. Kill if necessary." A glance at me, and she grimaced. "Just don't let them knock you off the line."

Then she strode three paces forward and placed herself between us and the pulse.

Talk about setting a low bar for me. Still, I had to do something, but with no magic. I patted my pockets, but couldn't find my sisters' special bottle of pepper spray . . . "Do you have anything I can use for a weapon?"

Maksim waved another finger, and a knife slipped out of his backpack to slide across the fate-line to me.

Scooping it up in trembling hands, I followed behind Geneva. My palms grew slick with sweat, more dampening a line down my back, but I retained the thick, heavy hilt. So what if the sharp point jittered around a bit.

"Move to your left," Shauntelle yelled. "Leave me a clear line."

I glanced behind and blinked. Her hands glowed so fiercely the light made my eyes water. Next to her, Maksim had an empty water bottle in one hand, ready to throw, and a pile of others nearby. Andrew stationed himself beyond, likewise with an array of bottles.

The cover of the pulse split into a million pieces revealing a dozen or more White men and a couple of women all carrying big knives or clubs. No guns, but they made up for that with their snarls.

Most appeared to be around my age or a little older, in Polo shirts, jeans, and sneakers.

Bob led them—looking more like the Bob from my time-line than the genial game player from Neil's. He waved a dismissive hand at Geneva.

"Out of the way, bitch!"

In answer, Geneva threw a water bottle as though it was a knife. She hit Smith, and he vanished in a pop, bottle rolling to the side. The men surged forward as she threw another bottle and nabbed a second equally cleanly. Andrew tossed more from nearby, while sparks flew through the air from Shauntelle and Monique.

Three more cracks broke the silence. Even the invading men stopped to glance behind as more immense pulses shattered. These each held three people, of a wide mix of ages, genders, and clothing styles except all wore shades of gray. Two-thirds were Black or Brown, with one in each trio appearing White.

A short, solid woman dressed in a dark gray jumpsuit and black hiking boots strode forward. Around her cherubic, sepia-toned face danced short, loose dark curls with only enough silver to make them glitter in light. Intricate, silver waterfall earrings also flickered. Holding up hands glowing with golden light, she yelled something in a liquid language I didn't recognize. Her voice, on the other hand . . . surely this was Tanisha.

Shoulder-to-shoulder with her stood a tall, thin man with long, dark-brown hair and a face so like Neil's it took three looks to be clear he wasn't. He'd opted for a thin, dark gray turtleneck and black jeans. His brows drew together as he yelled in a deep voice. "Give up, you're outnumbered."

The remaining White men hesitated, glancing in either direction.

"Now!" Maksim's voice might be weak, but it still carried.

Water bottles flew through the air, from him and Geneva and Andrew. Each hit its target, the bottles rolling off to the side but not falling, albeit only by a hair or two.

Sparks of some kind shot from Shauntelle and Monique's hands, shocking several more.

"You're supposed to let us relieve you." Tanisha rushed forward, her fingers snapping and clapping as she did. This time she spoke in English and sounded exactly as she had over the phone. A hint of perfume, tinged with cedar, and an aura of sweat hung about her as she stomped across the fate-line, her black boots leaving solid footprints behind.

Several of the people in middle split off to gather the water bottles and imprison the stunned attackers in additional bottles. They piled the bottles on a large piece of burlap that someone pulled out of thin air. The plastic chimed as one filled bottle bumped into another.

The three people at the back moved up. The mixed racial group took up stances around Maksim and Shauntelle.

"When you're ready." Tanisha gestured to Maksim from outside the triangle.

"Watch for the last." He dragged in a long, whistling breath and let it out almost as fast. "This lurked under a top layer of sleaze and nearly escaped me. I don't think there's a third hidden within, but fair warned is fair armed." He squeezed Shauntelle's hand and smiled up at her, then nodded at Tanisha. "Now would be good."

Energy began to swirl about them, obscuring Maksim and Shauntelle from view. Within moments, the odor of mold and rotting spinach started to fade. A light breeze gusted though, bringing a sweet celestial perfume instead.

Hairs all over my body stood on end, and I inched away before my leg muscles lost all strength and I crumpled to the fate-line. Swallowed several times, until my throat was clear, if dry. Andrew and Monique stared from their spots nearby.

Tanisha greeted Geneva with a quick handshake, then turned and crouched next to me, although her eyes flickered back to the banishment ritual regularly.

"They'll do fine." The Neil-look-alike followed behind, lips quirking. "It's hardly their first time. Trust them."

"If I didn't trust them, you and I'd be over there." Tanisha extended a hand to me. "Rose, I presume?"

"Yeah. And you're Tanisha?" Just to make sure.

"Well done." She shook my hand, grasp firm and warm in comparison to my chilly fingers.

"You remember me?" My mouth gaped like a fish. I couldn't even have said exactly what I meant, both timelines or the call or whatever.

"Always." Her gaze flickered sideways again. "We were nearly too late. A delay on the way that cost us, and will be investigated. Dhugal—"

"Make a note." The tall man heaved a long-suffering sigh and wrote on his hand. "Done, for the fifth time."

"That won't be all of them." Geneva pointed at the growing pile of bottle-prisons. "I only recognized Bob in this batch, but they had to have at least three directors to set a sleaze of this complexity. The question is, where are the rest?"

"A good question." Tanisha rose and headed over to the pile with Geneva in her wake.

"So you're Rose." The Neil-look-alike, Dhugal, remained and offered me a warm hand up. "I've heard a lot about you."

"From Tanisha?" I glanced over at Tanisha, keeping hold of his hand only until my legs turned steady enough to keep me upright.

"No, from Neil, my cousin." Dhugal rubbed his hands, an expression of pain flickering over his face for a moment. "In this timeline, but more the other. I remember both, if not so clearly as Tanisha though she's got three decades of practice on me . . . but where is Neil, anyway? I don't imagine he'd want you to head back in here without him."

"He vanished." Tears dampened the corners of my eyes. "I haven't seen him since before we got to this line."

Dhugal blinked and his mouth opened and shut several times. "Vanished?"

I nodded, but the gesture made me cough. He summoned an unopened water bottle with a flick of a finger and handed it to me.

Turning the bottle around, I checked for a figure before opening. Just in case. His lips twisted, but he didn't say anything.

Instead, he rubbed his hands together as I drank cool water.

After a few moments, he opened his cupped hands. Nothing appeared within his grasp as far as I could tell, but his expression grew darker.

"I can't summon his thread while in Fate, but it's dark wherever he is. I think,"—Dhugal glanced over at the pile of prisoners-in-bottles being wrapped up in the burlap—"it may be he's in a bottle?"

My stomach lurched, and I stared at the burlap covering the bottles. Neil hadn't been among the attackers. Could they have caught him? It made no sense.

"Perhaps they captured him." Dhugal's hands shook. "But—"

Before he could say anymore, an unearthly scream overrode every other sound. An immense tower of fire roared up from the triangle, engulfing Maksim and Shauntelle. Gouts of red, orange, and white flames entwined. The brightness grew so intense I closed my eyes and covered my face with my arms but still saw after-images.

A scorching heat flashed over me, followed by a cool wind.

When I dared open my eyes, Maksim and Shauntelle stood together smiling and untouched by the fire. They laughed and embraced as the three banishers crowded around them.

The fate-line gave a lurch beneath me.

"Places, everyone. We're surfing back!" Tanisha's words echoed up and down the line, and through my feet.

I swayed in place, numb and drained, but everyone else seemed to know what that meant. They lined up in groups of three-plus. The banishers kept Maksim and Shauntelle at the back. Geneva and Andrew joined the three in the middle. Dhugal led me to the front with Tanisha. A third person so shy all I ever glimpsed was a pair of deep brown eyes behind a waist-long veil of hair stepped back to form a three with Monique and another of Tanisha's team.

"What's happening?"

"The cleansing of Fate." Tanisha clapped a hand on my shoulder. Dhugal held onto my other side. "As soon as the banishment fully sets in the line beneath us, it will set up a tidal wave to cleanse from here to the future."

Even as she spoke, a light film formed a sphere around us. An immense wave of energy picked us up and sped us toward the present.

With Fate cleansed—but Neil still missing.

❧ 2 2 ❧

Riding a wave in Fate.

An immense force lifted me up—powerful and irresistible as the greatest of ocean waves yet buoyed gently, as though the most precious of cargo. The stars hung close enough overhead to seem within reach, though I had no chance to try and pluck them. Once raised high, the wave rushed forward with a sound reminiscent of whale song. Stars turned to streams of light, in rainbow colors on all sides. The celestial scent of the power beneath me cleared all physical aches from my body. Each inhale left me refreshed and energized.

It should have been one of the peak experiences of my life.

Yet I floated in a miserable daze. My arms pressed close against my side to the elbow, shoulders hunched and legs drawn up into protective curve. At most, I noted details and stored them away for use in some future dream.

Against the day I might dream.

My body might be returned to health after all the torments I'd put it through the last days, but not my spirit.

Neil's absence left a sore, as much because I didn't know who or what he was or might have done. Or was doing.

But also because I'd been wrong, so many ways. To suggest myself as a third for the banishment, thinking I had to bring back sorcerers or directors to free Maksim and destroy the sleaze when Tanisha would've made it all along, dragging Eli along with me, trusting Neil . . .

Warm hands clasped each of mine. The wave bore company along with me, to either side, preventing me from drawing further into myself.

"You did good." To my left, Dhugal squeezed my fingers. Although we rode the surge forward, his words sounded in my ears as clear as if we'd stood face-to-face in a quiet place.

"It's my fault the second sleaze escaped." I tucked my chin against my chest.

"How would you know?" A sharp-edged belly laugh reverberated down his arm and into me. "We don't ever even talk about assigning fault until a full debrief. Might've happened anyway."

"It's because I can't do magic." How many times had I said this in the last days? At least all the repetition meant it no longer hurt as it once had. Alas, the consequences still burned me. "They tried me as a third in the banishment, after Maksim and Eli, but we only managed to dispel the top layer sleaze, the one connected to the internet."

"Ah, well, it's true one participant having no magic reduces a banishment's power by a third,"—another squeeze —"but now that you know better you can do better."

Some of the warmth from his and Tanisha's hands seeped further up my arms. My muscles relaxed, no longer pinned quite so close against my torso. *Do better* . . . suggested I'd have a chance to do something in the future. Except, he'd said something earlier about remembering both timelines, so he might be mixing me up with the alternate version who'd worked for Atropos.

However had I managed it there? I still was only ninety-nine percent sure that me hadn't had magic.

Before I could ask, Dhugal snorted and beat me to it with his own question.

"Who is Eli and what is this about a double sleaze connected to the internet?"

"Eli's Maksim's stepson, who went with us into Fate. He was the second when we worked the banishment on the sleaze, a yucky poopy-looking thing with a thread leading off it that Maksim connected to a website." Words tumbled over each other as I tried to explain. Not everything made sense, even to me, but Dhugal and Tanisha teased important elements out until I'd given a reasonable overview, albeit lacking so many details.

But not stinting the problems we'd run into.

None of which troubled him as much as they did me, but then again he hadn't been there and lived through it.

Eli's loss of tangibility?

"There's a reason we travel in threes—teams of three and three teams for major banishments," Dhugal said. "It takes at least two people anchoring someone who doesn't exist in an alternate timeline to keep them from disappearing. Some-times more. Unless there's a strong biological or emotional tie between people. That balances numbers."

"Had you not returned to Maksim with Geneva and Shauntelle, the attackers would likely have overpowered and killed him." Tanisha's voice was calm and even, as though she didn't realize how much her words might mean to me—though her steady grip on my hand suggested otherwise. "Even three teams of three have sometimes gone astray and arrived too late."

"Good to know." I dragged in a deep breath and let it out

slowly. Maybe it was just my lack of experience with Fate and sleazes that had set me doubting, or all the slings and arrows that accompanied my learning.

"Even your being a third in banishment without magic is not unprecedented." Tanisha patted my hand. "It never works as well as three sorcerers, but good faith can carry you a long way. More, you say the sleaze was double-layered and set so the banishment of the top layer channeled power to the interior, which used not to be a common thing. Such usually require a banishment for each layer. It is a sign of an inside job, regardless of any other evidence." A snarl escaped her, raising the hairs along the back of my neck. "I'll happily cut the thread of any Lachesis employee who tries that again, subject to proper verdicts and judgments."

"I don't believe Neil was involved." Dhugal ground his teeth. "He can't have been. I suggested him for you to approach in that other timeline. Something must have gone wrong."

"We'll see what we find in Philadelphia. I've asked the wave to take us there, rather than Bermuda. I expect we'll find a welcoming committee of some kind."

An edge to Tanisha's voice gave him some kind of warning, based on the way he squashed my hand before almost releasing it and falling into silence.

"Welcoming committee?" I asked.

"There was only one person among those who attacked you whom I recognized as a director of the firm, and no other employees. I haven't spoken with Maksim yet about the men he captured earlier. Perhaps that encompasses all involved with the sleaze, but the numbers speak to a large operation, of which at least one leading member is unaccounted for."

My mind went first to Neil and trying to figure out how he played a part in this, so it took me a while to parse out her words.

Dhugal got there first, nodding so hard his arm vibrated. "There's always a fish that tries to get away."

That sent me in the right direction. "You think Bob will be there?"

"If we are fortunate, he will be there to confess and throw himself upon our mercy. Or, perhaps, he will be elsewhere and attempt to bluster his way out."

"Or he'll be there with friends to take us down and deny the whole, even restore the sleaze." Dhugal grunted. "Well, we're still fresh and ready to go."

"Don't be so eager for a fight." Tanisha leaned around me to pin him with a stern look. "I, for one, have hopes he will have become so secure in his place to forget certain salient facts about whose office it is. In which case, you may save your energy for all the paperwork this is going to generate."

A cross between a grunt and groan escaped Dhugal.

No wonder I lacked a sense of completion. Too many floating ends remained.

Not to mention, we were carried above the fate-lines headed toward a glorious sunrise in the future. Vibrant pinks, oranges, and purples striped the horizon, with bits of a sullen red peeping from between. The vista offered a balm of beauty, but not for long. The wave not only carried us to the present but deposited us in our world.

Dumped would be a better term, since I dropped two feet and landed heavily on the carpet. Tanisha and Dhugal managed to stay on their feet, despite being pulled to the side by our linked hands. All around us the others manifested in two group waves. It gave me little satisfaction to note that three others also tipped over onto their backsides.

By the whims of fickle fortune—or more likely Tanisha's arrangement—we wound up right outside the restrooms in what appeared to be the office I'd worked in for over a year. The hall had lengthened and now featured enough doors to restrooms to answer for all of us. That was one spell I wouldn't mind putting to use everywhere. My bladder sent me scrambling for a door, along with just about everyone else. Even Maksim seemed to have recovered some of his former vigor and heft as he dashed for a door.

I sprinted into the closest at hand, the first in the line, happy to see the room matched my memory of the office suite in every detail. Paint color, check. Layout, check. No shower, check!

But when I glanced in the mirror, my reflection spider earrings dangled from my ears instead of bells. I'd lost one of my favorite pairs to an alternate timeline and gained a new one. I didn't even know how the alternate me had obtained them—by purchase or as a gift?

I busted out of the room and slammed the door behind me.

The slam echoed a dozen times over. Or rather, bangs and crashes and shouts filled the long, extended hall. At first they seemed to come from everywhere, because others were also leaving the restrooms.

A musty odor hung in the air, vaguely familiar until dispelled by a sudden burst of smoke.

A bright red-orange object shot down the hall at an oblique angle. It sputtered and smoldered and gave off heat. I leapt back, but not quite soon enough. It scorched as it passed, leaving the stench of burnt hair and a hank shorter by a half-inch.

Two doors down, Dhugal caught the fireball in one hand. Closed his fingers, then opened them and flicked ashes onto the carpet.

"We've got company. Stand aside." Tanisha moved to the center of the hall and stretched her arms to either side. The walls moved to reveal a battle filling the reception area. My desk lay on its side, the chair rolled over into a corner. The chairs for guests were similarly overturned across the space, bearing a few rents and singed circles. Burn marks and splotches of thick, gummy substances marred the walls.

Despite the mist, the angle of the hall offered clear view of a half dozen or more white men ranged in front of the door. Most appeared older than the attackers in Fate. Jack Smith stood in the middle, dressed exactly as in the photo about discovering Atlantis that had started everything. One hand glowed with fire, the other held a miniature bolt of lightning. Two other men-of-a-certain-age matched him on either side, in shirts and shorts suitable for sailing on a yacht, plus four or five in matching white sailor uniforms. Most carried knives—no guns—with blades shining red or green.

Two more lay on the floor coughing.

Their opponents had their backs to us, and were divided into two distinct lines. The front included seven women somewhere around my age to Shauntelle's, all wearing casual dresses or outfits in pastel colors. Two had skin as White as mine or paler, and the rest shades from light to dark brown. They formed an irregular line, with an odd lump in the middle, mostly hidden by the women behind.

A tall, solid woman in a light blue dress, and with a crown of gray-sprinkled black braids pulled into a twist bun, pulled a canister of pepper spray from her matching purse. The angle of her body showed her face—and a distinct resemblance to Maksim.

Next to her, an older woman with a very short, stark-white afro leaned against a wall. A neon-pink purse hung from her elbow, matching her light pink dress and the russet highlights in her medium-brown skin. She cupped her hands before her face, blowing green-tinged bubbles that floated up and over the younger women.

None of them were dressed for a fight—every one wore

ample jewelry including matching sets of bracelets in pink, blue, and yellow.

And none of them could move from where they were, either, for the webbed carpet had risen to trap their feet and ankles in place.

Tanisha had inched up next to me, a scowl on her face. She bent down and grabbed a handful of webbing from the floor. "Give a warning," she called over her shoulder to Dhugal.

"Hold!" He cupped his hands around his face, the word almost visibly rocketing through the hall and reception area. "Surrender to the custody and mercy of Atropos—"

"Hah!" A deep, croaking bass rang out.

Another fireball arced through the mist. The women dodged easily, and Dhugal stepped forward to snatch it from the air. The dark gray of his attire shifted, turning his face into a stark plane of angles and contrasts.

Similar transpositions of light affected Tanisha and all those who'd come with her. Every inch of color bled out of them, turning them into beings made of shades of gray.

"Or we'll cut your lifelines short." Dhugal snapped his fingers, and the knife in the hand of the man to Bob's left jerked from his hold—he gave a choking gurgle—and flew through the air to land hilt-first in Dhugal's hand.

Tanisha yanked on the webbing. The carpet lurched, sending a wave through the office that trapped every person in spider silk up to their knees. Dozens—hundreds—thousands of spiders burst from the carpet and woodwork. Some patrolled the carpet. Others spun quick webs and dangled from the ceiling, until the mist vanished to be replaced by a living mass of spiders.

The oldest woman made some gesture—except a high cry from the lump in the middle of the women stopped her.

"No! They're friends."

I drew in breath so fast I nearly choked. Ducking to one side offered a clearer view of the lump as a gangling youth trapped in a sprawled position on the carpet—both feet showing socks. One shoe missing, and the other in his hands.

"Eli, Gramma." Shauntelle's scream echoed through the rooms.

"MOM!"

A moment later, the webbing around the women and boy dissolved.

Everything turned into chaos. A dozen or more voices talking. Groups of people moving this way and that. Yells from the still-trapped men. Orders from Tanisha and Maksim.

Coos. Cries.

All mattered, but nothing so much as watching Eli run into his mother's arms. The two rocked together, dripping tears and overlapping phrases none of which reached my ears. Within moments, they disappeared from view. First the oldest woman joined them, with Shauntelle frantically trying to hug grandmother and son at the same time. Monique and most of the younger woman formed a circle around to keep the rest of us away. Several wiped tears and exchanged smiles and high-fives.

The middle-aged Black woman and two younger who resembled her enveloped Maksim in a similar hug.

All went well that ended well.

Except this hadn't ended well enough. How many would have residual nightmares? Me for one.

Plus Neil still hadn't appeared. Not among the attackers, though that didn't prove anything, but nowhere else either.

I remained leaning against the wall, tears trickling down my face. Of joy, yes, and relief, and worry.

So much busyness. Tanisha and her team mustered to take the attackers into custody, plus the bag of water bottles containing captives that Maksim tossed to her. Bob kept yelling that he hadn't done anything she or Maksim wouldn't have done if they'd had a chance to tweak things and keep what was theirs by right. Andrew joined in, under Tanisha's direction.

Monique glanced my way, then left the group of women and headed over to me. Dragging in a deep breath, she offered her hand. "Thank you for helping bring them back together."

"Thank you for believing enough in me and Eli, even when you couldn't see him." A tremor rippled through me after we shook. It was over.

"Shauntelle always could talk me into almost anything." Monique frowned and shook her head. "And they did it all for nothing."

"You remember the other timeline?"

"Some, though it's getting foggy," she said. "A couple different presidents, a couple more laws about who can do what, but otherwise it was a lot like here."

Her words triggered memory of traipsing through the other timeline's streets and seeing newspaper headlines. A photo of recent presidents. "Were any of the different presidents there women?"

"Yeah, two." She stiffened, watching me close. "Why?"

"Things weren't that different for you, but there were two female presidents. The Philly office," I waved a hand at our surroundings, "wasn't a backwater as it is here but a regional headquarters. And Geneva was the head, not Bob."

23

Staring into Geneva's office gave me goosebumps and a flash-back.

For a moment, I layered over it the office I'd had in the alternate timeline. The window at the far end featured a view, albeit of other mid-rises and a river in the distance rather than City Hall. A faux leather sofa in blue sat against one wall, nearly opposite the filing cabinet in the far corner. A computer table positioned to look out the window and ensure no one could enter without the person in the steel-and-mesh chair noticing.

If I didn't know better, I'd have assumed my brain had made up my office using Geneva's as a blueprint.

Then again, the room differed in details. More art hung on the walls, mostly family portraits and scenic landscapes and all in elaborate gilded frames.

Plus, it was a bit of a mess. Overflowing piles of paper covered her desk with more atop the filing cabinet, where I preferred to pile papers in tidy piles—if I had to have them—and I filed or shredded them at the first opportunity. Six recyclable water bottles lined one side of her desk, some empty and others unopened. No reusable water bottle in sight, though that didn't mean she lacked one. Her backpack lay slumped on her chair, with protein bars in their bright wrappers spilling out and hinting at the additional supplies likely still within.

Geneva braced her hands against the desk, back rounded.

The carpet had muffled signs of my approach, but she turned her head around and glared at me. Her reddened eyes narrowed and her scowl increased.

"Happy now?"

"No." I stiffened and slipped sideways. Leaned against the doorframe to ensure the door stayed open, to allow Monique to listen from the hall. The hinges creaked as the door shifted to bang against the wall. Her shoulders were stiff and dislike poured off her, quite a change from past interactions. "Not all the way, but some." I wiped additional tears from my face with an exaggerated gesture. "Were you crying?"

"Why wouldn't I cry, or are you one of those people who think tears are a sign of weakness? They're not." She turned away, straightening and crossing her arms over her chest. "They're a perfectly appropriate response to loss."

"But we didn't lose."

"Speak for yourself. I didn't remember until now what it was like here." Her face twisted into a snarl. "This may be the right and proper timeline, but the other was better for me. This city was *mine*, the office was big and important and *mine*." Her fists jerked in emphasis. "Now I'm back to being number two."

"You'll be senior soon enough." I pointed a thumb at the foyer. "Bob's under arrest, so he'll hardly be put back in charge."

"Then there'll be some other man to get the power and the credit while I do all the work." Geneva paced over to the window to stare out, showing her profile—and hands still fisted. "Or maybe I'll get seniority, but I'll still be stuck here where the odds of winning higher place are against me. I'm old enough that if I don't get supervision of a regional HQ soon, I'll never escape this branch."

I licked dry lips, shivering in the blast of bitterness flowing off her.

"You should understand." She pointed a finger at me, right between my eyes. "The other timeline was better for all women. We were more equal. Respected. Finally gaining real power."

The anger in her voice resembled that in Bob's when he'd yelled about wanting to get and keep what was his.

They sounded similar. Not the same, but akin.

We'd banished not one but two sleazes—that weren't the work of one group after all. Maksim had said that often the people who created sleazes were selfish and wanted to exist in the other timeline to reap the benefit of their changes. Sometimes they also dictated that they, in particular, end up better off.

In the other timeline things had been better for women, with at least two women presidents in the newspaper I'd seen. Rather, things had been better for White women.

Geneva had benefited. Senior director of Philadelphia, a significant office rather than a backwater, and on the track to greater success.

Also, she'd stayed mostly the same between the version I'd known here and in the alternate. Neil was less shy and more outgoing and assertive. The other me had managed to earn a position with Atropos, so the score went to her for doing better work-wise. The few glimpses I'd had of Bob showed someone seemingly okay with a very different line of work. Granted, this was a very small sample.

Yet, she'd shown up in answer to Neil's spell seeking

someone to help us and would that have happened if she'd had anything to do with setting the sleazes?

Except, Monique had taken issue with how he'd worded it. He'd asked for whoever on the list was closest or could get there fastest. . . not bad criteria, but maybe he should've specified someone willing to help banish the sleaze, too.

Which she had.

Or had she? The attackers had shown up—and she'd gone after them.

Then again, they might've only set the outer sleaze. Maybe they hadn't even known about the inner layer.

Geneva straightened and turned away from the window, head lifted high in challenge. Something about my silence must've ticked her off. "What, you don't agree that women were better off?"

"Better for women, at least White women, but what about other groups? Undoing patriarchy doesn't mean the end of White supremacy or ableism or ageism or . . ."

"It's a start." She waved a dismissive hand.

"Yeah, but we both benefited there, so we're not the ones to judge how much the changes would've helped anyone else." I supported Maksim's hard line of no retrospective changes to Fate, lest helping one group make things worse for others in ways we were unable or unwilling to recognize. It focused the challenge: we had to work with improving the world the hard way, or else have the courage and conviction to change the past completely knowing that likely meant we'd never have existed.

Recognition flickered in Geneva's eyes, but nothing more. No confession or even anything admissible in any kind of court.

Rather than get caught up in a war of glares, I looked away. My gaze fell to her desk and the line of water bottles. From this angle, one of the full, unopened bottles had a distinct shadow on the label. A human shadow, identical to those on the water bottles holding prisoners.

But why would she have brought a prisoner here, and not have turned him over with the others to Tanisha's team?

An orb spider in gold and black clambered up the side to dance on the top. The spider who'd ridden around in my hair, and who'd gone off to search for Neil.

A stir of air and the soft shuffle of shoes against the carpet offered a moment's warning before Tanisha, Maksim, and Dhugal eased past me into the office.

"Bob has made a statement." Tanisha faced Geneva, matching her stance and posture.

"Of course he has, all bluster and no spine. He's taking the easy way and implicating anyone he can think of." Geneva's nose wrinkled and she gave a disdainful sniff. "Surely you don't take him seriously."

"He's made some allegations as to your involvement that warrant inquiry."

"I'm sure he'll babble all the bile he's capable, and stain as many others as possible." Geneva inclined her head a tad. "But that's all it is. Bile and mud."

After working with her for a year and a half, I knew better than to expect she'd admit anything no matter how long they dueled with words. We might suspect, but we had no proof.

Especially if she managed to get away with the bottle. It no doubt counted as tampering with evidence, but I couldn't wait any longer. The spider waved its legs at me.

I dashed across the intervening space and grabbed the bottle, although she lurched to stop me. The spider swung up onto my shoulder as I held it and backed away.

Twisted the cap.

Neil's body spilled out. He lay sprawled across the carpet, a limp and unmoving. He breathed, but barely. I dropped down and grabbed his hand. A weak pulse beat. From this angle, clotted blood marred the side of his head.

"Neil, no!" Dhugal fell to his knees on the other side, touching Neil's face and arms, anywhere except the wound.

"Let me by, I'm a doctor." Monique pushed past the others to join him. She pulled a first-aid kit from somewhere and started checking his vitals.

"Why?" I moved back to give her room to work, turning to watch Geneva's hands get bound behind her back.

"He was too smart, but not clever enough to hide it. Was I supposed to allow him to accuse me of trying to sabotage the rescue operation?" Geneva gritted her teeth as Tanisha and Maksim took her into custody.

Read her her rights, as an employee who'd broken core rules.

"Rose," Geneva said as she was marched out, "you should've left things alone. We were all better off in that timeline."

True for her. True for Neil. Maybe even true for me, but definitely not for Eli and probably not for Shauntelle or Maksim or Monique. I didn't have the right to speak for them, and neither did she.

"That wasn't your call to make."

24

Three months later, an immense wooden door with intricate carvings swung shut behind me. The thud echoed through the chamber. It reverberated off the dark-gray tiled floor, covered here and there with scattered throw-rugs of a dozen different colors of webs against white or black backgrounds. Likewise, it pinged off the dozens of bookcases lining the stone walls. All stood seven shelves high, made of metal covered in dark gray enamel and supporting dull, monochrome bound volumes. Skylights pierced the high ceiling at regular intervals, alternating with some kind of solar, motion-triggered flat lighting. All the same, the room seemed made of more shadows than light.

Spiderwebs adorned the stretches of stone between bookshelves and ceiling, their silken strands glittering in the light depending on where I stood.

Left alone in the library, I shivered at the sudden drop in temperature and humidity. A beige climate control panel—one of the few, even the only, such touches—proclaimed the temperature sixty-eight and the humidity level forty percent.

I'd dressed for late spring in Uruguay—seventies and

matching humidity according to my research—in dark green leggings and an amber-toned tunic of lightweight cotton. The tunic fell to my knees, belted with a twist of green cord, and bore a sprig of green ivy embroidered over one shoulder. Solid black walking shoes covered my feet. The thin layer of sweat dewing my skin under my clothes, after navigating my way over from the hotel, dried and left me chilled.

Not exactly recommended interview attire, but then again I'd not been asked to travel down for anything other than putting the final dots on Is and crosses on Ts after the mess in July.

Some deliveries evidently warranted the expense of sending a human courier across the equator. An all-expenses paid—granted, the budget for expenses was practical rather than generous—trip from the Webmasters office in Philadelphia to the Atropos enclave in Montevideo.

Lucky me to be the chosen one in this case. How could I turn it down, when I'd only ever traveled out of the country to Canada?

The plain gray messenger bag with matching Webmasters and Lachesis logos rested heavily on my shoulder. It shouldn't. I knew exactly what it contained. I'd packed the four hard-bound volumes myself.

My shoes clattered against the tiles, but made no noise when crossing any of the rugs. I only did so twice. Each time my feet sank into a thick, plush surface, the webbing began to glow. I stuck to the tiles.

Who knew where in Fate the webs led?

Not I.

For a library, this chamber was strangely devoid of furniture. It lacked chairs, tables, desks, anything. It only contained the rugs, shelves, and irregular arrays of books on the shelves.

And me.

A slender strand of spider silk dropped from the top of my head. A golden orb spider dangled in front of my nose.

It had insisted on coming with me, hidden in my hair all the long way. Over sixteen hours on various planes, but it had managed to remain whole and intact.

I'd asked Maksim, the first or fifteenth time I found it lurking atop my head, if it was a real spider or some type of magical construct. He didn't answer, only smiled, but it had to have or be some degree of magic to survive all the times I'd forgotten it might be around and combed my hair.

After three months, it had trained me to a degree. When it kept dangling in front of me, I turned one hand palm up.

With a flick of its spinnerets, it leapt to my palm and started dancing. Long legs directed me through the room. Avoiding the rugs made things take longer, but I navigated over to a range of shelves, none bearing more than two or three volumes and one being completely empty—a distinct contrast as most of the shelves held at least six or seven.

The spider tossed a length of silk and slid over to the second shelf from the bottom. There it began to spin a narrow web along the front of the shelf itself, not the air above.

"Is this where you want to be?"

It paused for a moment, but didn't answer any more than it usually did.

This close, I couldn't miss that many of the shelves had stretches of spiderwebs across their fronts—and each bore letters or characters. Some spelled out names in the Roman alphabet. Others used different alphabets or syllabaries. Greek, Chinese, Arabic, and more.

Within moments, the spider incorporated recognizable letters into the strip of web.

R . . . O . . . S . . .

Shades of *Charlotte's Web*. If a fictional spider could spell words in spiderwebs to save a pig otherwise destined for a dinner table, could this spider spin me a place in Atropos?

It evidently thought so.

The volumes sitting on other shelves bore bindings similar to that around the volumes in my bag. All were plain and undecorated, monotone cloth bindings. The spines, and those few front covers I could see without touching anything, held flat, printed text in colors appropriately contrasting with the cover.

The same kind of thing on each, although the details changed: a name and a date.

All of the volumes in my bag bore the same date.

Two had Maksim's name.

Two mine, each with the same contents: an account of my involvement in the banishment of the double-layered sleaze. I'd worked on it for weeks, in stray moments between my regular duties. Maksim refused to let me take it home to work on, and what he said went since he and I were the only employees left in the office until he'd arranged to bring over two directors. Both junior to him, but experienced enough to pick up their share of the labor quickly so he could spend more time at home with his family, not least his healthy infant daughter.

He'd also hired a new administrative assistant. Temporary for now, but given the way his lips quirked when he'd given me my discretionary budget for the trip, he wasn't sure I'd be back. At least not to stay.

The spider had finished my first name and started on my middle.

"Do my books belong there?" My fingers itched to touch the shelf and set the volumes in place.

"Perhaps."

I jumped, nearly cracking my head on the shelf as I

whirled around. My muscles shook and elbows clenched tight against my side.

Tanisha stood in the center of the nearest throw rug. Her face and general outline matched my memories—a short, solid woman with silver-touched black curls around a dark, mobile face. Instead of a jumpsuit and hiking shoes, she wore a light blue elbow-length shirt partially covered by a green and blue sari. A hint of cedar drifted about her along with her silks. Several gold necklaces hung around her neck, bracelets her wrists, and heavy earrings from her ears. Bare toes with nails painted red poked out below, as her feet were clad in gilded leather sandals.

"You're moving ahead of us, cousin. Wait your time." Tanisha's sari whispered as she approached and crouched down to speak to the spider.

It paused for all of two seconds before continuing to spin and weave.

"The spider has made its decision, but such as it aid and advise. They do not dictate." Straightening up, Tanisha held out her hands. "I believe you have some books for me?"

I offered her the bag, but she shook her head.

Undoing the clasp, I inserted a hand and found two stout volumes almost leaping into it. Maksim's narrative, with his name emblazoned in bright gold against black.

Tanisha accepted them. Curving an arm around, she flipped through some of the pages.

To verify I'd brought the right story? Both his and my versions had been sent by email several weeks ago. She'd already read them—and sent back suggested edits.

The movement of the pages raised a small, localized breeze. I quivered, wishing I'd brought a jacket or sweater of some sort.

All at once, she slapped her hands against the volumes and they vanished.

"What?" I jumped. Again.

"We'll add this to the library of directors' narratives."

"You mean this isn't the library?" I waved a hand at the lines of bookcases.

"We have many libraries, or at least many separate chambers holding different collections. Here"—she turned in a circle, hands out—"is where we keep our own tales. Accounts of the banishments and other actions taken by current employees. All new hires must select and read narratives at several points during their training, but we prefer to vary what they choose—whether those of other Atropos employees, other Lachesis firms, former employees . . . or outsiders."

"Where will mine go?" I removed the soft, dark green bindings with my name in a lighter shade and handed them to her.

"That decision has yet to be made."

An armchair rose out of the purple-on-white rug, a handsome affair of blonde wood and matching satin. Tanisha settled herself in it and opened one of the volumes. This time she didn't skim through the pages.

Fists tight against my thighs, and jaw set, I stayed in place. Shifted now and then from one foot to another, for the hard tile underfoot had no give whatsoever.

The spider had nearly finished my name. But it wasn't the spider's choice.

I'd applied for a place with Atropos less than a week after banishment. Long enough to think it over, and still be sure.

The firm-provided therapist had asked at every mandatory appointment if I remained certain of my decision.

One hundred percent? No, but in the nineties on a good day and seventies on a bad. Staying on as a receptionist no longer satisfied me.

The position at Webmasters had started as a way to support myself while figuring out a new plan for my life. I could've opted for all sorts of things less drastic than throwing my hat in for a job at Atropos that came with high odds of serious bodily injury or brain damage.

Neil understood. We hadn't dated that long—and certainly hadn't moved in together in the real timeline—but he was already planning to visit me here if I wound up starting training. He worked remote most of the time, so he could move wherever I went after, if we stayed together.

Tanisha glanced my way now and then as she turned the page.

The whole thing seemed a test of some sort, and silence the wisest course.

In the end, she spoke first. "You truly wish to join us?"

"Yes." My head jerked, spine crackling.

"Even though you have no magic?"

"Yes." I hadn't had any in the other timeline either, at least Neil never mentioned me doing magic there, but I'd somehow earned a place as liaison to Atropos there. Surely I could offer value in this timeline as well.

"Why?" She tilted her head to one side, gaze intent.

Another test? A deep breath filled my lungs. Letting it out slowly calmed quivering muscles. "Because I want to make a difference. Help keep Fate free of interference, by knowing what is and what isn't."

"You're willing to be among the least and last if necessary? To never be chosen for banishments?" She rose, and the chair sank into the floor behind her with a faint creak.

"Banishments aren't all you do. You also track potential dangers. Research risk-points. Infiltrate suspect groups." My shoulders slumped slightly. "And you require a support staff to provide all that your agents require. I have skills that may come in handy."

"A strong sense of the world, and stubbornness, can be as valuable as a deft hand at sorcery." A slow smile dawned on her face. "You won't be the first here without magic, though there aren't many. It will limit the work assigned to you, but not, perhaps, as much as you fear. And remember: all that we do is of value. You will be able to make a place among us. Welcome to the thread-cutters, the spider-trainers, the final judges."

She gave me one of the volumes with my name on it and kept the other. Together, we bent and set them on the shelf the spider had decorated with my name.

At last I had a new place and a purpose in life. Lacking magic, I'd never rise to lead, but that was okay. They valued people with the courage and stubbornness to follow their own convictions.

As part of Atropos, I'd make a difference. Though I could not undo any sleazes set in the past, I'd help ensure no further sleazes marred Fate.

I'd make a difference.

ORDINARY SORCERY

Adventure runs in the family—read on for a sample from *Swan and Shadow* where Rose's middle sister first discovers sorcery!

Viola values family and friends above anything else. After suffering abusive bullying in high school, she delights in a tight-knit group of friends at college.

Until the night she witnesses them meeting without her. The same night her younger sister calls with news their parents' marriage further disintegrated.

Running off into the forest, Viola witnesses sorcery and winds up tangled in a decades-old curse.

Lovely and poignant, *Swan and Shadow* mixes *Swan Lake* and *The Magic Flute* into to a gripping, emotional page-turner.

Chapter One

A swan turned into a man on the best worst day of my life. Everything sucked big lemons until that moment.

My sneakers pounded against the path around the lake, kicking up bits of gravel that skittered in my wake. Crushed pine needles scented the air and made me long for fall and cups of hot chocolate. The air lay still and warm, but I worked up a nice layer of sweat. My Arden College T-shirt and matching green shorts stuck to my skin, although my hair streamed back from my pony tail. Even my fingers pinked up where I held tight to my cell phone, making my skin rosy against the black case instead of the usual beige. Alas, every twenty steps or so my wire-framed glasses slipped down my nose no matter how many times I shoved them back up.

Varied trees grew along the path. Pine and maple, oak and sycamore. A few leaves showed signs of turning orange and gold, but most remained green. I ran through a world of deep shadows and flickering lights. Lampposts cast ovals of light on the path at regular intervals. Here and there blue lights gleamed from emergency phone towers.

Starlight reflected off the lake to my left, along with bits of moonlight from the waning crescent high in the sky. When the path moved farther from the water, the reflected light dwindled to firefly-flashes between thick foliage.

Across the lake, warmer yellow streetlights and lamps affixed to houses glimmered as though not-so remote stars flickered between branches. They grew closer and bigger as the path wound around to where the college's property ended and the suburb began.

The house at the edge of the development had a six-foot wrought-iron fence lining the path. Someone had cleared the ground between fence and lake. Or maybe it was like that to begin with: a rocky stretch with a clear view of the water and the bright lights of the college across the way.

Nothing burned so bright as an immense star blazing across the dark sky.

Pausing and panting, I backed up against the fence. My skin cooling as my sweat dried.

By then, the arcing light hove into closer view. Not a star but a swan, bright and radiant as it danced in the air. Drew near, moved far, and back and forth. It circled and sank down toward the surface. White wings widespread and neck arched in the air reduced to a blurry blob in the reflection mirroring the flight from below.

The swan landed close by and swam nearer. Ended up half-turned away from me a bare five feet from the beach.

So beautiful. The classic image of bright white plumage floating on an almost mirror-perfect surface. A few faint ripples marred the swan's reflection.

The swan reared up. Feet paddled hard, churning the waters, as it spread its wings wide. Wider. At least as broad as I stood tall. The gold-tinged beak sharpened.

A silvery aura outlined the bird against the dark waters and the distant shore.

In that moment, everything changed.

Wings shrank into human arms. The oblong body narrowed and lengthened to a broad torso. The beak dwindled into a nose, and the small white head expanded and grew brown hair. White feathers darkened to gold-tinged skin and shimmering lake waters lapped at a well-shaped backside.

The swan became a naked man.

My mouth hung open. Body swayed. Hands gripped the iron fence posts tight.

One blink, two, three. The bird didn't re-materialize. The man remained there, naked as the day he was born and in the spot I'd seen the swan a moment earlier.

Feathers floated on the water around his thighs. Another rested atop his head as he stared down at the lake surface.

Part of the feather's down tangled in the man's hair, but the shaft stuck out. It bobbled. Ridiculous, yet a sudden desire to hold the feather rose within me.

An instant later, a gust of wind blew it loose to dance on the breeze, wafting my way until it hovered above me. Letting go of the fence, I stretched out a hand. The wind died away, letting the broad, white feather float down into my palm—still warm from his body.

Physical proof a swan had flown in. I swayed, then slid down against the fence poles into a heap at the bottom. Wrapped my arms around my legs and hugged them to my chest. My lungs ached with every breath, as though the air turned to liquid ice.

The swan-turned-man failed to notice the feather's flight. Instead, he slapped the water, raising a great splash. Drops arced through the air, glittering as they fell back into the lake.

A moment later, he beat the surface of the lake full throt-tle. Shoulders flexed and arms lashed out. He fought the water as though an enemy bent on destroying him. Smacked the surface hard, each blow resulting in great waves and gouts. A few drops reached me despite the distance.

How did he resist crying out in pain? His hands must've hurt from the blows, yet he only huffed.

After a few minutes he ended as he'd begun—staring down. Head low and shoulders heaving.

My fingers stroked the soft feather over and over.

Then he turned and trudged out of the water.

Fine muscled legs, strong chest with a dusting of dark hairs, and . . . oh . . . even in the sharp contrast between light and shadow, he had an unmistakable face. An oval dominated by deep-set eyes and thick eyebrows. Angled cheekbones and stubble on his cheeks and upper lip. Starlight leached color from his skin, turning it silver-white against dark hair cut short.

Evan Roth.

Twice a week since the semester started—and all of last year before that—I had an excellent view of his face bent over a violin during orchestra rehearsal. One of the heart throbs of the orchestra, after the lead percussionist and the concert mistress.

Evan—a swan.

My fingers tightened around the feather.

Standing on dry land, he clapped his hands and a towel—white with red stripes—appeared out of nowhere.

He dried himself off with efficient snaps of the cloth against arms, legs, and torso.

Another clap, and the towel vanished.

More claps summoned clothes piece by piece. Dark brown shorts. Battered sneakers which he slipped on without socks. An Arden T-shirt matching mine only his had the Tree of Knowledge sprouting from a scroll of music instead of a book. Then a comb to run through his hair. He bent over the water once to check his reflection before he sent it back from wherever he'd summoned it.

Each spell made my hair stand on end as though I'd taken a too-big bite of mint ice cream.

Magic, magic, magic.

He still hadn't seen me.

I couldn't let him run off without talking to him, asking about it all, no matter that I'd meet up with him at the next rehearsal.

A fog seemed to have settled in around us. Not seen but felt. Certainty thrummed in my bones that I had this moment, this chance—if he went off, I'd forget.

I set my jaw and vowed it wouldn't happen.

"Hey, Evan!" Springing to my feet, I grabbed hold of the fence for steadiness.

He startled, arms pulling tight against his sides and hands

rising in fists. Then he got a look at me and relaxed. He gave me a polite smile, the kind meant to keep people at a distance.

"Hi, uh, Viola, right? Clarinet."

In other words, he found me familiar but not memorable. I gave him points for getting my name right—*Vi*-ola, like violet, because no way am I a stringed instrument. But while he got the general category of instrument I played right, he guessed the actual one wrong. Unsurprising because he ranked as one of the orchestra's good lookers with instrument or without. Not me, in part because no one looks good close up when blowing through an oboe, or other wind or brass instrument for that matter. Indeed, oboists often joked the instrument was an ill wind that nobody blows good.

He nodded, then turned to walk off.

I lunged after him and grabbed his arm.

"How'd you turn into a swan? From a swan into a man, I mean, but you must've turned into a swan first to turn back."

He stiffened, eyes staring right into on me—close enough to show thin, spiky yellow rings spread through the green.

"Are you a sorcerer?"

"What?" My turn to draw back. "A sorcerer? Is that what you call yourself?"

"You are, aren't you?" His hand wrapped around my wrist, holding tight enough the sinews made a crackling sound. He stopped the instant I winced. "Tell me you are."

I shook my head, glasses slipping down my nose until I pushed them up with my free hand.

He grimaced and cursed. Not magical curses, or even creative. A lot of f-bombs. After which he stared right at me again—still holding my wrist, though not so tight.

"There's still time. Forget. You saw a swan. Fine. You saw me. Fine. You didn't see me change shape, or anything else sorcerous. Forget before it's too late. You're only safe if you don't believe."

He pulled free, waved a hand, and ran off.

I gaped, then snapped my jaw shut and pelted after him . . . but everything that could go wrong did. I tripped on the second step and lost seconds righting myself. A sudden wind whooshed up fallen leaves from the underbrush and blew them across the path ahead of me, making me slow and bring up my hands to shield my face. Somehow I knocked off my glasses off. They fell into the bushes with a clatter.

After several minutes of searching, I found them—without a scratch.

Too late to catch him, so I gave up.

He told me to forget sorcery, but he shouldn't have used it to slow me down and keep me from following him. That made me believe all the more, though his warning rang in my ears as I headed back to campus.

You're only safe if you don't believe.

Be among the first to learn of new releases: sign-up for her newsletter at https://BookHip.com/PCSWMCK. Book recommendations, updates on stories, and snippets from works-in-progress—plus a free Dancing Princesses story for signing up!

ABOUT THE AUTHOR

Alea Henle writes non-fiction by day and fiction by night. Contemporary and historical fantasy, fantasy romance—and more! Check out her website www.aleahenle.com.

www.ingramcontent.com/pod-product-compliance
Lightning Source LLC
Chambersburg PA
CBHW061528210726
48287CB00006B/1884

9 781952 735240